PACI]

Amy Bess Cohen

For Rebecca and Maddy,
Nate and Remy,
and all of
their descendants

PART I: Isadore and Gussie

CHAPTER 1: IASI, ROMANIA
1899

Isadore and his brother David strolled home from school, passing through the narrow streets lined with houses and shops built shoulder to shoulder in the city. The walk from the school to their home on St. Andrews Street in Iasi didn't take very long, maybe ten to fifteen minutes, but Isadore and David liked to dawdle along the way.

Isadore was almost eleven years old, David nine and a half. The streets were crowded with people, many with familiar faces. The noise and commotion made Isadore smile. It felt good to be out of school and on their own. They loved to stop at all the shops along the way and see the food on display, the red and bloody carcasses hanging in the butcher's window, the smell of that meat mingling with the fresh aroma of cookies and cakes being sold two doors down at the bakery.

The peddlers lined the streets with their carts, filled with clothing, pots and pans, and fresh fruits and vegetables. Isadore's stomach growled as he thought about those cookies and maybe an apple. The shoemaker's shop smelled of fresh leather, like the horses that pulled the carts down the streets.

A peddler selling shoes and belts from his cart dropped an apple on the ground for the horse tied to his cart. Watching the horse twitch its tail and rub its head against the cart, Isadore wanted to take its bridle off and take it for a ride into the forest outside of Iasi. Such a beautiful creature, its hide so rich brown like the coffee his mother brewed each morning.

"Let's go see the blacksmith shop, okay?"

Isadore loved to watch the blacksmith Leon Marcovici forge the shoes for the horses, but when he then hammered the shoes onto the horses, it always made Isadore wince. Poor horses, having heavy metal shoes nailed to their feet. Yes, it protected their feet from the hard cobblestone streets, but it still seemed unfair. A horse should run free.

Beyond the narrow street where they walked, suddenly the cathedral bells pealed, ringing loud enough to be heard throughout the city. The golden spires of the cathedral loomed above them. Iasi was a beautiful city, a boy's dream. He and David and their older cousins Srul and Berl wandered through most places in the city, as long as they avoided certain neighborhoods where Jews were not welcome. But in Iasi almost half the people were Jewish, and certainly in their neighborhood, everyone was Jewish---all the shop owners, all the children, everyone in his school.

But there was the other half of the city, the ones who made the laws and ran the police force and the government. They had the real power in the city. The four large towers of the cathedral dominated the street where Isadore lived, St. Andrews Street, reminding him every day that he was an outsider in his own hometown, a Jew who did not quite fit. Its huge, rounded spires had only been completed a few years before he was born in 1888 and could be seen from almost anywhere in the city, the spires pointed on the top with globes underneath, shining brightly when the sun hit them. For Christians perhaps they were inspiring, but for Isadore, despite their beauty, they were intimidating and unwelcoming.

As they walked along the street, David asked him questions. Always with the questions.

"Izzy, are we going to the theater this weekend?"

"I hope so. We have to ask Papa."

Their father Moritz worked at the Yiddish theater as a lamplighter. He always came home with wonderful stories about the plays and operettas that were performed at the theater, and for special treats he would sometimes take the boys along to help. They'd sit all the way in the back, looking over the heads of everyone in the audience. The smell of tobacco and perfume permeated the air, and people chattered noisily while waiting for the show to start. Watching as their father dimmed the lights, the boys sat spellbound, counting down until the actors took the stage.

"What are they performing now? I hope it's not one of those boring love stories."

Isadore laughed. He and David had little use for girls or love stories and preferred the ones that told stories of adventure like Jules Verne's *Around the World in Eighty Days*. Isadore spent hours daydreaming about the play---imagining traveling around the world, seeing Paris, London, Rome, and New York.

But Isadore's favorites were the operettas---the ones with music, the sounds of the violins and cellos, merging together, crossing over, high and low. And the singers---oh, how he could listen to them sing forever. Their voices as clear as the morning sun reflecting off the spires of the Cathedral, piercing the smoke-filled air of the theater.

When they couldn't go to the theater, their father brought the theater home to them, telling the stories and acting them out for them. He tried to sing all the parts in the operettas and sometimes made them laugh so hard when he sang the high parts sung by the women or the very low parts sung by the big basso men.

Their father Moritz was a small man, not much more than five feet tall, but he was full of energy and spirit and always clowning with the boys. He'd fill their ears with gruesome tales of wolves and foxes and talking animals, raising his eyebrows high for the scariest part and whispering quietly to keep them listening carefully.

Mama didn't like it much when he got them all riled up.

"Moritz," she'd say, "stop making them so wild! They will never get to sleep."

Papa winked at them and then sat them down for a song or quiet story while Mama tended to Betty, their little sister, who was just three years old.

When Betty was born, Mama was thrilled.

"Finally a daughter for me," she'd exclaimed. Isadore remembered being a bit hurt by her words. Were her sons not good enough for her?

As they approached the blacksmith shop, Isadore and David heard a strange sound behind them, like thunder coming closer. Isadore turned back to see what was making that noise. People were running down the street. Lots of people. Men and women and children. The sounds of all those shoes hitting the cobblestones was deafening. They were all running towards where he and David were standing.

"What's happening? Where are you all going?" he shouted.

No one answered him. They just kept running past him, looking scared.

"Let's get out of here, David. Now. Something's wrong."

Mr. Marcovici, the blacksmith, heard the commotion and came to the doorway.

"Oy, it's happening."

"What? What's happening?" Isadore asked.

The blacksmith grabbed both boys by the arms and dragged them into the stable.

"The pogrom. It's happening. Stay inside."

With the door slammed shut, it was dark inside. The stable smelled of horse dung and Mr. Marcovici's sweat, and with the doors shut, the smell was overwhelming. Isadore coughed a bit, trying not to wrinkle his nose. David cowered in the corner, his lips quivering. Isadore put his arm on his brother's back.

"It's okay. We will be safe in here. Mr. Marcovici has his forging tools and the horses to protect us."

"Why are they doing this? What is going on?"

Isadore had heard his parents and his aunt and uncle talking. The students at the university---the non-Jewish students---had been having rallies and speeches about the Jews. The evil Jews who, they said, had killed Christ and taken over their city. The Jews had to go, the students said. They were ruining Iasi.

Papa and Uncle Yankel, Srul's father, shook their heads.

"Don't they know we Jews are the ones providing much of the trade around here?" Papa muttered.

Isadore had listened quietly to their conversation. He knew things were brewing at the university, but he didn't think the students would do more than talk.

Now something bad was happening. He left David's side and stood by Mr. Marcovici.

"What's happening?"

Mr. Marcovici peered through the small opening at the top of the doorway to the stable. Behind them the horses were beating their paws into the hay in their stalls nervously and making little neighing sounds.

"Shhh, be quiet in there," Mr. Marcovici whispered to the horses. He went to calm them down, and David went with him.

Isadore took the stool that Mr. Marcovici used to shoe the horses and pulled it towards the door. He climbed up and stood on the tip of his toes and then could see a slim sliver of what was happening in the street through the gap between the door and the sill above it.

People were still running, and there were also people screaming and glass breaking. Horse hooves crashed against the cobblestones. He couldn't see much right in front. He leaned up as high as he could and turned his head as far to the right as possible without falling off the stool.

Down the street where he and David had just been walking, he could see people lying all over the street, blood streaming from their clothes and their heads. A woman stood over a small child whose arms and legs were lying at odd angles from her body, like the rag doll that someone had given to little Betty. The woman was screaming, but the child wasn't moving. On the other side of the street all the meat from the butcher shop was thrown all over the street and the cakes and breads from the bakery were strewn all over as well.

The butcher was dragging something across the street, crawling along. What was it? Oh, no, oh, no---it's his dog.

The rioting students were getting closer to the blacksmith shop. Isadore felt dizzy and was about to step off the stool when he recognized his uncle Yankel trying to push his cart by hand down the street, away from the rioting students. Yankel was a painter and had a horse-drawn cart to carry all his paints and brushes and ladders. But where was his horse? Why didn't Yankel just run?

Then a young man on a horse rushed up to Yankel and smashed his back and then his head with a large pole. The cart of supplies toppled on to the cobblestones, and Yankel screamed out in pain, his head and face covered with blood.

"Oh, no---it's my uncle. I need to help him!"

Isadore jumped off the stool and was about to slide open the door to the blacksmith shop when Mr. Marcovici grabbed him, swung him around, and pushed him into the corner on the other side of the stable.

"Don't you dare! You want to get killed? You want us to get killed? Wait til they're gone. Then you can go help."

Isadore sank to his knees and started to cry. Softly.

9

David whimpered behind him. "I'm scared," he said. "I want to go home. I want Mama and Papa. What if they're hurt?"

Isadore pulled his brother closer.

"We'll be fine. They'll be fine also."

But he wasn't sure. All he wanted to do was take a horse, grab his brother, and ride that horse as far from Iasi as he could. He stood up and stroked the neck of the closest horse, feeling its muscles rippling under his touch. *If only I had that strength, if only I could run like a horse*, he thought wistfully.

Finally, when things seemed quiet, Mr. Marcovici let them out. Glass was everywhere, and Isadore had to tiptoe gingerly around the slivers of glass. And the blood. Then he saw his uncle lying on the ground, moaning and covered with blood.

"Uncle Yankel, it's me, Isadore. Are you okay?"

"What? Who? Where am I?"

"Stay with him, David. I'll go get help."

Isadore ran all the way home where his father stood outside the door, staring up and down St. Andrews Street, his mouth drawing a tight line across his face, his eyes filled with tears. When he saw Isadore running towards him, his mouth relaxed momentarily. Then it tensed up again.

"Where's David?" his father called out.

"Papa, papa, come quick. David's fine. But Uncle Yankel's hurt. David's with him."

The rest of that day and night was a blur. So many people had died, even more were seriously hurt. Uncle Yankel was very dizzy and tired. And sore and bruised all over. He kept asking for his painting supplies.

Srul paced up and down. "I'm going to get those bastards. They can't get away with this."

Papa looked at Mama and her sister Perla, Yankel's wife, and shook his head.

"They can and they will." His spirited, fun-loving father responded; he had nothing of comfort to say.

But once they were home, Moritz took David and Isadore aside.

"Look, boys, today was a very bad day. A terrible day. But we have so much to be happy about. We have the theater and the music. We have all our friends. Your school. Our synagogue. All our wonderful shops. Our beautiful city. We have our family. We have to put today behind us and focus on all the good things we have and all the good things to come. Don't let those who are evil make us evil also. Don't let them take away all that we love and cherish here."

Isadore listened, but for perhaps the first time ever, he wasn't sure his father was right. Hadn't those monsters already taken away so much of what they loved? Were there really good things to come in a place such as this that allowed innocent people---even children---to be killed in the street just for being Jewish? Maybe his father was just wrong.

Someday he would leave this place. Someday he would be free.

CHAPTER 2: NEW YORK CITY
1901

It was so cold outside that Gussie could not stand still or sit on the stoop in front of the tenement where she lived on Ridge Street in New York City. She kept stomping her feet and rubbing her hands together. When she sighed, her breath looked like smoke. She had never seen that before, and it made her a little nervous. Was her body on fire? If that was smoke coming out, why was she so cold?

She was only five and could hardly remember the winter before when she was four. She remembered seeing snow, though. It had been so beautiful that it made her street appear new and clean. The snow hid all the dirt and garbage. When she touched the windows from inside their rooms, the glass felt so cold, but her fingers left clear spots where she could see outside. It was magical. Her street looked like something from a dream. And when her big sister Tillie took her and Frieda outside to show them the snow, the streets smelled better also. She had wished for the snow to stay forever and keep everything clean.

Of course, a day later the magic was gone. The horses and the carriages and the men walking in the streets had turned the whiteness all gray and brown again. The snow was pushed aside, now just a slippery mess that made her feet feel numb. Her shoes were soaked through, and her stockings also were wet and uncomfortable from being splashed by the snow.

Now a year later, she was a little smarter and knew snow wasn't magical. It was just frozen rain, and it came and it went like the rain. And it wasn't snowing now. Just very cold. She wanted to go inside, but her big brother Hymie had said she had to stay outside. She did not know why. Frieda also was sent outside, and Frieda was also stomping her feet, rubbing her hands together, and blowing that mysterious smoke. Frieda was only three. She was too little to ask questions.

Her mother never made them stay out in the cold. Her father never even let them stay out in the cold. Her father was the kindest man. He never hurt anyone. And her mother? Her mother loved every creature that came by, the horses, the dogs, the cats that roamed the streets. She did not like the rats that ran around late at night, but who would? They were so ugly. And dirty. Ugh. Like the pigeons who ate all the garbage, the rats were disgusting. Gussie shivered with cold and disgust.

Her father had been coughing quite a bit lately. When Gussie asked him why he was coughing, he said, "Don't worry, little one. It's just from the coal." The coal. Papa was a coal man. Mama said he was important because without coal, the winter would be even worse. We needed the coal to warm the house. To boil the waters for baths. To make our food. Without coal there would be no soup. So Papa was important.

But the coal made him cough. And worse yet it made him turn as dark as the coal itself. He lugged the coal up and down the streets in his wagon, then carried it down in pails to the coal bins for each tenement. He got up early and came home late. And he was covered with coal dust when he came home. Gussie loved him, but she would not let him hold her until he was clean again. When she was even smaller, Frieda cried when he came home because she did not recognize him. Mama heated the water for his bath, and the children all went in the other room while he soaked in the bath. The metal tub would be so filled with blackened water after his bath that Mama had to rinse it five or more times before it could be used again. Washing his clothes made the tub filthy again. Poor Mama. It was such hard work. Tillie helped when she could, but she went to work every morning and was so tired when she got home.

In the warm weather it was easier. They stayed outside later, and it wasn't as cold. Gussie thought about the summer. She and Frieda sat on the stoop, playing with the other girls who lived on their street and in their neighborhood. Her Papa referred to the neighborhood as the East Side. There were big streets like Delancey Street and Orchard Street, and smaller streets that were quieter, like her street. She went with her mother to Orchard Street and helped pick out vegetables and fruits to bring home from the men with the carts. Mama sometimes needed Gussie to help her talk to some of the men with the carts. It was funny, but Gussie knew more words in English than Mama did, and some of the men did not know Yiddish.

13

Although the market area was smelly and the ground could be as slippery from squashed fruit and vegetables as it was from melting snow, it was still fun to see all the people and examine everything they sold. Next year when she was six, she was going to go to school, but now she stayed home with Mama and Frieda. And Sam.

Baby Sam had arrived in September. He screamed a lot. A lot. Gussie did not remember when Frieda was a baby. Maybe she had screamed a lot also? But Sam was such a cry baby. Mama said he would get better when was bigger, but so far he still cried a lot. Good thing he slept with Mama and Papa in their room. Gussie, Frieda, Tillie, and Hymie slept in the front room; Mama and Papa and Sam slept in the backroom, looking over the alley where the toilet was. Gussie was glad they got the front room so they could see Ridge Street, not the alley.

Gussie was really starting to get angry. Why couldn't they go home yet? Hymie had said to wait until he came to get them and not to come upstairs. But it was so cold, and it was starting to get dark.

"Frieda, let's go inside now."

"But Hymie isn't here yet."

"I don't care. I am bigger than you. You have to listen. Let's go."

Frieda shrugged. Everyone said Gussie and Frieda looked so much alike. Both had fiery red hair that curled around their ears. Both had dark brown eyes. So did Tillie. The brothers also had red hair, but not so curly. Mama's hair and even Papa's hair had some red in it though it was mostly gray. When Gussie looked at all the people on the street, she wondered why her family had red hair. Most people in their neighborhood had dark hair. Really dark hair. Her family was different. But everyone said her hair was so pretty.

Frieda was still too little to notice these things. Gussie grabbed Frieda's hand, which was so red and so cold, and they both walked up the stairs on the stoop, and then up and up and up the stairs in the building until they got to the fourth floor. As they approached the door to their house, Gussie heard a loud wailing. Maybe it was Sam. Then she could tell. It was not Sam. It was Mama. And Tillie. And even Hymie. Hymie was almost a man. He was seventeen. Hymie never cried.

"I knew something was wrong."

Frieda looked at her, frightened and confused. "What's wrong? Uh oh."

14

Gussie was torn. Should she go back outside? It was too cold. And there were so many stairs. Should she go inside? She was afraid.

"Let's stay here. Sit down."

Frieda sat. Gussie sat beside her. It was warmer inside, but not warm. There was no stove in the hall. But at least there was no wind. The two little red headed girls huddled together, holding each other to stay as warm as they could. Frieda started to fall asleep. It was past dinner time, almost bed time.

"I'm hungry, Gussie."

"Shhh. They'll come soon."

"All right."

They sat quietly for what seemed like a very long time. Finally, the door opened. Gussie turned around and saw Hymie. His eyes were red, his nose was red. He looked surprised to see the girls.

"Gussie, Frieda. Why are you inside?"

"It was too cold, Hymie. We were scared. And it's getting dark."

Hymie sat down next to them on the floor. He rubbed at his eyes and sniffled. "I was coming to find you. You have to go stay with David tonight."

Usually Gussie would be excited. A night with her big brother David and his wife Annie was always fun, and she and Frieda had more room to sleep since David and Annie did not have a baby. And David was teaching Gussie how to sew clothing; he was a tailor. But now Gussie knew something was not right.

"Why? I want to see Mama and Papa. We've been outside for a long, long time."

"Gussie, listen. Mama can't see you right now."

"Why? Is Sam sick?"

Gussie knew that babies sometimes died. Her friend Sarah had had a baby sister who had died. She wasn't sure what it meant to die, but she knew Sarah never saw her baby sister again.

"No, Sam's not sick."

"Well, then why can't Mama see me?"

Hymie took a deep breath. He said, "Hold on. I'll be right back."

Gussie watched him get up and go back inside. A few minutes later Tillie came out instead. She looked terrible. Her eyes were redder than Hymie's, and her hair was a mess. Tillie was never a mess. What was wrong?

"Tillie, what's wrong?" Gussie burst into tears. She knew now something terrible had happened.

15

"Gussie, Frieda, come here." Tillie gathered both little girls into her arms. Tillie was sixteen. She was almost a grown up, but still knew how to have fun. She could always make Gussie laugh. But not now.

"Papa was very, very sick. He couldn't breathe. His chest wouldn't open for him to breathe."

Gussie swallowed hard. *Would the doctor come?*

"He passed away." Tillie sobbed, choking on her words. *What did pass away mean?*

"What passed? Where?"

"Darn it, Gussie. He died. He's dead. Do you get it now?" Tillie was crying so hard that Gussie could barely hear her.

"No, you're wrong. He can't die. We have a baby. He can't die."

But Gussie knew. Tillie wouldn't lie. Gussie felt her heart sink into her throat. Frieda did not understand.

"But we'll see him tomorrow, right?"

"No, Frieda. We'll never see him alive again. His body is still here, but his soul has left it behind."

Frieda still did not understand, but Gussie did. She'd seen dead rats. Dead cats. Dead pigeons. She knew about Sarah's baby sister.

Gussie pushed Tillie and Frieda away and ran into their house. "Mama! Mama!"

The next day some men came and took her Papa away, and she didn't know where. No one told her what was going on. Mama went off with Tillie and Hymie and also her much older brothers, Max and David and Avram and her sister Toba, who were all married. When Mama came back with her brothers and sisters, they all had big rips in their clothes. Tillie said that people do that when someone in the family dies, but Gussie was too little. She didn't have to rip her clothes. Gussie was glad because she had so few dresses. If she tore one, what would she wear?

People were coming over, bringing food, sitting with Mama. Mama sat on the wash basin, the brothers and sisters sat on the floor. The visitors sat on the day bed where Gussie and Frieda slept at night. Shiva, Hymie called it. Sitting shiva. Was it like shiver? It was cold. Mama cried and rocked Sam, saying, "My poor fatherless baby. What will become of him? What will become of my little girls?"

The older brothers and sisters told Mama, "Don't worry. We'll be with you. We'll help you."

Frieda still didn't understand and kept asking when Papa would be back. And Sam---well, he kept crying but not about Papa. Poor

Sam. He had no Papa. He would never know him at all. There wasn't even a picture of him. Not one photograph. Other people had pictures, but not her family. Mama said it cost too much money.

Gussie sat and thought about Papa's face. It was round, like Mama's and like Hymie's. Sort of like Tillie also. They all had big cheeks that made them always look happy. Papa had dark brown eyes, like Gussie. He was sort of round and short, not like Mr. Weinberg from downstairs who was tall and skinny. And Papa's hair was mostly gray. Avram and the other brothers called him the old man. Papa was older than other fathers on Ridge Street. After all, he had a granddaughter already, Avram's baby girl.

Gussie remembered just a few months back, everyone had been at their house for Rosh Hashanah. They'd all squeezed into the kitchen and front room and eaten Mama's food. Chicken soup. Chicken fricassee. Or brisket. The house smelled of onions and meat. Tillie helped Mama, and Gussie had also. She scrubbed potatoes and carrots.

Papa and the brothers had laughed and told stories in Yiddish. They'd talked about things Gussie could not understand. About the old country. Then Papa said, "Enough! We are here now in America. Let's celebrate." Gussie sat on his lap, and Frieda sat on the other knee. Papa had hugged them both and kissed the tops of their heads. "My shayneh madeles. My pretty American girls."

As she remembered, Gussie felt hot tears racing down her face, dropping onto her neck and into her mouth. She gave out a loud sob. Max looked up and moved closer to her. He put his arms around her.

"You know, Gussie, I was about your age when my mama died. I thought life was never going to be better again. But then Papa married your Mama, and she became my Mama also. Life did get better again."

Gussie knew that Avram, David, Toba, and Max once had a different mother. Her name was Chaya, and she'd died when they all were living in the old country. Gussie did not know where this old country was. But she knew she lived in America. Papa had called her his American daughter. His first American daughter. Frieda was also his American daughter, and Sam was his American son, but Gussie, he would say, you are our first American child.

Gussie forgot for a minute why everyone was there. She felt better and almost happy. Then someone walked through the door. The door was open. She remembered now that Papa was gone. Forever.

She wanted everything to go back to how it was. But she knew it never would. No matter what Max said.

PART II Isadore comes to America: 1904

CHAPTER 3

Isadore touched the outside of each house, as he walked down St. Andrews Street, each house a different color, a different texture from the next. David was at school, but now that Isadore was fifteen, he was too old for school. He tapped his fingers on each house, counted the steps between each house. The cathedral bells tolled ten. What would he do today? Count the steps between his house and the blacksmith shop again? Watch Mr. Marcovici shoe the horses again?

It was five years since the pogrom, and the streets no longer were stained with blood, but the sounds and images of that day still haunted him. The screams, the moans, the children crying, the sound of glass shattering. Of his own teeth chattering. He'd never forget what he saw that lout from the university do to his uncle Yankel. Poor Yankel who still had nightmares and headaches. Whose cries woke his seven children every night as they tried to sleep. Well, six children.

His cousin Srul had left two years before for America. There was nothing for him in Iasi. Under the most recent laws, Jews were not allowed to vote or to own land. They couldn't be peddlers, journalists, craftsmen, or pharmacists. They couldn't sell tobacco, alcohol, baked goods or soda water. The baker whose cookies and breads had once tickled Isadore's fancy and his nose had left for America. Even the schools were being shut down.

When Srul left in 1902, Isadore couldn't have imagined leaving his family behind, going months without hearing from them, living on his own. But now? He was almost a man. But he had no job, and he was bored. He was ready for something to change his life.

Of course, the Romanian army would be happy to have him, though he could never be an officer. But Isadore did not want to fight in the army. That army did not exist to protect him or his family. But he might not have a choice. It would not be long after his sixteenth birthday in August before the army found him and drafted him into its ranks.

He turned the corner, hoping to find a way to fill the morning hours before he could go home for lunch, and spotted his classmate Hirsh. Hirsh saw him at the same time, and his face lit up with a broad smile.

"Hey, how are you? Are you busy?"

"Busy? With what? Counting the leaves on the trees?"

Hirsh laughed. He found Isadore's sarcasm refreshing.

"Actually, that sounds like fun. Let's go find a tree." Hirsh grabbed Isadore's arm and nudged him away from the crowded street towards the park near the National Theater. They found a bench under a tree, and Hirsh slowly lifted his eyes to gaze through the leaves at the blue sky above. It was April, and the air was chilly and a bit raw. Isadore pulled his collar up and his hat down over his ears, but Hirsh just kept staring at the leaves.

Isadore snickered. "You're in the clouds, aren't' you?"

A gang of tall, heavy-set boys their age passed by. Boys from the other side of town. They clustered together across from where Isadore and Hirsh were sitting. One yelled out, "Get lost, you dirty yids. Who needs you in our park?" Isadore clenched his hands and narrowed his eyes. He was short and wiry---like his father Moritz. Hirsh was not much bigger. There was no way they could take on this group of toughs, but how could they sit there and just take that abuse?

"What's the matter, Yid, you afraid of us?"

Isadore stood up. Hirsh pulled him back and whispered, "Don't mess with them. There are six of them, two of us. What's the point?"

"The point? We're almost men---we can't be treated like animals or babies."

Hirsh stood up and pulled Isadore by the arm, saying, "Come with me. I've got a plan. I'm leaving here."

Isadore's eyes popped open.

"You're leaving? How? When?"

"Not here. Let's go back to my house and have coffee."

The thugs were still hovering, moving closer like a herd of cows. Slowly moving towards them, fists raised.

"You can have your stupid park bench." Isadore shouted at them. "Only little baby boys fight over benches."

The gang started running towards them. Isadore grabbed Hirsh by the sleeve and pulled him with a jerk.

"Run, run as fast as you can," he yelled at Hirsh. *I might be small*, Isadore thought, *but at least I am fast*. Hirsh struggled to keep up, and the gang of toughs was still chasing them. Finally, Isadore turned a corner and pulled Hirsh into the butcher's store with him. As he caught his breath, he saw the group of boys run past the shop, not realizing he and Hirsh were inside. Hirsh laughed.

"What fools! We are faster and smarter than they are!" Hirsh said proudly.

Isadore wasn't feeling as proud. "Maybe we were stupid. Or cowardly. I hate running away like that."

Hirsh shrugged. "Who cares? We're safe."

They waited a few minutes and after looking up and down the street and seeing no sign of their tormenters, they walked to Hirsh's house. They sat at the table, sipping the coffee that Hirsh had poured. Isadore couldn't wait any longer to hear what Hirsh was planning.

"So when are you leaving, if you go? Where are you going? And how are you getting there?" he asked impatiently.

Hirsh responded, "Oh, I'm going. My brother bought me a ticket for the ship from Hamburg in October. You know he's in America? Philadelphia. I have to leave by July 15 to be sure to get to Hamburg in Germany in time to catch the ship. Maybe you can get a ticket also?"

Isadore shrugged and looked at the floor. He said, "I have no money since I have no work, and my father's earnings go to support the family."

Isadore wished he had a big brother in America. Srul was there, but all his earnings were to get his own family tickets out of Iasi. Then Isadore remembered that Mama's big brother Gustav was in America and her sister Zusi. Maybe they would help with the ticket for the ship.

Isadore then asked Hirsh, "OK, but how are you paying for the trip across Romania, Hungary, and Germany to get to the ship? Did your brother buy you a train ticket also?"

"Ah," said Hirsh, "I am going as a Fusgeyer! We earn our way across the continent by putting on performances for the citizens of the towns where we stop. I wish you could come with me---it would be fun, and we will get to America where we can live as free men and earn a real living."

Isadore's eyes lit up. A chance to perform? To be part of a theatrical troupe while seeing the world? It sounded too good to be true. He would finally get to experience theater from the inside, as a performer, after all the years of listening to his father's stories or watching performances from the back where his father worked the theater lights. And he would be able to pay most of his way to America, if only his parents could help out with the cost of the ship. How could he possibly not go?

Isadore responded, "I have to talk to my parents, but if they agree, I'm going with you, walking out of this place with you all the way to that ship and to America."

"One more thing, Izzy. If they see you are turning sixteen, they might draft you immediately. I won't be sixteen until long after we sail, but when is your birthday?"

Isadore frowned. The boat left not long before his birthday.

"August."

Isadore couldn't wait to get home and talk to his parents.

"Thanks for the coffee, and for the talk. I've got to get home," he said as he stood up to leave. He needed some time alone to figure out how to bring up the subject with his parents.

As he sat at the table in their house after dinner that evening, Isadore continued to rehearse in his head what he needed to tell his parents. He turned on the radio that sat next to the table. One of their few luxuries was a radio, and nothing soothed Isadore's mind like the music of the opera. As he sat there that night with the sounds of Puccini's arias playing on the radio, he thought about his family. His mother was cooking behind him, and his father was at work, expected home fairly soon. David sat on the other side of the table, reading something for school, kicking his feet against the table. Betty was lying on the floor, hugging her little cloth doll against her, and humming along with the music.

Yes, he had to go, but what would happen to his parents? His father had lost both his parents before he was even five years old and had no family aside from his wife and children. Isadore was his first-born child; he would miss him terribly if Isadore left for America. And Isadore had to admit that he would miss his father just as much.

And his mother? True, she still had her sister Perla with her in Iasi, but her older brother Gustav and her younger sister Zusi had already moved to America almost twenty years before. Isadore often saw her staring into space, tears forming in her eyes. He knew that

22

she was missing Gustav and Zusi and that she feared that she would never, ever see them again. It might be more than she could stand if her son left also.

He decided that he would not talk about leaving tonight after all. He would wait for the right time.

For three days Isadore tried to imagine leaving. He tried to imagine staying. It was impossible to stay. He had to leave. He decided he would try again to talk to his parents at Shabbos lunch on Saturday.

Not that Isadore cared much about Shabbos. Or God. What kind of God would let the Jews be treated as they were in Iasi? But he did love the peacefulness of Shabbos. No radio, just reading and eating and talking.

His father came home after shul, and his mother served a big lunchtime meal for the whole family. Moritz lifted the Kiddush cup filled with wine and chanted the Kiddush prayer. His musical voice filled the room, and everyone echoed Amen when he was done. After the prayer over the challah, his father passed a piece to each of them. It melted in Isadore's mouth, the eggy sweet dough so familiar. How would he live without it?

"Mama, Papa, I need to have a talk with you."

His mother looked at him suspiciously.

"I'm listening," she said. His father nodded at him as well.

Isadore took a deep breath. He avoided his mother's eyes and looked at his father.

"I have been thinking about going to America. Soon."

His mother put down the ladle she'd been using to serve the soup to the family. It clattered into the pot. No one said a word. Then his father cleared his throat.

After a few seconds, his father said, "Why? Why now? Why so soon?"

"Because I'll be sixteen this summer, Papa, and I don't want to be drafted into the army. I don't want to serve with those bastards."

Moritz shook his head and said, "Isadore, it's Shabbos, and your brother and sister are here. I don't disagree with you about the army, but let's try to maintain a calm and civil tone here."

Isadore apologized under his breath, and then said, "If you agree with me, does that mean you'll help me go?"

His mother put her hand on her husband's hand and turned to Isadore.

"Not yet. Your father should go first. He can earn money and then send for you and the rest of us. You are just a boy."

"If the army thinks I am old enough to be a soldier, then I am old enough to go to America."

"Don't talk back to your mother. And anyway, how will you do this? How will you get there?" said his father.

"I will go with the Fusgeyers. Hirsh is going, also."

"What is a Fusgeyer?" his mother snorted.

Isadore explained, "We will go in a large group---it will be safe. We all walk together. And we will make money along the way by putting on plays and selling tickets."

His father's eyes brightened when he heard about the theatrical aspects of the group. His mother just sat quietly, avoiding Isadore's eyes.

Isadore said, "But I'll need your help to pay for the ship's ticket. I need to be able to purchase the ticket before we leave because without a ticket, I won't be able to cross into Hungary or Germany. No one wants more Jews moving into their country. They want to be sure we're leaving."

His mother shook her head. "No, we have no money. You aren't going."

Isadore knew that once his mother had spoken, his father would not contradict her. Isadore took another bite of the challah, now tasting bitterness hidden inside of it.

His father turned his attention to David. "How's school, David? What are you learning this week?"

Isadore knew the conversation was over.

CHAPTER 4

A week went by, then another. It was getting closer to May, and Hirsh was leaving in just five weeks. Isadore couldn't stand to listen to him chattering on about the upcoming trip. What would Isadore do once his friend left? Counting the leaves seemed like his only choice now. Or perhaps the cobblestones. How would he get out of Iasi now?

He once again found himself in the park, this time alone. It was warmer now than when he'd been here with Hirsh, but the skies were cloudy and dark. Storm clouds rumbled in the distance beyond the forest outside the city, but Isadore hardly noticed.

Who cares? he thought. *So I get wet. Who will care? I will die anyway, staying here.*

He picked up a few stones and leaves lying on the ground and made a pattern on the bench, then wiped them off with one hand, watching them scatter to the ground.

"Hey, yid, we told you to stay out of our park."

Three of those thugs from the last time were standing ten feet away, one with his hands on his hips and a snarl on his face. The other two had their hands behind their backs.

I am not running this time. What's the point? Isadore thought. He turned to the group before him and said, "It's not your park, you jerks."

The thug in the front moved closer, sticking his face almost into Isadore's.

"Yeah, you think so, you stinking kike?"

Isadore stood up. The thug who'd spoken stood over him, at least nine inches taller. Isadore wasn't budging this time. He took one of the rocks he'd found and grabbed it in his fist.

Suddenly, the three toughs jumped him. All three all over him so that he didn't know where to turn or kick. Someone's fist smashed into his nose so hard that Isadore felt his teeth shake. He saw blood running onto his shirt, but before he could wipe it off, he felt the toe of a boot land on the soft part of his stomach. He vomited, but he refused to cry, he refused to plead with them. He felt the rock in his hand and swung his arm as hard as he could, landing a solid hit with the rock on the head of one of his attackers, who yelped in pain.

But the two others only got angrier, kicking Isadore over and over, hitting him with sticks and rocks. He heard a loud crack after one of the toughs swung a large stick against Isadore's arm. Isadore curled his body into a ball, giving in to the beating and hoping it would stop.

Finally, it stopped. He heard the one who had first attacked him mutter, "We're done with this one. Let him go. He's just a little rat anyway. Look at that long hooked nose. Those beady eyes."

The three toughs got up, kicked him each one more time, and walked away. They didn't even run. They had nothing to hide, no one to run from.

Isadore groaned and felt the rain start to fall on his face. That was the last thing he remembered.

When he woke up, he was home. *How did I get here?* He thought. He started to sit up, but when he moved his arm to push himself up, he gasped. An excruciating pain surged through his arm, spreading throughout his body. Everywhere he touched his body or his face made him wince with pain. He couldn't even turn from one side to the other.

His father came in to see him and helped him sit up on the bed. David had been sleeping in the front room so that Isadore had more space. Isadore felt dizzy as he tried to hold himself up in the bed. His father could barely look at him.

"Do I look that bad?" Isadore asked. Moritz grunted and brought over a mirror. Isadore groaned when he saw himself in the reflection. His nose, already large enough, was broken and purple and swollen. His eyes were black and blue, and his whole face was swollen like a balloon.

His father rubbed his hands together, looking at his wounded child, and said gravely, "Why were you alone in the park? Don't you know better than that?"

Isadore sat up as tall as he could, "I can't live like this anymore. This is our city, and I should be able to go anywhere I want. And when they came after me, I decided I wasn't going to run, Papa. Not anymore. It's not manly."

"Well, that was pretty foolish---to get yourself hurt like that. Being a man isn't about pride. It's about responsibility."

Isadore snorted. Responsibility? For what? He wanted to be free of responsibility, not saddled with it.

Moritz pulled a folded piece of paper from his pocket. Then he said, "This came yesterday right before we learned you'd been beaten. So your mother and I talked and we agree. It's time for you to go."

Isadore took the paper from his father. His draft notice. He'd have to report to the army in August when he turned sixteen.

"But how, Papa? What about the ticket?"

"Mama sent a telegraph to your uncle Gustav. He helped your cousin Srul come to America, and he said he will help you also."

Isadore gulped. Did he really want this? Couldn't his whole family come with him?

Then his father cleared his throat and put his hands on his son's head, looking right into his eyes, saying, "Isadore, when you get to America, you will be our representative. Our sponsor. You will work hard, save money, and then we will find a way to join you there. Lots of our friends are leaving, and even Perla and Yankel are talking about leaving. After all, their Srul is already gone. And Gustav and Zusi--- your mother aches to see them again. We all hope to get to America as soon as we can. So yes, you can leave. We place our trust and hope in you and in God and know that we will see you again in America."

Isadore felt his eyes fill with tears.

"Mama is really agreeable to this?"

"Ask her yourself. When you can move a bit, we will have a family talk."

The next day Isadore slept late, but when he woke up, he was hungry and realized he hadn't eaten at all since the attack. It was Shabbos, and everyone was home. By the time he managed to get out of bed and limp into the front room, he'd missed the Kiddush and challah, but was in time for the soup.

"Mama, can I have some soup?" Isadore asked with hesitation. It even hurt to move his jaw.

She wouldn't even look at him, his face was so bruised and purple and broken. His father helped him to his chair, and Mama placed the bowl of hot soup in front of him. His eyes teared from the sting as the hot soup touched against his split lips. David grimaced when he looked at Isadore's face, and Betty just stared at the table.

"Mama, you're all right with me leaving?" Isadore said quietly, looking at his mother, who still wouldn't look at him.

"No, I'm not happy about it, but what choice do I have? To see you beaten like a mule or shot in the army is no choice. But a deal is a deal. You must go and work. No time for playing or girls. You have a job---to earn money so we can all come to America. Do you understand?"

He nodded.

"One more thing," said his father, wiping a drop of soup from his son's chin. "The army. If they see your name and age on the ticket, they may never let you leave the country. We need to consider what will happen then."

Isadore had been avoiding thinking about that. He'd take his chances. He'd get away.

Before they could say anything else, David spoke up. "Look, I won't be sixteen for almost a year and a half—not til next November. Maybe Izzy can use my name, my birth date. Who would know? Then I will try and come myself long before next November when I will be sixteen."

Isadore looked at his brother and laughed. "But David, you are taller than I am, and we don't look alike at all. Who would believe that I was David Goldschlager?"

David chuckled, "True, you are a little guy. But what do those stupid officials know? They don't know you or me. There's no pictures on the ticket. Those bureaucrats probably won't care---one less Jew for them to worry about, one less troublemaker. It's worth the risk--- what other choice do you have?"

Isadore nodded, but then said, "But what if you can't get out before next November? What will you do then? I'd never forgive myself if you were arrested or drafted instead of me."

David sighed. He was fourteen. Life still seemed easier to him. He still had school and a life in Iasi. He wasn't ready to leave or even to think about leaving.

"I have over a year to figure this out, and who knows? Maybe things will change. We have to get you out now."

Isadore turned to his brother. He rubbed his head and punched his arm. If his body hadn't ached so much, he would have wrestled David to the ground and kissed him. David didn't think what he was doing was such a big deal, but Isadore knew that it was.

Betty, who was only eight years old and who'd said nothing during this whole time, stared at her brothers. Isadore knew she was a bit jealous of their closeness. She was so much younger and had no siblings close to her in age. But Betty had a special place in her parents' hearts. She was their girl---their princess. She was their baby. Everyone pampered her, even her brothers. To her, life in Iasi probably seemed fine.

Betty finally spoke up. She turned to Isadore and said, "You are ruining our family! You're making everyone sad. I hate you!"

Isadore was stung by her words. He looked at her and said, "Betty, I'm going to go to America where you'll be able to have lots of dolls and nicer clothes and live like a real princess. I'm going to make sure that you get to live in a place that is so much better than Iasi. I promise you."

He knew Betty was not convinced. From her eight year old perspective, what could be better than her little house on St. Andrews Street with the view of the cathedral spires? What could be better than her mother's soup? What could be better than her father's stories about the theater and his music? What about her cousins? What friends would she ever have who would be as dear to her as they were?

She looked back at Isadore and said, "I don't know. I just know that right now I am really angry." And with that she ran from the table in tears.

Isadore looked at his family. His mother still wouldn't look him in his eye and his father hadn't said another word. David was slurping his soup, but his parents weren't scolding him. Isadore shrugged and tried to get some soup past his tender lips. He would be leaving soon. His sore lips curled up in a slight smile, but his hands felt cold against bowl of hot soup.

CHAPTER 5

Isadore had his ticket, purchased by his Uncle Gustav. Gustav was a big success in New York, where he had his own painting business. He'd been trained by Uncle Yankel when he was a young man. According to Mama, Uncle Gustav had many children, some of whom were close to Isadore in age. They were born in America. Real Americans. He couldn't wait to meet them all.

A few days before he was supposed to leave, his father explained to him that Aunt Zusi's husband Moshe Mintz was to meet him at the boat, not Uncle Gustav.

"Why can't Uncle Gustav meet me?"

"He's busy working. He has a large family to feed, you know."

"Doesn't Zusi's husband have to work?"

"I don't know. Maybe he works nights. I don't know anything about him at all. Your mother hardly hears from her sister Zusi. But Gustav said he'd get Moshe to meet you. You'll be fine."

"All right. I've never met either of them anyway, and I can hardly remember Zusi. I was just a little tyke when she left Iasi." What difference did it make who met him as long as he got there?

He pressed the ticket tightly to his chest, silently thanking his brother again for taking this risk. He'd told everyone to call him David, not Izzy, and he hoped he would remember to use that name whenever stopped by a police officer or any other official. He had a canvas duffel bag to use to take his few items of clothing. Since they would be walking, he could not carry very much. There were about seventy-five others in their group, and they would pile their supply and food bags in one horse-drawn cart so everyone was limited to one bag. Isadore was glad that there would be a horse accompanying them. This horse would not be as magnificent as those in Mr. Marcovici's stable, but he still remembered how strong that horse had felt that day of the pogrom. A horse would be good to have along.

He went to say goodbye to Aunt Perla and Uncle Yankel. His uncle, who always had seemed somewhat confused after the injuries he'd suffered during the pogrom, just stared into space, tears in his blurred blue eyes. Aunt Perla hugged him and told him to be careful and to be prepared for things not to be as he might expect.

"In his letters home, Srul said that life was hard there, too," she warned him.

He didn't know what Aunt Perla meant. He had no expectations---did he? Life might be hard in American, but it couldn't be worse than Iasi.

The next morning Isadore woke up before sunrise. He'd tried to sleep, had tossed and turned for hours, finally dozing off only to wake up again a few hours later. No one else in his house was awake. He glanced around his room. David was sound asleep on the other side of the bed, not a care in the world. Betty was on the little bed just a few feet from there. David would be happy not to be sharing a little bed with him anymore. In the dark Isadore could not see too much, but in his head he catalogued all the things in this small room. He wasn't leaving much behind---a few school books, some clothes, that was it.

The night before his mother had made a special dinner for him, all his favorites. Eggplant salad with tomatoes, cucumbers, and radishes. Kreplach. Pickled chicken feet. Would he ever taste these treats again? Did anyone make them in America?

The meal had been wonderful, but the tension around the table was hard to ignore. Betty didn't look at him once. David, who was usually cheerful, was very quiet, rubbing his hands together nervously and hardly eating a thing.

His mother had not said a word, other than, "Eat up. You don't know what you will be eating after this. Eat." His father had tried to make conversation about anything other than the fact that Isadore was leaving.

Isadore pulled himself quietly out of bed and walked out of the bedroom into the front room. He touched the table, the chairs, the stove and the radio, trying to store some images in his brain. He walked out the front door. No one was on the street. He looked up at the spires of the Cathedral. Would he ever see it again? Was this his last time on St. Andrews Street? He'd lived no place else his whole life. This narrow street with all the houses lined up against the street, a Jewish family living in each one, was not beautiful or grand, but it was home. But he was ready to go.

When he walked back into the house, his mother was awake. She sat down with Isadore at the little table and sipped her tea.

"Isadore, remember. Be careful. Follow your own good instincts as you travel and when you get to America. There will be lots of temptations wherever you go, but we are relying on you. We are looking for you to be there for us, to work hard, to save money. We want to be with you as soon as we possibly can."

"Of course, Mama. I won't let you down. I promise."

His father entered the room, looking somewhat disheveled, more so than usual. He put his hand on Isadore's shoulder. "You should go soon. I can't bear to watch you go, so please make it quick. Go wake up David and Betty and say your good-byes. Then go. Before we ask you to stay."

Isadore opened the bedroom door. David stirred. He was now done with school for the year and probably for good. He was going to train to be a hat maker. He didn't want to wake up this early. Isadore took the pillow and slammed it on his brother's head.

"What are you doing? I am sleeping!"

"I am going, David. It's time."

David slowly sat up, rubbing his eyes. "Now? It's so early. Why?"

"Papa wants me gone. He says a long goodbye is too hard. He's right. I'm ready."

David stared at his brother, looking at his deep-set dark brown eyes, his long nose, his quirky smile. "Well, you may be ready. I'm not, but I never will be. When I next see you, I hope you are the mayor of New York or a star in the opera. Save me some of the pretty girls in New York. I hope to be there before next November. And don't do anything to embarrass me---since you are now David Goldschlager!"

Isadore gave him a quick hug, looking into his brother's eyes that were shaped so much like his own, but a beautiful clear blue in color. David was taller, more handsome, more easy-going than Isadore. Isadore would miss him. But he had every reason to hope that he would see him in just a few months.

He then turned to Betty, sound asleep, and tickled her arm. "Bets, I am leaving. Don't wake up---just say goodbye."

Betty opened her blue eyes, looked at her brother just as intensely as David had done, put her arms up to him for a hug. "Don't forget me."

"Never. I will be there to meet you when you get to New York. Just don't grow up too fast, and keep away from trouble, princess."

Betty turned her head into her pillow and sobbed. Isadore left the room, not looking behind him, his eyes filling with tears.

His mother grabbed him to her and kissed his head, tears dropping into his hair. Then his father did the same. Isadore grabbed the canvas bag at the door, walked out, closed it behind him, and walked with his eyes forward down St. Andrews Street for the very last time. He would, in fact, never see it again.

CHAPTER 6

They'd been on the road a little more than a week, walking, rehearsing, walking, rehearsing. Tonight was their first real performance. It was the story of David and Goliath, and Isadore had been cast as David—not because he was any better than the others, but because he was the shortest and looked the most youthful.

He fidgeted in the back of the barn, biting at his finger nails, hearing his mother's voice in his head, nagging him about ruining his nails. He pulled his fingers from his mouth and tapped his feet instead.

"Stop doing that, David." One of the older girls in the group scolded him.

David. They called him David. And now he was playing David.

He pulled the slingshot he was carrying out of his pocket and practiced pulling back on the sling. With nothing in it, of course.

But another member of the troupe saw him and called out to him to stop.

"It's not loaded. Really? Do you think I'm stupid?" he responded.

He listened to what was going on in front of the wall that separated him from those on stage. The first skit was a comedy, some farce about two men who are chasing the same girl who likes a third man. The audience was laughing. The room was full---children and adults.

Isadore's heart pounded. What if he failed at this? What if he hated it?

He heard applause and realized that the silly skit was over. First King Saul went on stage and did a long speech about the wars they were losing to the Philistines.

Then it was his turn.

The room was silent. All eyes turned to him.

"Your majesty, King Saul, I am the shepherd David, here to serve you. I can defeat the giant Goliath, leader of the Philistines."

Everyone laughed. The soldiers. King Saul. And the audience. Isadore knew he looked nothing like a warrior. He knew why they were laughing.

Saul then launched into another speech, and the other actors took their turns speaking their lines. Isadore looked out again at the audience. Their eyes were on him. They knew the story. They knew he was the hero. People were smiling at him, waiting in anticipation for his next line.

He took a deep breath and smiled, his shoulders relaxed. He was going to be just fine. This was going to be fun.

Isadore felt the warmth of the sun on his face before he opened his eyes. It took a second to remember where he was. He was lying on the ground about eight miles from their next stop, the town of Targu Mures in Romania, about two hundred miles from Iasi. He stretched out his arms and legs from the scratchy blanket that he had wrapped around his body when he went to sleep the night before.

He sat up and looked around. He and his fellow travelers had been on the road for over three weeks now. They'd passed through the mountains between Iasi and Targu Mures, and at times the climbing and the heat had been draining. It was officially summer now. When he looked around him, he had to smile. In three weeks these people had become like family to him.

About twenty feet away were five young women, all about two or three years older than Isadore. Most of them had older brothers traveling with them so that they would be protected. Isadore had not known any of these girls back home, although some looked familiar. Now they were his friends.

He'd never had a close friend who was a girl before. He was fascinated with how they were able to talk to each other and to him and the others about all their feelings and fears and thoughts. Although Isadore missed his family terribly and spent hours at night, wiping his tears and wondering how they were all doing, he never said a word to anyone about being homesick. The girls, however, were always consoling each other, talking about how much they missed their mothers, their fathers, even their younger siblings. Isadore wished he also could share his feelings.

But beyond his envy of their closeness to each other, he was fascinated by their eyes, their mouths, the legs, their bodies. Especially Malke. Her thick red hair was almost like mahogany, not

35

as orange as many red heads. She had an oval shaped face and full lips, eyes that had a mix of green and brown in them. Her eyes had a bright and piercing look, and her lips often curled into a half-smile as she talked. Her nose was long, but only made her eyes and lips stand out even more. She was eighteen, two years older than Isadore, and an inch taller than he was, which wasn't very tall at all. Her older brother Reuben was also part of their troupe. Although Isadore had hardly yet said a word to Malke, he found that he could not stop thinking about her.

He turned over onto his stomach and breathed deeply. It was hard being a young man surrounded by young women with no parents around to chaperone. Day and night, they were together. He remembered his mother's words about resisting temptation and staying focused on his goals. Was this what she meant?

Just then he heard someone whistling. He sat up and saw Isaac, one of the older members of the group, gathering some wood for the fire. Isaac was almost thirty. He and his wife Rivka were in charge of the theatrical productions. Isadore was glad that there were people like Isaac and Rivka who were worrying about the details. There was also the other leader, Marcus, who was overseeing all the other details---the money, the arrangements for the posters and tickets to be sold in the towns before and when they arrived, the routes they would follow, and the timetable they needed to keep to be sure that they arrived in Hamburg in time to catch their boat by October 1.

They performed in barns, in fields, in homes, and in shuls. In some towns the crowds were quite large; in other towns perhaps only ten or twenty people would show up. Isadore loved performing. It made him forget about home and escape into the story he was telling. The girls in the audiences always giggled whenever he sang or danced. It made him blush, but he did enjoy the attention.

But the performances weren't just for fun. They used the money they made from selling tickets to buy food and supplies to get them to the next town, and sometimes people would donate food and other items to them. They never traveled on Shabbos, observing it as a day of rest wherever they were. Wherever they went, families invited them to their homes for a Shabbos meal or even just a breakfast.

Isadore stood up. It was time to start another day of walking. They had to get started as soon as possible because they had a performance in Targu Mures tonight. Every day was getting him closer and closer to America. Everyone was getting up. Time to break up camp again and get moving.

Five hours later, the hot summer sun was almost unbearable. His clothes, already getting a bit faded and tattered from the weeks of walking and sleeping outside, were soaked with sweat, and he was constantly wiping his face and forehead with his one handkerchief.

His fellow Fusgeyers were cranky and uncomfortable also. There were only sixty-eight of them after seven had left the group, finding the traveling too hard or finding leaving home too hard. They usually walked about ten miles a day, but today's heat was slowing them down. Although they had planned to get to Targu Mures by nightfall, it was looking less and less likely that they would make it in time.

Isadore turned to Hirsh, grumbling about his sunburn and his aching feet. Hirsh just grinned and said, "Remember---soon we will be in America where the sun is never too hot, the rain is never too cold, and the beds are soft as a kitten."

Isadore rolled his eyes.

Then suddenly, the skies opened on them. Thundershowers started and cooled them off, but left them soaking wet. His shoes squeaked from the water that burst through the open seams with each step he took. He was tired and hungry, sun-burned and chilled, and the mosquitoes were relentless whenever they walked near puddles or water. Why had he done this? Was it worth it?

Finally, at eight o'clock, the group leaders decided to stop walking before it got too dark. They found a clearing in a nearby woods, and they all settled down to try and sleep on the wet and soggy forest floor. Isadore tossed and turned, unable to get comfortable as he felt all the rocks and sticks under his blanket roll and felt bugs crawling up his pants legs and buzzing around his ears.

Then Malke started singing in a soft, delicate voice. The refrain of a Yiddish folk song his father used to sing to him when he was a child. Others joined in, and Isadore felt suddenly comforted.

He drifted off to sleep, hoping tomorrow would be easier.

Two weeks later, he finally had a chance to talk to Malke alone. Malke had been cast as Gretel to his Hansel, and they had spent time together, rehearsing. During their first performance, Isadore took Malke's hand as he pulled her away from the witch in their play. His heart pounded as he felt her warm hand in his.

37

Afterwards, he said to her, "That was a good performance. But it made me miss my little sister. You're lucky---your brother is here with you."

Malke replied, "Yes, but my little sister is still at home with my parents. I miss them all. Should we go talk about our next performance?"

The two of them then found a spot near the place where the horse and wagon were tied and exchanged stories about their families and rehearsed their lines a bit. The horse whinnied at one point, and Isadore stood up and rubbed the back of the horse's neck.

"You like horses?" he asked Malke.

"Yes, yes, I love animals. I miss my dog so much." Her eyes became misty.

Isadore touched her arm and said, "I don't have a dog, but I used to spend a lot of time at Mr. Marcovici's stable, helping with his horses. I've been taking care of this old girl also." He patted the horse on the rump as he spoke.

"Maybe I could help you? Taking care of her, I mean?"

"Sure! I'd love to have your help," Isadore said with a smile.

And so he and Malke took on the responsibility of caring for the group's horse. Every day they fed and brushed her, making sure she had enough water and a warm blanket on nights when it was cooler, especially in the mountains. Sometimes they even took the horse out to an open field and took turns riding her. Then they would sit and talk while the horse cooled down. They named her Chocolate because of her dark brown hide, but it was a name that they didn't share with anyone else.

After another two weeks went by and they'd been on the road for two months and had walked four-hundred miles, they were finally near the border with Hungary in the town of Salonta. Tonight would be their last performance in Romania. Tomorrow, they would cross into Hungary. Isadore had been feeling a bit anxious and excited all day. It was almost his birthday. He wanted to be out of Romania before he officially turned sixteen, even if his ticket said he was only now fourteen.

He stood towards the side of the stage, waiting to enter for his big scene. They were doing the story of Joseph and his brothers, and Isadore was Benjamin, the little brother. He had to tell his parents, Jacob and Rachel, that their son Joseph was gone. It was a hard scene to play; every time, Isadore would think about leaving his own parents and how sad they were, how brave they were to let him go. Too often he would choke up a bit as he delivered his lines in this scene.

But now he was watching the audience, looking at the people who were watching the show on stage. They were spellbound, quietly watching the story unfold---Joseph showing off the wonderful coat his mother had made for him, the other brothers jealously complaining about him, then conspiring against him to punish him for his arrogance. Isadore always thought about his brother David during that scene, David who had loaned him his name so that Isadore could leave without being drafted. Sure, they'd had their moments of rivalry, jealousy, arguments and squabbling. But never had they betrayed each other as Joseph's brother did to him. Isadore felt his ticket in his pocket and muttered a thank you to David under his breath. What if his brother had been jealous and spiteful like Joseph's brothers had been?

Isadore looked across the stage and saw Malke. So much had happened in the last few weeks. More and more, Isadore dreamed about Malke, both sleeping dreams and dreams before he fell asleep. He dreamed of holding her and kissing her, and in his sleeping dreams, sometimes he dreamed that she loved him and that they were riding off on the horse together. But more often he dreamed that she was mocking him and his feelings for her. He would wake up agitated and confused. He had never touched her for real---except on stage when he had to hold her hand as they escaped from the witch. He hadn't told her how he felt. He didn't want to risk losing her friendship.

He found himself staring at her now and looked away before she caught his eye. He noticed that the scene before his big scene was ending. It was almost time to go onstage. It was almost time to be Benjamin, breaking his parents' hearts.

CHAPTER 7

The next night Isadore stood with Hirsh, each clasping their papers tightly, each breathing loudly. Marcus was standing at the front of the group, talking to the Romanian guards who protected the border, asking for permission to cross into Hungary and leave Romania behind. The Romanian guards were lined up, five of them, all on horses that made the Fusgeyers' little horse look more like a pony or a mule. They had their pistols in holsters. Not one had a smile on his face. Not one would make eye contact with Marcus, although two of the guards were watching the young women, leering at them and chuckling.

Suddenly, the five guards all jumped off their horses, pulled out the guns, and charged towards the bedraggled and exhausted group of young people waiting to cross the border. The guards grabbed their bags and duffels and emptied everything on the ground, pushing and yelling at them all. They tore through their food and papers, looking for jewelry or anything of value. No one was allowed to take anything of value out of the country without permission.

Isadore held his breath the entire time, fearing that the police would question him about his ticket, his name. His birthday was this week. What if they knew who he really was? Everyone in the Fusgeyers called him David; he had insisted from the beginning. Most did not even know his real name.

A large guard, at least a foot taller than Isadore, approached him. He stared at him intently, making him feel naked and two years old. The guard's large bulbous nose was red and pimply, and his teeth protruded through his lips. Isadore stood as still as he could, keeping his eyes straight ahead, saying nothing.

The guard said, "Papers. Where are your papers?"

Isadore reached into his pocket, his precious ticket tight in his fist. He pulled it out, the guard breathing down on him, stomping one foot impatiently. The guard grabbed the papers from Isadore's hand before he even had a chance to hand them over to him.

"When is your birthday?" The guard growled at him.

"November 4, sir." David's birthday, not his birthday. He swallowed hard.

"What year, you imbecile? Did you think I was going to send you a gift?"

"1889." David's birth year. Stay calm, stay focused.

The guard stared at the papers for what seems like ten minutes.

"What is your father's name?"

"Moritz Goldschlager."

"He let you go. You must be a worthless good-for-nothing for a father to let his son leave. He must hate you a lot." The guard pushed against Isadore's arm, the one that had been broken by those thugs in Iasi. Isadore winced.

Isadore counted under his breath. He would not let this monster get him angry. His arm throbbed. He said nothing, but rubbed his arm, letting out an involuntary whistle.

The guard looked at Isadore. "Are you mocking me, you little shit?"

Before Isadore could say anything, the guard smacked him across the head, causing him to fall to the ground, kicked him once in the back, but then told him he could go.

"Romania doesn't need little kikes like you who can't work, too small for the army, and bound to be another useless beggar. Leave before I kick you again."

With that, the guard tossed Isadore's ticket to the ground. Isadore grabbed it, stuck it back in his pocket, and scurried along the ground to where Marcus and the others who had passed inspection were gathering.

Isadore wiped off his pants, bent over in pain, and vomited facing away from the group. No one said a word. Everyone just remained motionless.

When he turned back around, the guard was now questioning Malke, but with a different approach.

"You want to leave our country? Perhaps you have already slept with too many men here, you whore. Give me a kiss or I will put you right back on the streets of Iasi."

Malke kept her head down, saying nothing. Isadore wanted to jump forward to protect her, to kick that guard as hard as he had been kicked. Marcus, as if reading his mind, grabbed his arm, saying, "Stay still. You go near her, and it'll make it worse. Malke will be all right."

Reuben also wanted to go protect his sister, but Isaac held him back.

Malke just stood in silence. The guard looked over her ticket, asked her questions, standing so close to her that she must have felt the sweat dripping off that ugly nose. He put his arm around her waist, and she did not move at all. He kissed the back of her neck and then pushed her forward.

"Ugly Jewess bitch. You aren't good enough for me. Go screw around with those losers over there."

Malke grabbed her papers and walked quietly and calmly to her brother Reuben, who held her against him.

"Is that your beastly husband?"

"I am her brother," Reuben answered.

The guard spat at both of them and turned back to harassing another member of the group. Malke caught Isadore's eyes looking at her, and then they both looked at the ground in shame. Humiliated.

And then the guards took their beloved horse. Chocolate. The one he and Malke had brushed and care for every day. The small brown horse whose large, sad, dark eyes had matched his own large, sad, dark eyes. The horse could not cross the border. It was Romanian, they said. It was valuable. Malke gasped as they grabbed the reins and yanked the horse over to their side, tying it to a tree. Isadore could not look at Malke or at the horse; if he did, he might call out. Then the guards would torment him so more. Maybe even arrest him. All he could do was hope that the guards would treat the horse better than they treated the Jews.

After all was said and done, only one member of the group, Bercu, was arrested and taken away. He had lied about his age, and the guards did not believe he was only fifteen, given his size and the whiskers that were sprouting on his face. They accused him of trying to escape the draft, tied his hands behind his back, beat him with sticks, and threw him into the police wagon. Isadore wanted to fight back, defend Bercu, but Hirsh and Marcus held him back. It was wrong. It was just wrong. He hated Romania, and he could not wait to cross the border. He would not stand for this kind of humiliation again.

As he actually crossed into Hungary, however, he felt his stomach jump a bit. Now he could never return. Now he had placed a barrier between his family and himself. It might be a hateful place, but the people he loved were still there. He swore he would work hard to get them out, and then he would never, ever look back at this place, his homeland for almost sixteen years. He would wash his hands of Romania forever as soon as he could.

Things were different once they entered Hungary. The language was different, the people were different. And they found that their mission had changed. While in Romania, they did not need to explain to their fellow Jews the reasons they were leaving home. Everyone knew. But in Hungary, everyone asked, "Why would you leave your home? Why would you walk out?"

The Fusgeyers were determined to educate everyone and anyone they met about the conditions back in Iasi. The group now started the performances with a short speech describing conditions back home and asking for support for them and for their families still in Romania. It was no longer just fun and games. A somber air hovered over the group wherever they went.

Isadore spent a night with a Jewish family in Budapest when they stopped there five days after crossing the border. In Budapest, the Jews had to live in one particular neighborhood, but conditions otherwise for Jews were not too bad. So the family was puzzled as to why a young man would leave his family and his home. Sure, things weren't good for Jews anywhere, but no one knew what things were like Romania.

Isadore explained. "It's not just that people don't like us there. It's not just that we are poor. The government hates us. The government and the police hate us. We have no rights. We can't work, we can't vote, we can't own property. They beat us, they kill us."

The father shook his head, "Here things are bad, but we do have some rights. The goyim may hate us, but we get some protection from the police. From the State. And I own my house and store. I didn't know that Romania was so different."

Isadore sighed. Why was he born in Romania? Why had his family ever settled there? He had spent so much of his childhood in innocence, not knowing there were other choices. When he saw the attacks in 1899, he woke up to reality, but still assumed that that was just the way the world was. Now he knew it did not have to be that way.

He thought about sitting in the park that day with Hirsh, the day they had run from that gang. And then crossing the border just a week before, the beatings and the abuse he and his fellow Romanian Jews had suffered. He remembered how Hirsh and Marcus had silenced him.

"When I get to America, I will be free," he announced to the family. "When I get to America, I will not be silent any more. I will not let the government or anyone else pick on me or on others simply because we are Jewish or poor or foreign. I will be a man."

After another day of walking after leaving Budapest, Isadore was tired and emotionally drained. He sat by himself away from the group, throwing sticks and stones as far as he could. His shoes had holes, his clothes were torn. He'd had enough. He wished that his time as a Fusgeyer was over.

Malke saw him sitting alone and walked over to him.

"What is going on? Are you all right? You don't seem like yourself."

"I'm myself. What do you mean?"

"You're sulking a lot. By yourself a lot. You don't talk to me or tell me stories anymore."

It hurt him to hear her say it, and he tried to explain.

"The world is evil, Malke. I'm angry. Angry with the world."

Malke suddenly took him by the hand and said, "But you seem angry with me, not just the world. What did I do?"

Isadore pulled his hand away.

"We've been talking and talking for weeks. You are as close to me as anyone I've ever known. But this is the first time you've taken my hand except as part of our stage roles. I can't go on this way. I don't want to be just friends anymore."

He leaned in to kiss her. She put her hands to his lips, and said, "Wait. You can't just kiss a girl like that."

Isadore put his hand on her hand, moving it off her lips. He squeezed her hand against his chest.

"Why not? The world is going to hell, and we don't have much time."

He took his free hand and pulled her closer to him. She bit her lip and started to lean towards him. Isadore leaned in again to kiss her.

But then he suddenly pulled back.

"I can't do this. We have no future, and you're not that kind of girl, I'm not that kind of boy. And we all have bigger worries right now. Like getting to America."

Isadore stood up and walked away. He did not look back. He did not see that Malke was still standing in the same spot, shocked.

CHAPTER 8

Finally they boarded the train for Hamburg. Hirsh rushed up behind him.

"Grab a seat fast. We don't want to stand all the way to Hamburg."

Hirsh pushed past him, moving into a seat by the window.

"Here, sit here. Hurry!"

Isadore grimaced. "What's the big deal? There are plenty of places to sit."

"I wanted a window."

Isadore looked at him quizzically. "But now I don't have a window."

He sat down, stuffing his canvas bag at his feet.

Hirsh started tapping his feet on the floor.

"Stop it, Hirsh. You are making me nervous with all your fidgeting."

"Sorry, Izzy. Just excited."

Isadore said with exasperation, "David. I'm David. Remember?"

"Yeah, yeah."

It was going to be a long ride. Isadore was not sorry that his time with the Fusgeyers was coming to an end. As the traveling drew to a close, they were all tired of performing and tired of sleeping on the ground. At least on the train he had a seat, even if next to Hirsh.

He looked around him and saw his comrades all crowding onto the train. He wasn't sure he'd see most of them ever again once they got to America. Some were going to New York like he was, but many were off to other places. Philadelphia, Boston, Baltimore, Canada--- all places with musical and magical sounding names. Places he'd never heard of before. He had no idea how far any of them were from New York.

Up in the front of the train car he noticed Malke and her brother Reuben were looking for seats. He'd barely talked to Malke in the last few weeks since their last conversation. He didn't even know where she and Reuben were heading. Last time they'd talked about it, she hadn't known. Maybe some place called Ohio or Michigan. Some place where Reuben could have land.

Malke and Reuben were approaching him as they continued to look for seats. He looked up and made eye contact with her. She looked away.

"Malke? Please. Can we talk?" Isadore inquired, grasping her hand as she was about to pass by.

"Not now. We have to find seats. Maybe on the ship," she said in a cold voice, pulling her hand away. Reuben looked at Isadore and shook his head. The two of them pushed on, into the car that followed theirs.

Isadore kicked at the bag at his feet. Perhaps he'd been too hasty that day. Was it too late to make amends? He might never see her again.

Isadore stood against the rail on the wharf, looking at the gray and green water below. He'd never seen the sea before. There was water as far as he could see in front of him, rushing in and out of the harbor in gentle waves, seagulls hovering over the water looking for fish. Isadore sucked in the air with his nose. The salty spray tickled his nose, and he sneezed. And even though the sky was as cold and gray as the water, he could almost feel himself being across the ocean, some place warm and happy and free. He couldn't believe they had made it to Hamburg.

Although his clothes were so worn that beating them with soap and water no longer got them clean, he felt proud to be standing in this seaport city in Germany, hours away from leaving Europe behind. Hundreds of fellow immigrants roamed the streets, sleeping under bridges and in alleys. Jews and Italians and Slavs. The noise and the mixture of languages excited him. He grabbed the rail, feeling his pulse beat against it. He was finally leaving for America.

The ship was in the harbor, and loading would start later that day. It had been almost three months since he'd left home. His parents would be dismayed by his appearance. He had always been a careful dresser, keeping his clothes as neat and unwrinkled as he could. Now he looked like a pauper. His whiskers were scratchy and long; he desperately needed a shave, but barbers were expensive, and his money was running low. They had not performed since boarding the train, and so the expenses now were just draining what was left of their earnings. He worried about how he would look to Uncle Moshe and Aunt Zusi, getting off the boat in America looking like a ragamuffin.

He looked up, and walking towards him he saw Malke and Reuben. As they got closer, Isadore walked towards them and Reuben again sneered at him.

"Reuben, I'd like to talk to Malke---alone, if it's all right."

Reuben eyed him suspiciously.

"Sure, I suppose, if it's all right with Malke."

Malke nodded, and she and Isadore walked off the pier, finding a spot along the water where they could talk. The crowds were growing, the noise increasing, so they stood close by and tipped their heads closer together.

"Malke, I'm sorry. So sorry. I was hasty and angry and stupid. I ruined our friendship, and now I will always regret not having this time together."

Malke's eyes filled with tears. "Will we ever see each other again once we get to America?"

"I don't know. Where are you going?"

"I'm not sure. Reuben decided we'll go to Chicago. From there we'll work and save money to buy land somewhere cheap, he says. I guess we'll see."

"Well, I'll be in New York. I don't know where Chicago is. Maybe it isn't too far."

Isadore grabbed her hand again. This time she didn't pull away. She looked him in the eyes, and he felt his pulse quicken, his body drawn to hers. He put his other hand on her cheek and bent his head towards hers. She took her free hand and touched his lips.

"Not now. Not here. It's really too late."

"Just one kiss?" Isadore put his arm around her, the old injury causing a twinge of pain.

She tilted her head towards his and kissed him on his mouth. She didn't move away when he held her closer to him.

Then suddenly she pushed against his chest, freeing her lips from his.

"That's enough." She said, though her eyes suggested otherwise. "For now, let's enjoy our trip across the ocean."

Isadore pressed her hand in his. "Yes." Then he reluctantly released her hand.

Isadore rolled over on the floor of the ship, adjusting his duffel under his head. Sleeping on the ship was impossible. The crowding, the crying, the smells, the coughing, sneezing, the filth. It had not been what Isadore had expected. If he thought sleeping on the ground as a Fusgeyer was uncomfortable, sleeping on the ship was far worse. It was dark down below where the steerage passengers slept. It smelled like a latrine--- urine and worse. Vomit everywhere from people who were seasick or just plain sick. No decent food to speak of, and not enough water. So many people were sick. Rolling on their stomachs in pain. Babies crying, old people moaning.

Someone was touching his shoulder. Isadore grabbed for his papers deep inside his pocket and looked around to see who was there. Reuben stood above him.

"Malke is sick. So sick. I don't know what to do." Reuben wiped sweat from his brow.

Isadore stood up. He'd barely talked to Malke on the ship. It was so crowded and dark in steerage that it was hard to find anyone. He and Hirsh had remained together, but Malke and Reuben had stayed across the ship where more of the women were sleeping.

Isadore walked over with Reuben to where Malke was lying. Her skin was a pale gray, her lips colorless. She seemed delirious, not recognizing Reuben or Isadore.

"I don't know what to do either. She needs a doctor." Isadore said as calmly as possible.

Isadore had no idea if doctors even came to steerage or if there was any doctor on board at all. A woman nearby called out, "Take her to the sick room. And hush. We're trying to sleep down here."

After asking where the sick room was located, Reuben lifted his sister from the ground and carried her in his arms.

"I will take her there. Thank you for helping. I just didn't know what to do." Reuben said to Isadore.

"Glad to help. Please let me know how she fares." Isadore watched Reuben carry her away.

Four days later, he stood on the upper deck. The sky was lit up with stars, though the sky itself was black. The water was calm, and the breeze was gentle and not too cool. He could see some lights ahead at the horizon. His long trip to America was almost over. His new life would begin, and he would never, ever look back again. It had to be. But what had happened to Reuben and Malke? He hadn't seen them again after that night when Malke had taken ill. He didn't even know if she was still alive.

48

PART III New York City
1904-1909

CHAPTER 9

As the sun rose, he watched the light bounce off the water and then noticed the giant statue standing in the water, a green goddess with her arm raised high. Liberty, he'd heard others call her. Lady Liberty.

Now they were right under her, and the boats in the harbor in front of them were starting to come towards them as fishermen and barges entered the water for a day's work. Isadore looked up at Lady Liberty, her armpit just over his nose. Liberty. What did that mean? Her face was serious, not smiling. Was this his welcome to America?

Then she was behind them, getting smaller again. He turned around again as the ship's engines slowed. Before he realized it, they had docked at the pier. The engine noise sputtered and then cut out, no longer drowning out the sounds of the people around him on the ship's deck. Everyone was pointing and shouting at the city ahead of them. Some were weeping, some laughing. Isadore could hardly breathe with all the people crushing around him. He looked across the pier at the city. There were even more people, rushing by on the street or standing at the pier, gazing at the ship. So many faces, so many people. No one smiling. Like Lady Liberty, everyone looked serious.

It seemed an eternity before the first and second-class passengers disembarked. Isadore rushed to disembark. But no, they weren't going ashore. The guard put up his hand and said sternly, "No, steerage must go through Ellis Island. Wait for your barge."

Now what? A barge? What was a barge? Then he saw a large flat boat almost as big as the ship. Everyone was rushing now, pushing and shoving to get on the barge. Once the barge pulled out, several people panicked. Were they taking them back to Europe? Isadore ran to the edge of the barge and spotted an island that looked like it had a castle on it. Or maybe a prison? Isadore was not sure.

"What's that? Why aren't we going on the land? Where are we going?" he shouted to the man who happened to be standing next to him, trying to be heard over the crowd.

"That's Ellis Island. Don't you know?"

Isadore felt a bit embarrassed. "Why are we going there?"

"Ha! You think they just let anyone in? You think they don't want to inspect you and make sure you are acceptable? Are you a fool?"

Isadore gave the man a dirty look and walked away. What did the man mean by "inspect"?

"Isadore!" He turned around and saw Hirsh, his hat flying back, running to him. "We are here, Izzie, we are here!" They hugged each other, slapping each other on the backs, and snorted with laughter.

"Yes, but what is Ellis Island? What is that? A castle? A prison?" Isadore said with concern.

"It's where they inspect us and make sure it's all right for us to go to America," Hirsh stated with assurance.

"Now? Now that we have traveled for months and puked and suffered on that ship? Now they decide if we can come?"

"Don't worry. You're young and healthy and strong. You're not going to be a burden on America. And you have family here. You are not going to have any problems getting through. You still have some money saved, right? Don't worry."

Isadore breathed more easily. As they talked, the barge pulled up to the pier, and the crew was now tying it down, getting ready for them all to disembark. Isadore grabbed his duffel and for the millionth time since he'd left home, felt for his papers tucked into his pocket. He was all set.

But where were Malke and Reuben? He had not seen them since that night when Reuben had taken her to the sick room. As Isadore and Hirsh moved forward like cattle being prodded along by a dog, moving closer to the gangplank, Isadore felt his hands getting sweaty. What if he didn't see Malke and Reuben before they got off the barge? What if they had died?

Hirsh tapped his arm, as if reading his mind. "Look, down there, Malke and Reuben. They are just getting off." He saw Malke scanning the faces until she saw him waving at her.

Isadore yelled over the edge of the barge. "Wait for us! We're coming!" She smiled faintly and waved back.

But she also kept moving forward. She had no choice. The guards were quietly moving people along, saying, "Keep on going. Don't stop.

There are too many of you. You will find each other on the mainland. Just keep going." They were firm, but not at all angry or mean like the police and the guards in Romania.

Isadore sighed. He would find Malke once they were done with Ellis Island. There were just too many people between them. Finally, he and Hirsh reached the gangplank and started to walk down towards the red building on Ellis Island. They also were pushed along by the guards until they reached the front of the building.

First, they climbed a long and steep staircase. Some people were tripping and out of breath, dragging their luggage up the stairs. Guards were gently pulling them aside. What would happen to them?

Once they got to the top, they had to wait in a line. Why? Where were they going? No one would tell them. The line snaked along until finally Isadore could peer into the room ahead. People were undressed, wrapped in white sheets. What was this? Then he saw that each person was waiting to be examined. He shivered. Was it nerves or was he cold?

Hirsh tapped his foot, whistling. He was nervous also, despite his seeming confidence. Every few minutes they lifted their bags and walked a few feet closer to the door. It seemed like an hour, more before they got to the doorway and then were told to step to the back of the room, get undressed, and then wait on yet another line. Isadore and Hirsh shrugged at each other and did as they were told.

"Hirsh, I'm scared. What are they looking for? Are they going to throw us out when they see we are Jews?"

"Come on, they'd be sending back half the ship. No, they just want to be sure we aren't sick."

As they approached the front of this line, Isadore stared at the doctors and nurses, hoping he got the friendly-faced doctor with the dark brown eyes and black hair. Although his face was serious, his eyes had a kind look. But no, Isadore got the one with the crooked teeth and small, beady eyes.

First, he listened to his heart, made him cough, touched his back and his stomach, and then took a long metal instrument with a hook on the end. What in the world was that?

"Ouch!"

He had pulled the hook under his eyelid and lifted it. Isadore was afraid to move, to ask anything, though he certainly was thinking a few unkind things. The doctor tugged at his other eyelid. He looked Isadore right in the eye. What would he say?

"You can go. Follow the line to the Great Hall." The doctor spoke Yiddish, but with a different accent than Isadore knew.

But he had passed! He grabbed his papers after the doctor stamped them, ran to the back of the room, got dressed, and looked around for Hirsh. Where was he? Had he passed?

He couldn't find him, but he figured he'd see him in the Great Hall, whatever that was. He followed the line. Isadore had never seen such a huge hall. It felt as big as the city park in Iasi that surrounded the National Theater and the other public buildings. And the hall was teeming with people. All those people from the ship now in one place. Though he'd known that there were hundreds and hundreds of them onboard, he'd never realized just how many until he saw them lining up in the hall, waiting their turns to be questioned and inspected. People everywhere. Sitting, standing, even lying down. Children, old people. He couldn't even see the people all the way across the hall.

There was no room to move freely. People were crammed in everywhere, and the smells of urine, body odor, and stale clothing filled the air. There were so many voices talking that no words were discernible, just endless babbling.

Isadore didn't care; his smile stretched across his face, his cheeks almost hurting from smiling so widely. He was in America. Just a few more hours, a few questions, and then he would be in New York. Uncle Moshe would be here to greet him. He would meet Aunt Zusi and Uncle Gustav. He would meet his American cousins. He could hardly stand still at all.

But where was Hirsh? Malke? Reuben? Anyone he knew from the Fusgeyers? The room was so big and so crowded that he could not see anyone. Then he caught sight of Hirsh's cap.

"Hirsh! Over here!"

Hirsh rushed over to stand with Isadore.

Smiling broadly, he said, "We made it through one more step. We're almost there!"

They sat cross-legged on the floor, standing every so often to inch slowly towards the front of the hall every few moments. Then they sat back to back, leaning against each other for support. Each time they stood up, Isadore looked to see if he could locate Malke or any of his Fusgeyer friends. Nothing. The room was too crowded, the people too closely packed for him to see.

As the hours dragged on, and the crowds seemed to get bigger, not smaller, Isadore's excitement turned to boredom and hunger.

"Hirsh, you have anything to eat?"

"What? Are you crazy? What would that be? Did you see any free food as we left the ship?"

Even Hirsh was getting cranky.

After six hours of waiting, they finally reached the front of the room. Hirsh went up to the immigration officer first. Isadore strained his ears and his eyes to try and find out what they were asking Hirsh, but he could not hear. Hirsh took out his papers, and the man in the cage looked them over very carefully. Isadore heard Hirsh say his brother's name, Marius Goldenberg. The man stared back at the papers and then at another document. Finally, Isadore thought he heard the man say, "Marius Goldenberg, yes. He has signed for you. You may now go."

Hirsh turned around and smiled at Isadore. "You're next! See you outside."

Isadore moved up to the man in the cage. The man had a kind face, though his chin was rather sharp. After several minutes of staring at papers on his desk, the man looked at Isadore. He spoke a rather strange form of Yiddish, but familiar enough that Isadore understood.

"Name and date of birth."

"David Goldschlager, November 4, 1889." Maybe this would be the last time he would have to call himself David.

"Father's name."

"Moritz Goldschlager"

"Home address."

"St. Andrews Street, Iasi, Romania."

"How much money do you have?"

"Ten dollars."

"Person who is responsible for you in the United States."

"Moshe Mintz."

"Address"

Isadore studied the paper in his hand. "124 East 108th Street. New York."

The man in the cage pulled out a document and studied it, looking over it several times. Isadore's stomach grumbled, and his heart pounded. Would he now be caught for using David's name? What would happen?

The man looked up at him. "There is no one named Moshe Mintz on our list. There is no one here taking responsibility for you. You cannot enter. You must go to the detention room."

Isadore's heart almost stopped. He started to protest. "But I know he is here. He's my aunt Zusi's husband. He lives here. So does my uncle, Gustav Rosenfeld."

The man said, "Look, boy. Move over to detention before you get arrested. Don't make trouble or you will be in trouble. Go now before the police hear you arguing with me."

Isadore picked up his duffel and walked slowly in the direction he was told to go. His heart now was beating too fast. He thought he was pass out or throw up. He was feeling more numb than alive. As he crossed the hall, he saw Hirsh, waiting outside the door.

"Izzy, where are you going?"

"Don't know. Something called detention. It's a big mistake. I'll see you in a little while."

"All right. It'll be fine. I'll wait for you." Isadore saw Hirsh's brother standing next to him. Behind them, he saw Malke and Reuben. He knew they wouldn't wait. Couldn't wait. Would he see them all ever again?

"Malke, Reuben!" He shouted, but it was too noisy and too far for them to hear him.

"Hirsh! Please tell Malke and Reuben I said goodbye, and tell her I..."

Just then a guard came over and slammed the door shut.

"Trying to get out without permission, kid? Get a move on before we send you back where you came from."

Isadore was stunned. This was it? Would he never get to tell Malke how he felt? He dragged himself across the rest of the hall and was amazed at how long it took for him to walk to the detention room. He had to ask several guards along the way. Some didn't speak Yiddish and answered him in words he could not understand. He made several wrong turns. Finally, he reached the room. His heart sank when he saw what was inside. Hundreds of people. Old people. Children. Men. Women. Jews. Others. All with the same horrified expression on their faces. All pale, teary-eyed. Some crying. Some just quietly staring ahead.

He sat down next to an old woman. He asked her why she was detained.

"No husband. No husband here."

"Your husband is back home?"

"No, husband here in America. But not here."

"He sick?"

"Don't know. Just know he not show up here."

Like Uncle Moshe. Isadore was not alone. He sat down next to her.

He sat and he sat. He'd been off the ship now for ten hours. Six hours on one line. Four hours in detention. It was seven o'clock, and he hadn't eaten all day. And he realized as the hours went by that no one was left. Reuben and Malke would be long gone, maybe on a train to Chicago already. Hirsh was off with his brother, heading to Philadelphia. Even if they were all still in New York, he had no idea where they were. He could never find them. He had no address. He would never see them again. He felt so alone. He missed his friends. He missed his family. And where was Uncle Moshe? Why hadn't he shown up? What if they sent him back to Iasi? He was too scared and too confused to cry. Breathing alone was a struggle.

Then the man up front stood up. "No more processing today. Time to close. You will all go to the dormitory where you will be given a bed and a meal. We will reopen at seven tomorrow morning. Follow me." Another man stood up and spoke in another language, maybe Italian? Then another in another language. That one he couldn't understand at all. Was it English?

Again, Isadore lifted his bag, which felt like it was getting heavier each time he picked it up. It felt like he'd put rocks inside, though it still only held his clothes and a few personal items. He followed the line of fellow detainees. They separated them, men on one side, women another, and then assigned them a bare bed from the two long lines of beds running down the room with less than a foot between each bed.

Isadore was put next to an old man, shorter than he was, with a sad look in his eyes and a crumpled hat in his hands. Isadore tried to speak to him in Yiddish, but the man shook his head. Then he tried Romanian. The man raised his eyebrows.

"Italiano?" the old man asked.

"No, Romania."

The man answered him again, using words that sounded similar to Romanian, but different enough that Isadore couldn't really understand.

Then the Italian man pulled a pen from his bag and an old newspaper. He wrote some words, and Isadore found that the Italian words when written were easier to understand. He wrote back in Romanian, and the Italian man smiled and nodded his head, giving Isadore a reassuring pat on the head.

Across from him was a man, about thirty, with a bad limp. Then there was a skinny young boy, maybe twelve years old. He didn't say a word. Isadore tried to speak to him in Yiddish after noticing that the boy had a Hebrew prayer book clasped in his hand.

"So how are you? Where are you from?" He asked the boy, but the boy just shut his eyes and went back to his prayer book.

A guard appeared and signaled for everyone to line up again, and they took all of the men to a large room with long tables. Isadore could smell food and his stomach growled. They were feeding them! By the time a surly guard slapped a plate of food on the table in front of him, Isadore was so hungry that before he even thought about what he was eating, he had cleared his plate. So had everyone else. Only the boy did not eat. He just sat and stared. Isadore wasn't the only one who eyed his plate of food, tempted to eat it. Probably not kosher, he thought.

Through sign language and writing, some Romanian, some Italian, Isadore learned that the Italian man was detained because he had no money, no job, and no one to meet him. And he was old. The man with the limp just pointed to his leg and shrugged his shoulders. The boy wouldn't talk. Maybe he had that eye disease? Isadore felt himself shudder and move further away.

They returned to the dormitory. The lights went out, and Isadore put his head on his duffel, as he had done on the road with the Fusgeyers and as he had done on the ship. He turned on his side away from the boy. And slept. At least it was quieter than the ship.

"Everybody up. You will be given breakfast and then moved back to the detention area."

Isadore rubbed his eyes. He couldn't believe he'd actually slept through the night. The relative quiet and stillness after the nights on the ship had made this dormitory with its bare beds seem comfortable. Then his heart sank. He remembered where he was and why he was there. What if no one came to get him? What if they sent him back to Hamburg? What would he do? Could he even go home?

He felt last night's meal come up through his stomach to his throat. He swallowed the bitterness of it and got up from the bed.

Around him the other men were also getting up and down at the other end women were also moving around, getting ready to go downstairs. Some men were davening, their tallisim and tefillin wrapped around them. Isadore hadn't been to shul or even prayed for months. His tallis and tefillin were in his duffel, but he'd not touched them since leaving. He only took them to please his parents. The pogrom and then the beating had made him angry with God. Who needed prayers? Watching the men pray now, Isadore wondered whether having that kind of faith would make him feel any better. He picked up his duffel and moved to the front where a line was already forming.

Once settled back in detention, Isadore sat quietly. He had no desire to talk to or even look at anyone. His heart was pounding so hard that he thought it would explode. Or burst out of his chest. His stomach was cramping, but he did not want to move to the toilet area. What if they called his name?

The men in the front standing behind the desks occasionally called out a name. People walked up to them, got their papers stamped, and then left the room. Where were they going? Were they free to go to America? Or were they being sent home? Or somewhere else? He didn't know, and he was afraid to ask. So he just sat, rubbing his hands, breathing deeply to try and slow his crazy heart. And hoping his stomach would hold on just a little bit longer.

Finally, around 11 o'clock, he heard, "David Goldslayer? David Goldslogger? Are you here?" At first he did not respond. Goldslayer? Goldslogger?? But then he realized that the official just could not pronounce Goldschlager. And he was still David. He picked up that duffel again and walked up to the front.

The man looked up at him and asked, "Are you David? How do you say it?"

"Gold Sh logger."

The man's Yiddish wasn't very good, but it was good enough. He smiled at Isadore. "Thanks! Well, you're one of the lucky ones. Your aunt Zusi Mintz is here to get you. She is waiting outside in the welcome area. Good luck, and welcome to America!"

"Really? Really? I can go! Thank you, thank you, thank you! But first, can I use the toilet?"

The man laughed. "Sure. Third door on your left as you walk towards the exit."

"Thank you, mister. Thank you."

Isadore again picked up his duffel, which felt lighter than it ever had, ran to the toilet, relieved his stomach, and then looked in the mirror as he washed his hands. He was so dirty, so grimy. What would Aunt Zusi think? He washed his face as best he could with the icy water, wiped it with his dirty shirt, and looked again. He was smiling from ear to ear again despite the dirty face. He looked awful, but he looked happy. He was as happy as he had ever been.

He walked out the bathroom door, he walked down the hall, he opened the outside door, and he was in America. Finally.

CHAPTER 10

Isadore rushed out the door and searched through the crowd gathered outside for the woman meeting him, his aunt Zusi Rosenfeld. He didn't remember her at all from when she'd lived in Iasi, and she certainly didn't know what he looked like. As he scanned the faces, he saw a woman who resembled his mother and his aunt Perla. She had the same deep set dark eyes that were set at a slight angle. She had a stern look on her face and was quite thin, unlike his mother and other aunt. She was tapping her foot, pacing anxiously on the pier.

"Aunt Zusi? Excuse me, are you Zusi Rosenfeld?" Isadore touched her elbow lightly.

The woman yanked her arm back and turned to look at him.

"Susie now. Susie Mintz. You are Isadore, I assume?"

Isadore reached out his hand to greet her and said, "Yes, ma'am, I am. Nice to meet you, and thank you for being here."

Aunt Zusi looked him over critically and said, "You sure are a dirty one."

Had she forgotten what it was like on those ships? She didn't even hug him.

"Where's Uncle Moshe?" he asked tentatively.

"He disappeared. He left me."

Isadore put his hands in his pockets and decided not to ask any more questions. He just followed where she led. They took the ferry from Ellis Island across to New York City, Zusi barely talking and Isadore pacing back and forth, staring at the buildings and boats ahead of them. Once on the land, Isadore wanted to stop and ask a million questions about all the tall buildings, the strange street names, the street vendors, the people, but Zusi just kept walking, faster and faster. Isadore stared up at the buildings---some were more than twenty stories high! The horses and carriages, the trolleys, the people running here and there. A few times he almost lost Zusi as she ran from corner to corner, not looking back. She didn't seem to care whether he followed her or not.

Finally, they arrived at a street called Forsyth Street. Zusi stopped at a building and opened the door and started up the stairs.

The hallway was dark and smelled of cigars and onions. Isadore followed her up to the third floor and dropped his duffel on the floor. The rooms were tiny, smaller even than in their house in Iasi. The walls were gray, and there were no curtains on the windows.

Zusi pointed to a daybed in the first room.

"I sleep here. You will sleep over there. On the floor. My cousins sleep in the back. They're not home now, but it's their apartment. So keep quiet and keep it clean while you're here."

Isadore didn't know who these cousins were and was afraid to ask. Isadore looked around the front room. There was a stove and a sink. No toilet.

Zusi barked at him, "The toilet is in the backyard. Be sure you clean it after you use it. We share it with everyone in the building. You can sleep here tonight. Gustav will be here in the morning to get you. I have to work now since I have already lost several hours this morning. There is food on the shelf over the sink. Make yourself something and go find something to do outside. But be sure to wash up first before you touch anything, and be sure to clean up when you're done. Now I have to go work."

Isadore was too happy to let her ruin his day. He grabbed some bread and walked back down the steep and dark stairs to the street. The streets were filled with vendors selling fruit, vegetables, clothes, shoes, meat, almost anything he could think of. Everywhere he looked there were people buying and selling. There were many people speaking Yiddish, many with long payes and beards, but many others without. He could see kosher butcher shops and many little shuls with Hebrew inscribed above the door. The air smelled like bread and rotten fruit and smoke and sweat. It was noisier than Iasi ever was. Isadore felt almost dizzy with excitement and confusion. He did not know where to go or to look first.

He could see off in the horizon a beautiful structure. Was it a bridge? He'd never seen such a big bridge. He decided to walk closer to get a better look. He walked down Delancey Street, passing streets with names like Norfolk, Suffolk, Clinton, Attorney, and Ridge, and he could see the water as he got closer. Five more blocks, and he was at the water. The bridge was so huge that even if he turned his head all the way up, he couldn't see it all. To his right he could see another bridge, another beautiful bridge, spanning this river in front of them. Such a big river. Miles across. What was that on the other side?

A boy who looked about twelve came up and stood beside him.

First the boy said something Isadore did not understand. He said to the boy in Yiddish, "Yiddish?"

"Whatcha doin? Why you looking at it?" The boy's Yiddish was very funny. But understandable.

"Never been here before."

"Oh, that's the new bridge. Williamsburg. Just finished last year. It's nice, huh? Not as clunky as that old one. That's the East River Bridge. This is modern---hangs instead of being heavy like that old one."

Isadore thought they were both magnificent.

"What's that over there?" he asked, pointing across the river to some land and hills that looked almost country-like.

"That's Brooklyn!" The boy laughed at him. "Dontcha know nothing about New York?"

Isadore blushed and smiled, "No. I just got here today."

"Today!? Well, that's something. I was born here."

"But you speak Yiddish?"

"Sure, my mom and dad came from the old country. Near Lemberg. But I speak English also."

"Let me hear."

The boy said some words that Isadore could not understand at all.

"I hope I can learn that English soon also."

"You will. Just go to night school like my dad. His English is pretty good now, but not as good as his Yiddish. And my mom doesn't know English much at all."

"Good idea."

"Well, I have to go now. My mother needs me to help her in the market. Some of the vegetable sellers don't speak Yiddish."

"Nice meeting you. Thanks for telling me about the bridges."

The boy ran off, and Isadore turned once more and looked around him. "Williamsburg, Brooklyn. Already I know some English."

As he walked back along Delancey Street to get to Forsyth Street, Isadore passed by Ridge Street. Two little girls, maybe eight or nine years old, both with dark red hair, sat on the stoop outside one of the buildings. They could have been Malke as a young girl; her hair was also that color. He remembered her lips against his. Malke, would he ever see her again?

The next morning Isadore woke up rolled on the floor next to the stove. Aunt Zusi had given him a rough blanket and pointed at the corner furthest from her. He'd never seen the cousins, who must have come home after he'd fallen asleep. As he turned over on the floor, he heard whispering and saw a tall man standing near Aunt Zusi.

Isadore sat up and cleared his throat. The tall man turned around and looked at him.

"Isadore, you are awake! Welcome to America. I'm your Uncle Gustav."

Gustav walked over to Isadore, and Isadore jumped up to greet him. He reached out his hand to his uncle, but instead of taking it, his uncle reached his arms around Isadore and hugged him so tightly that Isadore couldn't catch his breath.

"Isadore! My nephew! I am so, so happy to see you. You must tell me all about my sisters, my other nieces and nephews, and my dear brothers-in-law Moritz and Yankel. You must tell me how things are in Iasi."

Gustav hugged him again. Isadore had almost forgotten what it was like to be hugged. He'd forgotten what it was like to be loved. He rested his head into the chest of this man, an uncle he'd never met before, and perhaps for the first time in months, he felt his shoulders relax. Uncle Gustav felt like home.

Gustav had gray hair and a thick moustache that curled over his lips. He was tall---well, tall compared to Isadore---and he had the same deep set eyes that Isadore, his brother David, his sister Betty, and their mother had. Aunt Perla and even Aunt Zusi had them. They were Rosenfeld eyes, his mother had said. Deep and slanted and large. Soulful eyes, his father would say. Looking into those eyes, Isadore felt his own eyes start to fill with tears.

Gustav patted his back, "It's all right, Isadore. You are with family now. I'll write to your mother and tell her that you are here and that I will take care of you. Everything will be fine, and soon they will be here also. Now let's get you up and fed and on your way. Zusi has no room for you."

"Where are we going? To your home?"

Gustav shook his head. "I live in Brooklyn, but we are too many to take you in. I have a friend uptown who says he has room for one more. We'll go there now."

Isadore's face must have shown his disappointment.

"Don't worry. You'll come to our house every Shabbos. I insist!"

Isadore nodded, got his duffel, and said goodbye to Aunt Zusi, who touched his arm and wished him well, but did not move from the chair where she was sewing in the corner. Something in her was broken, and all the good cheer from her brother Gustav was not going to fix it. Isadore knew how sad his mother would be to see her little sister Zusi now.

Gustav and Isadore walked down Forsyth Street, and Uncle Gustav stopped and bought Isadore a bagel and an apple. Isadore had never tasted anything so good in his life. The apple was crisp and juicy; it almost hurt to eat it, feeling all the sensations in his mouth. The bagel was hot and chewy and a perfect contrast to the apple. Isadore was so excited that he almost laughed, choking on the food in his mouth.

"Slow down, boy. There's lots of food in this city."

"All like this?"

Gustav laughed. As they approached Rivington Street, Isadore saw the long staircase leading to a platform rising above the street. He looked up, and then he jumped back when he heard a loud booming noise.

"What is that?"

"That's where we are going. For a train ride uptown."

They climbed the stairs, people running up and down around them, pushing each other as they rushed on their way. Gustav paid the fare, and when the next train came to a screeching halt, Isadore followed his uncle on to the train. They had to squeeze into the crowded car. It smelled like burnt rubber and garlic on the train, but Isadore was too busy looking out the windows to care. So many buildings, so many people. Horses, carriages, policemen, stores all over. It was endless. The first time the train stopped, Isadore stood as if to get off.

"Not yet, Izzy. We've got a long way to go."

Isadore sat back down. "Uncle Gustav, what is wrong with Aunt Zusi? She hardly talked to me, and she just seemed so sad."

Gustav sighed. "It's a sad story. She has reason to be so unhappy."

And Gustav told him about Zusi and Moshe. Moshe, who was Harry in America, and Zusi, had had twin babies. One died shortly after he was born. Just a month old. Zusi had been devastated. She refused to eat, she refused to take care of the other baby. She didn't sleep. She just would sit, stare at the floor. Her hair was a matted mess, she smelled, she would just talk to herself, cry, and stare. Finally the city police came and took away the other baby, whose name was Nathan. They took Zusi to a hospital.

Slowly she had improved. She started to eat and to take care of herself. The doctors helped her. When she was strong enough, they let her leave. But Harry was gone. And the baby Nathan was in an orphanage. And Zusi had no money.

Gustav tried to help her, gave her money, and found her a place to live with a kindly young couple from Iasi who had room for a boarder, the so-called cousins whom Isadore had not even met in his short stay on Forsyth Street. They were distant cousins of some sort, but no one knew how. So Zusi was living with these cousins and hoping to someday be reunited with her little boy, who was now seven years old. She visited him all the time, and as soon as she could save enough money as a seamstress to take care of him, she was going to get him back.

But for now, Zusi had to work hard and fight to stay healthy so she could get there.

Isadore had listened quietly to Gustav's story. He thought about the dead baby, the little boy in the orphanage, and Aunt Zusi all alone. No wonder she was so harsh, so unfriendly. He shook his head. Would Aunt Zusi be happier in Romania? He didn't know.

He looked up at Gustav. They'd been on the train for close to an hour.

"Are we still in New York?"

"Yes, we're still in New York. We're in a neighborhood known as Harlem. Well, East Harlem. We're still on the East Side of the island."

"You mean there is a whole other side? Just as long as this?"

"Yes, and a whole other river."

They passed 100th Street, and Gustav said, "Next stop."

Isadore followed his uncle off the train and down the stairs. They walked a few blocks up Second Avenue until they got to 2213 Second Avenue at 116th Street.

"This is it. This is where my friend Rico lives."

"Rico? What kind of name is that?"

"Italian. He's from Italy."

"Jewish?"

"No, Catholic. Good man, hard worker. He sometimes works with me on jobs."

Isadore asked Gustav about his painting business. Gustav explained that he mostly painted inside buildings in Manhattan and in Brooklyn. He also sold paint. When he worked in Manhattan, Rico would work for him.

"Does he speak Yiddish?"

"Well, a little because he works with me. But no, he speaks Italian. Some English. It will be good for you."

"But are there Jews here?"

Although Isadore had his doubts about God and about prayer, he'd never had a friend who wasn't Jewish. In Iasi, Jews stayed with Jews. Christians had no use for Jews.

"Sure, Isadore. There are Jews. There are Jews everywhere in New York. More in some places, like where Zusi lives now. But I lived up here when I first arrived, and Zusi lived up here also. It's good. You will learn English faster. You'll be a real American, living with people from all kinds of places. Besides, it's cheaper here than down where Zusi lives. And the streets are wider. And also, Srul lives up here. He's a good worker, doing wallpapering for me. You'll like having a family member in the neighborhood."

Isadore nodded. Yes, it would be good to see Srul, to live near his big cousin.

They entered the building. Gustav knocked on Rico's door. A small child answered, followed by a woman with long dark hair and eyes so dark that Isadore could see no light in them. Isadore had never seen such a beautiful face. He couldn't help but smile at her.

Gustav spoke quickly to the woman in Italian and then turned to him and said, "Isadore, this is Gina. She is Rico's wife. They take care of the building. It's called a superintendent here, or super. Gina says that Room 1C is available for $5 a week. You can move in now. There's a bed. A stove, a sink. The toilet is out back."

Isadore followed Gina and Gustav around the corner. The room was small, which Isadore expected it would be. The bed almost filled the room. The stove and sink were close enough to the bed that Isadore could cook and wash while sitting on the bed. There were no blankets, no pots and pans. Nothing. How could he live here? The walls were dark brown, the floor was almost black it was so dirty. The one window was tiny and fogged over with grime.

He had less than $10 to his name after they took money for his two meals on Ellis Island. That was not even enough for two weeks. Then what? How would he buy food? A blanket? A pot? Some clean clothes? All he had in his duffel were a few shirts, two other pairs of pants, a coat, and some underwear and socks. Most of those were so torn and worn after his months of traveling.

Looking at the empty shelves and bare bed, Gustav said, "Let's go find you something to eat and maybe a pot." Gina looked in, with her little girl at her side. She and Gustav talked a bit. She walked away and then returned with a blanket and a pillow.

"Gina says that you can keep these as long as you live here and pay your rent on time."

Isadore smiled at her and nodded. He felt so silly, not being able to talk to her.

He and Gustav then walked to a little grocery around the corner. Gustav opened the door and spoke to the bald chubby man standing behind the counter, "Mr. Greenberg, how are you?"

Gustav knew everyone, it seemed. "Ah, Mr. Rosenfeld, how are you? The neighborhood just is not the same since you moved to Brooklyn. Who's this? A son I haven't met? He looks a lot like you."

At least Mr. Greenberg spoke Yiddish so Isadore could understand.

"It's my nephew. My sister's boy. Just got here yesterday from Iasi. He's the first to come, and he's here to work hard and bring his mother, father, brother, and sister to America. He's a good boy."

Gustav asked Mr. Greenberg for a loaf of bread, some potatoes, some carrots, some other groceries. Mr. Greenberg took the items from the shelves and placed them on the counter. Gustav paid Mr. Greenberg, and Mr. Greenberg placed the groceries in a box.

Gustav pointed at Isadore and said to Mr. Greenberg, "So what do you think?"

"Is he strong? He looks pretty skinny." Mr. Greenberg frowned.

Isadore was not amused. Why was Mr. Greenberg talking about him like he was a horse?

"He's strong enough. At least as strong as my boy Abe. And remember, a greenhorn will always work harder than an American born boy," his uncle replied.

Isadore was confused. Who was Abe? And what was this all about? And what is a greenhorn?

Mr. Greenberg looked him over. Mr. Greenberg was small and round, with round spectacles that made it almost impossible to see his eyes. He wore a big white apron over his clothes, and his hands were wide and chubby. He was serious, but not unkind looking.

66

"Well, I can give him a try. Let's say we will start this week for two weeks and see how it goes. How about $8 a week?"

"Well, Izzy, what do you think? Eight dollars a week will cover your rent and leave you something for food and something to put aside for your family. It's better than a sweatshop."

Sweatshop? That sounded terrible, though he had no idea what it was.

"Yes, but tell me what I will do."

"You will be here at six in the morning to prepare the store. I arrive at seven, and I need everything opened and put away so we can open the store when I get here. There will be deliveries starting at six—milk, eggs, newspapers, and such. You help me in the store---put things on shelves, sweep the floors, wash the windows. If you're smart and work hard, you'll learn English and Italian and you can help customers soon. Then I'll pay you more. Maybe nine, then ten dollars a week. I go home at seven, you will stay until eight to clean up and close the store."

"Thank you. That sounds good."

Gustav and Mr. Greenberg chuckled, shook hands. Mr. Greenberg said, "Can you start right now?"

Isadore would have liked more time with his uncle, but he knew he had to say yes. "Yes, now is good."

Gustav looked at him. "You're going to be just fine. I will be back to check on you in a few days and will take you back to Brooklyn for Shabbos. Right, he gets Shabbos off, Greenberg?"

Mr. Greenberg looked at Gustav, "You know Saturday is my busiest day. How could I let him off on Shabbos? He can leave early on Saturday and have Sunday off. The store is closed then."

Gustav sighed. Being Jewish was not so easy in this country, but like others, he had learned to adapt. So had Greenberg. So would Isadore.

"Izzy, I will come by on Saturday around six and take you back to Brooklyn. You can sleep over and spend Sunday meeting your cousins. Yes?"

Isadore missed his mother's wonderful Shabbos meals, the candles, the challah, and the songs, but he did not really care about working on Shabbos. It was America, and he had to do what he had to do.

"Sunday will be good for a day off."

"All right then, I have to get back to work. If you need anything, talk to Rico—he knows enough English---or to Mr. Greenberg. I will take the box back to your room now so you can get right to work."

"Thank you, Uncle Gustav"

Gustav shook his hand, smiled, and winked at him. "You work hard and bring my sister here to America. You don't need to thank me."

And so Isadore's life in New York, in America, began.

On Tuesday, Isadore was moving canned goods onto the shelves when the bell on the store's door rang. He almost fell off the ladder when he saw his cousin Srul standing in the store.

"Srul? Srul!"

"Yes, that's right." Srul tilted his head at Isadore and smiled. He looked good. Taller and more muscular than he had two years ago when he'd left Iasi. He had a moustache, more a dark shadow under his nose, and his skin was darkened by the sun.

Isadore jumped off the ladder and grabbed his cousin's hand. It turned into a hug.

"How are you? How are you doing in New York?"

"Well, I'm working a job with Uncle Gustav; I'm sure he told you. We're painting a big apartment on Park Avenue. Rich people who want fancy wallpaper. You know what wallpaper is?"

Isadore shook his head. Srul explained about patterns and glue and rollers.

"Uncle Gustav found someone to teach me. I work with him. Name's Schneider."

"You making good money?"

"Eh, it depends. When we have a big job like this, I can make twelve dollars a week. But many weeks there's no work. So then it's not good."

In the back, Mr. Greenberg cleared his voice. Isadore gestured to Srul, shrugging his shoulders in apology.

"I've got to get going anyway. Don't want to be late for work."

"Come by later? We can go for a walk?"

"Sure, see you later.

When Srul came by later, it was dark out. Isadore wished he had a place they could go sit and talk, but his room was no place for visitors, and Srul explained that he was a lodger in someone's apartment, sleeping in the kitchen. So they walked and then found a bar to sit in. One beer wouldn't be too extravagant after almost a whole week of work.

"Here's to America," Srul toasted, lifting the beer to his mouth, the foam covering his moustache so that he looked a bit like a horse after running.

"Tell me about America---what have you seen? Do you know English? Have you made friends? Met girls?"

"Girls? Who has time? All I do is work, work, and work. When there's no work, I look for work. What have I seen? The inside of lots of buildings. Not much more." Srul wiped some of the foam from his moustache.

Isadore took a large gulp of his beer. Srul did as well, and then he asked Isadore, "Tell me about home. How is my father? My mother? My brothers and sisters?"

"I haven't been there for months myself. You've probably heard from them more recently than I have. But they were doing all right back in June."

Isadore wasn't used to beer, and he felt his muscles relax a bit as he finished most of his glass. Srul also seemed to be feeling the effect of the drink. He leaned back and started to reminisce.

"Right now in Iasi, we could be going to the Yiddish theater. Or listening to your father sing to us or tell us stories. Or remember how we'd play in the forest? Berl and I would run, and you and David would chase us? I miss those days. Being a boy. So much time to play and explore. So many trees and horses."

"Aren't there trees and horses here? And theater?"

"Not like home. Nothing like home."

"Well, I'm going to Brooklyn this weekend, seeing Uncle Gustav and all the cousins. Across the river. Have you been there? Is it nicer there?"

"Yeah, I did that once. It's so far. And those children are so wild and rude. Not like we were. Not like children back home. They think they own the world here."

Isadore shrugged. He looked around at the bar and saw all kinds of men, old, young, heavy, thin. There was laughter throughout the room and a mix of languages and voices. Srul was the most somber looking person in the bar.

He tried again to talk to his cousin.

"Have you learned English?"

69

"Of course! I need to know English. I took a course at night. Uncle Gustav paid for it. I worked all day, then went to school. You must do it also."

A large man in a green-checked jacket, smoking a cigar, walked by their table and bumped into Srul's chair and spilled some of Srul's beer. Srul said something sharply to the man in what Isadore thought was English, and the man glared back at him and said something back, just as sharply. Isadore didn't know what he'd said, but he could tell the man was being nasty and sneering at them.

Srul turned red and turned around in his chair, facing the table. Isadore stood up, looked right into the man's eyes, and cursed at him in Romanian, saying, "You've got the face of a donkey and smell like one also." The man shoved and responded in English, but Isadore didn't know what he'd said. Srul pulled at Isadore's arm.

"Shh, let him go. We don't need a fight."

Isadore uttered one last curse at the man and took his seat. The man muttered something back, but walked away. Reluctantly, Isadore sat down.

"What did he say to you, Srul?" Isadore asked.

"Nothing, just nothing. Learn to ignore ones like that."

They finished their beers, and then they walked back uptown to head home. Isadore felt weighted down, his shoulders stiff, his head aching. The calming effect of the beer had disappeared, leaving behind only a stale taste in his mouth. Srul didn't say a word as they walked, just kept his eyes on the ground, sighing.

Isadore's first few days in Mr. Greenberg's store were a challenge. The job was easy enough, lifting boxes, sweeping the floor, putting things on and off the shelves. But the languages? The first morning an older woman dressed all in black rushed into the store, talking so fast that Isadore had no idea what language she was speaking. Mr. Greenberg had stepped out, so Isadore raised his hands to stop her and then raised them with a questioning look.

"Slowly," he said in Yiddish. The woman frowned.

Speaking more slowly, she said, "Dove Signor Greenberg?"

It sounded like the Italian he'd heard at Ellis Island, so he tried a little Romanian.

"Not here," he said as slowly as he could in Romanian.

The woman shook her head and said, "Pollo?" and she clucked like a chicken.

The chicken delivery hadn't yet arrived. So Isadore said, "No. Later." In Romanian.

The woman clucked her tongue and resumed speaking quickly so that Isadore had no idea what she was saying. Fortunately, Mr. Greenberg walked in and greeted her.

"Buon giorno, Signora," he said to her, and then they both spoke Italian, filling her order.

After she left, Isadore turned to Mr. Greenberg and said, "How did you learn Italian and English? How will I learn?"

Mr. Greenberg smiled at him and said, "Signora Rinaldi said you were a smart boy. That you spoke something to her, I assume Romanian? You will learn. Just listen and you will learn."

Isadore felt his shoulders relax. He would learn. And each day that week he picked up new words, some English, some Italian. He read the labels on the canned goods and the advertisements in the newspapers, asking Mr. Greenberg for help now and then. By Saturday, he knew many words, especially those for the grocery items that Mr. Greenberg sold. He beamed every time a customer came in now and asked for chicken or eggs or cheese or fruit or bread—in English or Italian. Now he understood. He knew how to say hello and goodbye. If the customers spoke slowly, he could sometimes understand even more. Mr. Greenberg said on Saturday, "See? You are one smart boy. You will be just fine."

But now his first week of work was over. At six o'clock on Saturday, Uncle Gustav appeared at the store, right on time as promised.

"Uncle Gustav---so good to see you! Can I go now, Mr. Greenberg?" He called out to the storeroom behind the store.

"Sure, sure. You want your pay first?"

Right, payday! Isadore walked to the back, and Mr. Greenberg gave him a five-dollar bill and three singles. One would go in the jar for saving for his family's tickets, one would go for food, and one for savings for clothes and other expenses. The five-dollar bill was for rent.

"Let's go, I'm ready!"

Uncle Gustav chuckled. "You taking the broom with you. And that apron?"

Isadore laughed. He put the broom down, took off the apron, and picked up his hat and his torn duffel. He planned to stay the night in

Brooklyn and had taken some clean clothes and some candy he'd purchased from the store as a gift for his cousins and aunt and uncle.

They walked to the elevated platform to catch the train, and as they rode the train downtown to Brooklyn that October evening, Isadore asked Gustav about his cousins.

"Well, there are quite a few of them. Even I can't always keep track, and they're all mine! There are nine of them all together, last I counted. Where should I start?"

"Oldest first, of course." After all, Isadore was himself a first born child.

"Oy, do we have to start with my oldest?"

"Not if you don't want to." Gustav frowned, and Isadore waited.

"Ach, okay. My oldest is Lilly. She was born in Iasi, was just a little girl when we came to New York. Her little sister Sarah was also born in Iasi. All the rest starting with Abe were born here in New York."

Gustav rubbed at his chin and his moustache. Isadore waited for him to go on.

"Lilly is now 21. She lives with us, but she was married. Her husband died just last year, just three years after they got married. My Lilly was only seventeen when she married him. Before he died, they had a little boy Billy. He's three now. Lilly and Billy are both living with us now in Brooklyn."

Isadore had a feeling there was more to know about Lilly, but the frown on Gustav's face warned him against asking more questions about her.

"How about Sarah? Is she married?"

"No, not yet. She's seventeen, still helping out at home. Next comes Abe. He's just a little bit younger than you are. Fifteen now. Then comes Beckie---she is just eleven. Then Jack---he's ten. Robbie is eight, Morris is seven. Then two more girls---Lizzie is five, and the baby is Rachel. She's not yet a year old."

As the train bumped on the tracks, Isadore tried to imagine this family. There were nine of them, five girls and four boys. They were as old as 21 and as young as, well, not yet one. And there was Billy also. And Gustav and his wife Hennie, of course. Where did they all sleep? Where would he sleep?

"So did you see Srul?" Gustav inquired.

"Yeah, yeah, we got a beer on Tuesday."

"Did you have a good time?"

Isadore gave Gustav a look. He shrugged and said, "He seems homesick."

"Well, keep your head about you. Keep focused on what's to come. Don't get pulled down into the past. It's not good."

Isadore nodded. He had to look forward, not backward.

After the long train ride downtown and then a trolley across the bridge and a walk of several blocks, Gustav announced, "There's our house. My boys are already gathering outside to meet you."

Standing outside, tossing a ball around, were four boys, one taller than Isadore, the others smaller. And they seemed to be everywhere. Just four of them, but three younger ones were chasing after the ball together as the oldest, Abe, tossed it down the street.

Abe looked up and noticed Isadore standing next to him. "Look! It's our new cousin!"

The whole gang charged up to him, all staring at him, smiling and sticking their hands out while announcing their names.

"I'm Morris." "I'm John, but call me Jack." Abe stuck his hand out and said, "I'm Abe, and it's good to finally have a guy my age in the family." Isadore shook each of their hands. Robbie stayed back a bit, somewhat shyer than the others, but waved and quietly said, "I'm Robbie."

Morris then asked, "Wanna play some ball?"

Gustav interrupted, "Morris. He just got off work and then traveled from uptown. Maybe he's tired."

"It's okay," Isadore responded quickly. "I haven't played ball--- or anything else---in months. Is it okay if we play a bit?"

Gustav said, "Sure, I will let your Aunt Hennie know we're back."

They tossed the ball for a while, Isadore feeling like a boy in ways he hadn't felt in years. Running, shouting, chasing after the ball. If only his brother could be here.

When it finally got too dark to see the ball, they went inside.

"That was fun. Thank you for playing."

Uncle Gustav's apartment was huge compared to his dark little room uptown. There was a kitchen separate from the living room, not too big, but big enough so that three girls could work in there with their mother. As he walked in, they were all rushing around, putting food on the table and stirring pots on the stove. The aroma of chicken soup filled the air. His stomach growled, and his mouth watered. Eggplant salad in a white ceramic bowl, just like home.

His aunt first noticed him after calling to her boys to get ready for dinner. She wiped her hands on the dishcloth, walked over, and hugged him. "So glad you're here. Your mother was always such a dear to me. I miss her so."

Her embrace felt like warm bread, and she smelled like his mother.

Hennie then lined up her daughters. "These are my girls, Sarah, Beckie, and Lizzie." Sarah was beautiful. Such long dark hair, such large dark eyes. Just a little older than he was. Beckie and Lizzie were reminded him how much he missed his sister Betty, who was about the same age as Beckie. They each nodded at him and quietly said hello.

Lizzie said, "You don't look green."

Isadore wasn't sure how to answer.

"Lizzie, hush! He's a greenhorn, a newcomer, not green.

"Oh, I thought he'd be green with horns."

Her sisters giggled.

But there were two missing, Isadore realized.

"Aren't there more? I thought Uncle Gustav said five girls?"

Aunt Hennie said to Sarah, "Take your cousin into the living room and introduce your sister to him."

Isadore followed Sarah and there sitting on the floor was another dark-haired young woman, holding a baby in one arm while playing with a little boy. '

"Lil, this is Isadore, our new cousin." Lilly looked up and gave Isadore half a smile.

"Hi. Nice to meet you."

Lilly didn't stand up or smile at him, but just went back to rocking the baby. Billy, however, stood up.

"Who are you? Another uncle?"

"A cousin. Just a cousin."

"Oh." Billy turned back to the box of clothespins he'd been playing with.

Morris then came charging into the room, jumping on Isadore.

"Can we show you our room?"

There were two bedrooms. One for Gustav and Hennie and the baby Rachel. One for all the boys, including little Billy. Isadore would sleep in there as well, sharing a bed with Billy since he was the smallest.

"Where do the sisters sleep?" he asked.

74

"In the living room, of course." Four girls in the living room. Lilly slept with Beckie, Sarah slept with Lizzie. Two daybeds that turned into night beds at night. Twelve people in three rooms. Plus Isadore tonight.

In Iasi, his Aunt Perla and Uncle Yankel also had a large family. Three boys, four girls. In a somewhat larger home, but still very crowded. But their house was not so loud, the children not so energetic. This was something new, something different. Isadore could not remember so much laughter among children at any time during his childhood in Iasi.

It must be good to be born in America, Isadore thought. It makes you happy to be a child.

CHAPTER 11

The October air was brisk, but the sun was strong and made their red hair shine with golden flecks. The coolness in the air made Gussie think about winter, and that always brought her back to that day almost four years ago when Papa died. Although they managed with Tillie still helping Mama at home and working in a sweatshop, the house still didn't feel right without Papa.

Mama worked at home doing piecework, sewing garments for one of the sweatshops. That way she could take care of Sam, who at four still needed Mama's attention. He was a quiet boy who didn't laugh a lot. Mama said he was sad because he had no Papa. Sam was the only boy in the house now since Hymie had married Sophie in March, just seven months ago.

Gussie missed Hymie, but now there was more room in the Ridge Street apartment. Mama slept in the backroom now with Tillie since Papa was gone and Sam was too big. Sam, Gussie, and Frieda shared the front room, which felt big and spacious with only three children in there. Frieda and Gussie still shared the daybed, and Sam slept either on the floor or on the chair with his legs curled under him.

Before she'd left for work that morning, Tillie had brushed Gussie and Frieda's hair and put matching little clips in them to keep the hair out of their eyes. Now the two younger sisters sat on the stoop outside their building on Ridge Street, ready to walk to school, but waiting for their friend, Ida. They went to school two blocks from their home on Ridge Street, Gussie to fourth grade, Frieda to second grade.

Gussie liked school most of the time. Last year her teacher, Mrs. Smith, was strict and never smiled. She wore her gray hair tied back in a tight bun and wore heavy gray stockings and gray dresses. But Gussie learned how to add and subtract numbers and even could multiply. She also learned how to read bigger words. Now she could help Mama read notices and newspapers. She felt like she was helping now also, like Tillie.

Gussie's teacher this year was Mrs. Curtin. She was younger than Mrs. Smith and pretty and kind. She had blond hair tied loosely up and a warm smile. Mrs. Curtin read stories to the class when they had finished all their work. Gussie loved the stories, and she loved listening to Mrs. Curtin's voice. Sometimes they sang songs. And they talked about America. They said The Pledge to the flag, though Gussie had no idea what most of the words meant. She'd asked Tillie what allegiance meant and republic, but Tillie didn't know either. Maybe she would ask Mrs. Curtin.

"Hi, Gussie. Hi, Frieda," said Ida as she approached the stoop where the sisters were sitting.

Ida, who lived down the street, had two little brothers and one older brother and no sisters. Gussie felt sorry for her, surrounded only by boys. But Ida had a father, and Gussie didn't so maybe they were even.

"Hi, Ida. I guess we'd better get to school. Come on, Frieda. Let's go."

As they walked to school, Ida, Gussie, and Frieda held hands and talked about school. Gussie was telling them about a book Mrs. Curtin was reading called "The Secret Garden" about a girl and a boy who become friends trying to solve a mystery in an old garden locked by a key. Gussie had a hard time picturing in her head what the garden looked like. She'd never seen a real garden or a big house like the one in the book.

"Let's go look at the river!" Frieda suggested.

They ran along Delancey Street down to the newer bridge, the Williamsburg Bridge. There was Brooklyn across the wide East River, and there were barges and boats passing under the bridge.

"When I am ten, I am going to walk across the East River Bridge and go to Coney Island," Ida announced proudly.

"By yourself? You can't do that!" Gussie was indignant. Brooklyn was far, the river was wide, and Coney Island was a wild place, so she heard.

"No, silly, with my papa and my big brother. They promised. I want to see the ocean and ride the rides. You can come, too. For my birthday next June."

Gussie tried to imagine walking across that bridge, taking a trolley out to Coney Island. She squeezed Ida's hand. "Yes, I want to go! You won't forget, will you?"

"Course not, silly. You're my best friend!"

"What about me?" Frieda stomped her feet.

"When you are ten, we'll take you also." Frieda frowned. She didn't like always being the little sister.

"I'll get Max or Hymie to take me. Or maybe Avram or David. They won't make me wait til I am ten."

Gussie suddenly felt a pang in her stomach. If Papa was alive, they wouldn't have to rely on the brothers. Ida was lucky. Gussie withdrew her hand from Ida's hand and folded her arms across her chest. She turned her head away from the water, looking back down Delancey Street. She took a deep breath.

"You all right, Gussie?"

"Sure, I'm fine. Let's hurry up. We'll be late for school.

Gussie was quiet now, but Frieda and Ida continued chattering on about school and beaches and bridges. Gussie thought about what she'd have to do after school. She'd help in the kitchen, give Sam a bath, and wash the floor after dinner. Then she and Frieda would be able to sit in the front room and maybe read a book from the library. Her favorite right now was *Little Women*. It was about sisters who lived in the country. Their Papa was gone away at war, so they also just lived most of their time with their mother. Gussie could almost imagine what their lives were like.

Two months went by, and the days were shorter. It was getting colder and colder. The gentiles were having Christmas soon, a holiday that Gussie's family did not celebrate, but Mrs. Curtin and many of the children in her class did. The class was learning Christmas songs and talking about Santa Claus and reindeer and someone named Jesus. Gussie and the other Jewish children would sing also, but they did not get to see Santa Claus or know about Jesus.

A boy named Tom in her class came up to Gussie after school one day and said to her, "You know, you're going to burn in hell because you don't believe in Jesus."

Gussie didn't know what to say. She just stared at him and then ran home and rushed into their home, asking Mama right away, "Am I going to hell? Why don't we believe in Jesus?"

Mama put down the potatoes she was peeling, and said, "Where did you hear that?"

"Tom. A boy in my class," Gussie shouted in frustration.

Mama said, "Don't listen to that boy. People believe different things. We believe in God, and He won't let us burn in hell."

Gussie wasn't so sure. God didn't protect Papa. But she felt better. Mama pointed out all the holidays they got to celebrate that the Christians didn't, like Rosh Hashanah and Passover and Purim and Hanukkah. Gussie liked their holidays, but no one at school sang the songs from those holidays or told stories about Moses or Esther or the Maccabees.

Frieda was practicing her letters, and Gussie began doing some work with numbers. She soon forgot about Tom and Jesus and hell.

Then suddenly Tillie opened the door to their apartment, letting in a big gust of cold air. Gussie shivered and yelled, "Shut the door!"

"Oh, Gussie, don't be so grouchy." Tillie was smiling broadly.

Gussie looked up at her big sister. "Why are you so happy?" Usually Tillie came home tired and a bit grouchy herself.

"No reason. Just happy." Tillie responded, but her eyes twinkled, and she twisted her hair around her finger.

Mama overheard all this and asked Tillie, "Is there something you want to tell us? Gussie's right. You seem a little too cheery for so late in the day."

"Well, you know that nice young man at our shul, Aaron Bernstein? He met me at work a few days last week and walked me home."

Mama already knew that, but it was news to Gussie.

"So? What's so great about that?" Gussie interjected.

Tillie went on with her story, ignoring Gussie. "Well, today he brought me flowers and walked me home. He even held my hand. I think he would have kissed me, but I was so cold...and a bit nervous. So I just squeezed his hand and ran upstairs."

Gussie wasn't even sure she knew who this Aaron was. "What does he look like?"

"Oh, very distinguished. He's twenty-five. He used to live with his sister Lena and her family on Delancey Street, but now he lives on Henry Street. They came from the old country around the same time we did. He works as a cutter in a men's clothing shop. He's saving money to start his own business someday soon."

Gussie nodded at Tillie, but inside felt her stomach jump a bit. What if Tillie married this Aaron? What if she moved away? Gussie could not imagine life without her big sister. She loved Mama and Frieda and even Sam. But Tillie was the one who made her happiest. Tillie was the one who made everyone laugh. No matter what happened, no matter the weather, no matter the what---Tillie could cheer them up. She told great stories, she knew games to play with cards, she could even talk about baseball and other things that most girls didn't know about. Tillie was even more fun than Mrs. Curtin.

But Gussie looked up at Tillie, and said, "I'm sure he's nice."

Mama smiled at her girls and said, "Almost time to eat. Potatoes and carrots for dinner."

The wedding took place in March, 1905. Tillie was 21, ready to be a wife and a mother. They were married in the apartment on Ridge Street, and as with Hymie and Max and David and Toba, the families gathered for a big dinner after the ceremony. The apartment was bursting with people, some in the hallway, some in the backroom, the kitchen, and the front room. Some of Aaron's family were out on the stoop, getting some fresh air. Everyone had some wine, some brisket and potatoes, and vegetables, and there was even a cake for dessert. Gussie was both excited and scared. She loved having everyone there, but one by one, her older siblings had married and moved on. They were living on their own. Avram and Beatie now had three little girls, Ethel, Sadie, and Ruth, and there were whispers about new babies being planned soon by the others.

Who would take care of Sam and Frieda and her now that Tillie was gone? How would Mama pay for them without Tillie's job to help? Who would help her with her school work? Mama's English was getting better, but not good enough to help Gussie with hard words and with writing. Despite all the good food she had eaten, Gussie's stomach felt queasy and empty.

The Ridge Street apartment, once packed with David, Max, Hymie, Tillie, and Gussie plus Mama and Papa and then Frieda and Sam, would feel so empty now. Just Mama and the three younger children. True, there would be more room. But Gussie felt lonely already even though as she looked around the room, she was surrounded by her whole family and Aaron's family also. They had all left her behind. Now she was the oldest. Mama had already told her, "Well, Gussie, now you are my big girl, and you will have to help me cook and clean and care for Frieda and Sam."

It didn't seem fair at all. Gussie did not want to be the big girl. She wanted to be little, small again, sitting on Papa's knee, playing with Frieda on the stoop, laughing at Tillie, listening to stories, reading her book. She drifted into a whirl of memories that made her feel warm and safe. She looked up and saw her sister Tillie laughing with abandon, leaning into her new husband's shoulder, and smiling at him with her eyes. Aaron was so proud, sitting with his new wife, wearing his best clothes, and puffing on a cigar. Max and David and Hymie were teasing them, talking about married life.

Gussie wanted to be happy for them. Sam was bouncing around, clapping his hands and being tickled by his big brothers. Frieda sat on Mama's lap, giggling at Sam and the big brothers. Everyone was so happy. Gussie sighed. Maybe it would really all be all right after all.

Frieda called out, "Avram, tell us again about the old country."

Frieda never tired of the stories of Galicia, where Mama and Papa had lived before coming to America. Avram remembered it best since he was the oldest, and he was already a teenager when he and David had taken the boat to America over fifteen years before. Papa had already left, leaving Mama alone with the other children. Max left a year or so after Avram and David, and then finally Mama had come with Hymie and Tillie.

"What story do you want to hear?" Avram asked Frieda.

"Tell us about the village."

"Well, when I was a little boy, Papa and my first mother, Chaye, lived in a little village near Dzikow. Papa had a little shop. A food store. The farmers would trade with him, and he would sell food in the town. It was a nice little store. And we always had good food at home."

David chimed in, "But we did not have a lot. So Papa said we all had to work hard to make money so we could come to America. Avram and I would make a few cents by bringing our neighbors firewood. And sometimes we would deliver food if we really needed the money."

"Did your house look like our house in New York? Were there tall buildings?"

"No, silly, we've told you before. Everyone had their own house, their own building. We did not have to go up any stairs at all."

Max then added, "It was beautiful there. We had trees and fields and open skies where you could see forever. And the air was clean--- no rotting garbage in the streets, no noisy trams or trains."

Frieda was confused. "So why would you ever leave? You had a house and trees and fields and everything was beautiful. Why did you leave?"

Avram and David and Max turned to look at each other. How could they explain to a seven-year-old how much the Jews had been hated by their gentile neighbors? How could they explain the ways that Jews were humiliated and sometimes beaten or worse? Why frighten a seven-year-old child?

Toba, overhearing the conversation and fearing her brothers would scare Frieda, responded, "Because we wanted a change. Papa thought things would be even better in America."

Avram gave a loud snort. "Ha! Streets paved with gold!"

Hymie, who'd been just eight years old when he'd left with his mother in 1891, had been quietly listening to his big brothers. But now he jumped into the conversation.

"Avram, America is good to us. Yes, it is crowded and smelly here, and yes, we are working as hard as Papa ever worked in the old country. But here we are people with rights. We can own a real business. We can send our children to a real school."

David smiled. "We love it here also, Hymie. You know we do. We just sometimes miss the quiet and the open spaces we knew as children."

Gussie listened to all this with half an ear. Unlike Frieda, she did not find the stories of the old country very interesting at all. Why should she care about a place she would never see? What mattered was that Mama and Papa and the brothers and sisters had left that place and come here. She was born in America. She was her Papa's first American child. Whatever that old country had been no longer was important. At least not to Gussie.

Mama clapped her hands as if she had read Gussie's mind. "Enough of the old country. It's a wedding today. Let's talk about the happy times. Let's have some cake in honor of our bride and groom, my Tillie and her Aaron. Mazel tov!"

CHAPTER 12

Isadore leaned against the door of Mr. Greenberg's store. The summer air was hot and damp, and the store was even hotter. He needed a bit of outside air to cool down.

He'd been in New York almost a year. Where had the time gone? He'd hardly been anywhere out of East Harlem, except for his trips to Brooklyn to see his cousins and aunt and uncle. He still worked every day but Sunday. His days were long, but they went by quickly. The store was always busy, and Isadore knew most of the customers well by now. New York felt like home.

Where was that skinny little boy who'd nervously walked out of his house on St Andrews Street for the last time? Sure, he was still skinny and he was still short. But he was no longer a boy. He had his own apartment, tiny as it was. He had a job and was slowly saving money to help bring his family to join him. It wasn't much, but he was proud of the jar hidden under his bed as it slowly filled with dollars.

Things had gotten easier since those first few weeks. His English was coming along. Mr. Greenberg said he'd never known anyone to pick up English as quickly as Isadore had. Mr. Greenberg said, "You've got one smart head on those little shoulders of yours." Isadore wasn't sure whether to be insulted or flattered.

But it was true. In addition to understanding English, he found that by spending time with Rico and Gina and their children, he'd been able to pick up a lot of Italian. In fact, Italian was easier than English since it was so close to Romanian. And it was a good thing that he could speak some Italian because many people in the building, in fact in the whole neighborhood, were Italian. Mr. Greenberg was very pleased because Isadore could talk to the Jewish customers in Yiddish, the Italian customers in Italian, and the suppliers and other locals in English.

"Buon giorno, Signor Petruzelli!" Isadore called out. The old man who lived across the street looked up and smiled at Isadore. He walked across the street.

"Are you open yet?" he asked.

"Si, si. Andiamo." They walked into the store where Isadore watched as the old man picked out his Italian newspaper as he did every day and a small bottle of milk. Another morning in America was beginning.

"Good morning, Izzy. Any fresh eggs today?"

Isadore turned around. There was Mrs. Silverstein, speaking to him in Yiddish, but with a Galician accent, not a Romanian one. Mrs. Silverstein lived in the building over the store and was often his first customer.

"Hello, Mrs. Silverstein. The eggs have not arrived yet, but maybe by ten. Can you wait?"

"Well, I guess I'll have to wait. No eggs for breakfast today. Oh well. I'll buy some flour and some sugar when I come back so I can make some cookies later. Should I save you some?"

Isadore felt his mouth water. "Yes, please! I love your cookies!" They were almost as good as his mother's, but not quite.

"My niece Sylvie is coming uptown today to visit with my sister. Maybe you would like to meet her?"

All the Jewish mothers in the neighborhood wanted to mother Isadore; they all had a niece or a daughter for him to meet. But he had no time for girls now. He was just seventeen---still too young to get married and still working too hard to save money for his family.

"Sure, Mrs. Silverstein. But I am so busy."

"Oy, don't worry. You don't have to marry her or take her to a show. Don't you need a friend?"

Isadore would love to have some friends, but who had time? Plus he had no money to do things with friends.

"Sure, Mrs. Silverstein, bring her to the store."

"All right then. I'll be back later when the eggs come in."

The store's door closed behind her, and Isadore looked up at the clock. Five minutes to eight. Things would be getting busy soon. He swept the floor and wiped the counters, checked the shelves, and waited for the next customer to walk through the door.

The morning went by quickly. At least ten customers came through that door, and the delivery man came with fresh eggs, cheese, and milk. Isadore chatted with each of them, flipping between Yiddish, English, and Italian. The sun was out, and the leaves were starting to fall from the trees. Customers dragged in leaves every time they entered the store, meaning Isadore had to keep sweeping it up over and over again.

Around two in the afternoon, Mrs. Silverstein returned for her eggs, milk, sugar, and flour and brought Sylvie with her. Isadore had two customers in the store at the time, so Mrs. Silverstein had to wait. Sylvie smiled at Isadore when he caught her eye. She was a tall girl, taller than Isadore, and she wore a dull long skirt and long sleeves. A greenhorn, Isadore thought. Just off the boat.

Finally it was Mrs. Silverstein's turn to be served. She handed Isadore her shopping list and said, "So this is Sylvie. Say hi to Izzy, Sylvie."

"Hello."

"Hi, Sylvie. When did you get to New York?"

Sylvie blushed. "Just last Tuesday."

"How do you like New York?"

"It's nice, I think. I came from near Krakow in Galicia, so I am used to a city. But New York is so big and so noisy. And so dirty."

"Yeah, but you will get used to it."

Mrs. Silverstein jumped in. "Maybe you could show her the sights, Izzy?"

Isadore laughed to himself. *What sights?* He'd barely seen anything himself.

"Well, I work every day except Sunday, and then I visit my family in Brooklyn. I don't have much time to myself."

Sylvie blushed again. "I'm sorry. I don't mean to impose."

Isadore felt ashamed that he had embarrassed her. "No, I'm sorry I don't have more time. If I did, I'd show you New York, or at least the parts I know."

"OK, Sylvie, let's go. Maybe Izzy will find some time soon before the winter comes. You don't have to go to Brooklyn every Sunday, do you?"

"Maybe not, maybe not. Maybe another week I will be free on Sunday."

With that Sylvie smiled, and so did Mrs. Silverstein. "Thank you. Now we'll go make the cookies. I'll bring you some later."

"Thanks---I can't wait."

They walked out the door. Isadore felt a pang of regret. He really missed having friends. He missed his family; he'd get a letter once a month or so, but they took so long to arrive that the letter written in June had arrived in July. It had been over a year since he'd seen his parents, his brother and sister. Would they know who he was now, the American boy hardly a greenhorn anymore, speaking English, riding trains and trolleys all by himself to Brooklyn?

And he had no real friends. He'd spend time with Srul now and then, but they both worked so hard, and being with Srul often left him feeling lonelier. And even his Fusgeyer friends who'd stayed in New York lived and worked too far away and for too many hours. He didn't even know where they were and had no way to find them except by wandering the streets. Once he'd run into a former Fusgeyer, Baruch, but Baruch worked nights, Isadore worked days, Baruch lived downtown, Isadore uptown. It was impossible.

Isadore often thought about Hirsh. Hirsh had settled with his brother in Philadelphia, which was almost a hundred miles away. There was no way that they'd ever get to see each other. He'd been lucky to get one letter from Hirsh, which had gone from Hirsh to Iasi back to New York because Hirsh didn't know where to find Isadore in New York. Imagine that! The letter crossed the ocean twice. Isadore had written back, giving Hirsh his new address. But he'd not heard from him again.

And Malke? He had no idea where she was. He'd never seen her again after they left Ellis Island, and he didn't even know where she and her brother had ended up. Were they in Chicago? Or did they end up on a farm, like her brother had planned? Isadore had written to his parents to ask Malke's parents where she lived, but by the time his parents received his letter, Malke's parents had left Iasi, and no one knew where they had ended up either. It was useless. America was too big, and there was no way to find someone in a different city. There just was no way to find someone in America unless you knew someone who knew someone who knew them. People just got swallowed up in this big country, never to be seen again.

Maybe he shouldn't have been so quick to let Sylvie go. Maybe he needed to work harder at finding some friends. Maybe going to Brooklyn every single Sunday wasn't such a good idea. He'd have to think about it.

When Mrs. Silverstein came back a few hours later with the cookies, Isadore asked, "Where's Sylvie?"

"She went home. She said you had no time to spend with her."

"I'm sorry. She seems very sweet. I---I---I just wasn't thinking. I'm not used to girls anymore."

Mrs. Silverstein looked at him sympathetically. "I understand. I really do."

"But I'd like to take her around the city. Maybe next Sunday? I can't this Sunday since my family expects me, but I'll tell them I'm not coming next Sunday."

"I'll check with Sylvie and let you know."

Isadore waited several days before Mrs. Silverstein came back with an answer. "Her mother says to come by their house on Delancey Street on Sunday so she can meet you first."

"Sounds good. Thank you, Mrs. Silverstein."

Isadore took the train downtown that Sunday morning and met Sylvie's mother and father. Then they walked through the streets of the Lower East Side. Sylvie was very pleasant, and he told her all about his trips to Brooklyn and his job and his family. He talked so much that his mouth became dry. Sylvie was very, very quiet. Mostly she just listened or looked like she was listening.

After an hour, he brought her back to her home on Delancey Street.

"Maybe we can do this again sometime?" He knew that he wanted to go back to Brooklyn next Sunday and wasn't sure when he'd want to come downtown again to see Sylvie. He'd rather spend time with his cousins.

Sylvie nodded and looked at the ground. She shook his hand and went up the stairs to the door to her building. She turned and waved good-bye.

Isadore put his hat on his head, walked down Delancey Street back to the train. Sylvie was too shy. Conversation shouldn't be so hard. He passed Ridge Street, Attorney Street, Suffolk Street, Norfolk Street. Almost a year ago he'd been here that first day. He'd walked down Delancey Street to see the river where the boy had explained to him what Brooklyn was. He hadn't known any English then, he'd never seen such a big bridge or such a wide river, he'd been hungry and excited and more than a little scared, at least until Uncle Gustav rescued him from Aunt Zusi.

As he approached Forsyth Street, he thought about Zusi. Was she still living there? Had she gotten back her little boy Nathan yet? Was she still as unhappy? Isadore shook his head as he remembered chasing her through the streets that first day in New York City.

Isadore climbed the platform and got on the train, remembering his first ride uptown. Now he knew the trains and trolleys by heart, could read the station signs, understand the conversations others had on the train. He could read the newspapers. He was sometimes lonely, but learning to like being alone.

87

CHAPTER 13

Another school year was about to begin and Gussie was excited. Much as she loved the warm weather in the summer and the long, long days, she was ready to be back at school. Summer days could be pretty dull. Sure, in the old days she could stay outside, playing on the streets, walking through the neighborhood. Now that she was almost ten years old, Mama let her do a lot more things on her own. But she also had more work to do. She no longer was the little sister; she was the big sister. She had responsibilities.

It wasn't too bad when Tillie first left. Tillie and Aaron still lived in the neighborhood on Henry Street, and Tillie would stop by every day on her way home from work to check on Mama and the children. Friday nights she and Aaron would come for Shabbos dinner, and sometimes one of the brothers would come with his wife, but not as often.

But now Tillie was going to have a baby, and she'd not been coming around as much over the summer. She was so tired after work and feeling a bit sick to her stomach. Her tummy was still pretty flat, but Gussie could see that the buttons on her shirtwaists were tugging a bit.

Gussie was working so much harder since Tillie was not around to help. Now it was her job to wash the floors, to hang the laundry, to scrub out the tubs and the sink, and to help Mama cook. The last job she liked---standing close to Mama, watching her chop the onions until her eyes teared. Seeing Mama's eyes tear made Gussie's eyes tear also. Gussie liked to help Mama make the soup---boiling the meat bones to give it that rich flavor, adding the onions, the parsnips, the carrots. She also liked to help with the brisket or the chicken on Shabbos and holidays---whatever Mama made tasted delicious, and Gussie was proud that now she knew all Mama's secrets. Even Frieda said that Gussie was getting to be a good cook.

But it was so hot in the summer up in their apartment. The air did not move, and Gussie often felt like she could scream from being so uncomfortable. Her hair would stick to her, and her clothes felt like wet cloth clinging to her arms, her legs, everywhere. Sometimes she would sit by the window near the fire escape, wishing for a breeze to come up from the river, but it hardly ever did.

So Gussie was ready for fall, ready for school, ready to get out of the house and back with her friends and her new teacher. Fifth grade was going to be hard, but she would learn so much now. She knew her numbers well from fourth grade, and she could read even very big words. In fifth grade she would learn about history and science and read new books. She was excited for the new year to being.

She brushed her hair, pulled it back just like Tillie used to do it, and felt proud that she no longer needed help. She then called to Frieda.

"Frieda, we need to do your hair."

"Gussie, I can do it."

Gussie wished she would. She looked at Frieda sternly and said, "When you do it, it falls out by the time you get to school. And then it will be in your eyes all day. Let me do it."

"You don't do it like Tillie did. You just think you're so big now. But you are just mean. I want Mama to do it."

"Mama is getting Sam dressed. She has to go to Mrs. Levy's house and get some work to do." Mama was taking in more sewing jobs. She would pick up dresses from Mrs. Levy and repair the dresses. She also took in laundry jobs now. Mama never complained, but Gussie knew she missed Papa and her older children. So did Gussie. Frieda hardly remembered Papa and did not remember a time when the brothers lived with them. But she missed Tillie just like Gussie did.

So did Sam. Poor Sam. Almost five now. The same age Gussie was when Papa died. Sam clung to Mama all the time. He never knew Papa, and he had never lived with his big brothers. They did their best to take him places and to be fatherly to him, but they had their own lives and wives and jobs and children. Sam was such a good little boy, almost too good, Gussie thought. He'd do anything Mama said. It was good that next year he would go to school and make some friends of his own.

Gussie grabbed Frieda by the arm, tugged her hair back tight, and tied the ribbon through it. It was not perfect, but it would do. Frieda turned and stuck out her tongue at Gussie, then ran off to find her friends and go to school.

"Mama, I'm leaving," Gussie called out to the back room. "See you after school."

"OK, Gussie, but no dawdling. Today is laundry day, and you need to help me do the wash and hang it out. And you need to watch Sam so I can finish my sewing."

"All right, Mama. I will."

Gussie sighed, blowing the air out loud enough so that Mama would hear. But Mama ignored it. Gussie picked up her books and slammed the door behind her before she ran down the stairs and out to Ridge Street and off to school.

I'm free! she thought to herself. Well, at least until three o'clock.

The new teacher was Mrs. Wilson, and she had dark brown hair and dark blue eyes. She might have been pretty if she smiled. She walked around the classroom, making loud noises as her heavy black shoes hit the hard wood floors in the classroom. She carried a ruler with her, and every few minutes she would hit a desk with the ruler, making Gussie startle in her seat. She didn't like loud noises.

"This is fifth grade. You are not little children any more. You are in the upper grades here at P.S. 47. You must work very hard or you will not make it all the way to 8th grade. There is no time for games or fooling around. You will have school work to do at home, and there will be no excuses for not doing your work. Do you understand?"

"Yes, Mrs. Wilson," the class said in unison. Gussie looked around. Her classmates looked nervous, and Gussie felt her stomach making all kinds of jumps and twirls. She threw up a bit of her breakfast into her mouth. Maybe being at school would not be so much fun this year after all. She already missed Mrs. Curtin and her blonde hair tied back in a bun and bright blue eyes that sparkled. Gussie eyes filled with tears.

"Young lady, what is your name?" Mrs. Wilson was looking right at her.

"Gussie Brotman, ma'am."

"Stand up, please, when I address you."

Gussie stood up. "Gussie Brotman, ma'am."

"I did hear you, Miss Brotman. Can you tell me the sevens table?"

"Yes, ma'am."

"Well. Go ahead then."

Gussie was so nervous that she thought she would throw up. She looked down at her desk and tried hard to remember the sevens table. "7, 14, 21, 28, 35...."

She hesitated for a second. Was it 42 or 46? She couldn't think.

"Well? What's next? Can someone help Miss Brotman?"

Michael from Attorney Street raised his hand.

"OK, young man. Tell me your name, and tell me what comes next."

"Michael Weinberg, ma'am. 7, 14, 21, 28, 35, 42, 49, 56, 63, 70, 77..."

"That's enough. Miss Brotman, was Mr. Weinberg correct?"

Gussie hadn't heard anything Michael said because the noise in her head was too loud. "Yes, ma'am."

"All right, Miss Brotman, you may sit down. But next time you'd better know them all."

Gussie sat down, her face feeling as hot as one of those long summer days. She couldn't wait for the day to end.

She wasn't sure now which was worse: doing chores at home or being at school.

By January, Gussie was more used to Mrs. Wilson, but she still didn't like her. There was no talking during class, no day dreaming. Mrs. Wilson seemed to know when a student wasn't paying attention and would bang that ruler on the desk, sometimes hitting the student's hand. Her tests were very hard, and she gave a lot of homework.

Gussie had to admit that she was learning a lot. They were learning about America. Now Gussie better understood why Papa and Mama had come to this special place and left Galicia behind. Gussie loved the stories about the cruel king from England and how the colonies had been fed up and thrown the tea in the water rather than obey him and pay taxes. She liked to hear about the Pilgrims and the Indians, about the explorers. Mrs. Wilson told them how free everyone was in America.

But Gussie didn't feel too free. She was working so hard. Working at home, working at school. There was never a break. Maybe America was better than Galicia, but everywhere she looked, people seemed in a hurry, heads down, rushing to work, rushing home. Maybe there were rich people somewhere who were free, but in her neighborhood, people were poor. They didn't live in big houses and have big parties like the people in some of the books Gussie read. Some of the children in her class had relatives way uptown in East Harlem and said that they'd passed large fancy houses while going uptown on the trolleys to visit their poor family members in East Harlem. But Gussie had never been out of her neighborhood in the whole ten years of her life.

Mrs. Wilson said that in the spring the class would take a trip uptown. They would go to the big museum where they had dinosaur bones and Indian hatchets and sea shells and animal hides. And maybe they would have lunch in Central Park where there were open fields and trees and even a zoo with real living animals like zebras and tigers. They would ride the trains there and back together. Gussie could not wait. Mrs. Wilson said that if you didn't do all your homework and pass all your tests, you couldn't go, so Gussie was determined to work hard and do well so she could go. Nothing would stand in her way. Not if she could help it. Mama would just have to understand that her school work was just as important as her chores.

CHAPTER 14

Gussie rolled over in bed. It was getting lighter every morning, and she could even hear the birds chirping outside. Although the mornings could still be cold when she first got up and the fire in the stove was not yet lit, it was definitely spring. There were even some fresh flowers being sold on Orchard Street for Shabbos again, so colorful to see after the long gray winter. Gussie remembered when she thought snow was magical. Ha! Not after this winter. She hoped she'd never see it again, but she knew she would.

In a few weeks her class was planning to take the trip uptown to the museum and to the zoo in the park. She couldn't wait. She'd been excited about it ever since Mrs. Wilson had told the class about it back in January. And Gussie had been working very hard to keep up with both her chores and her schoolwork. She had almost no time for play now. She was either helping her mother with Sam or helping her cook and clean or she was doing her homework and studying for tests. She had no time to read any books except her school books. No time to play with Frieda or Ida or anyone else. But now the trip was coming closer, and Gussie was counting the days. June 15, just another two months.

"Gussie! Get up!!"

Mama was yelling---but it was still early. It was Sunday. There was no school. Gussie rolled over and covered her head. Couldn't she just get a little more sleep on Sunday morning?

"Gussie! Now!!" Her mother opened the door to their room. "The baby's coming! I have to go help Tillie. You need to get up and watch Frieda and Sam."

Gussie put her feet on the floor and dressed quickly. Mama was already out the door, and Gussie was left to start the stove and boil some water and make some breakfast for herself and Frieda and Sam.

Another baby! Gussie had to admit she was excited. Sure, she had lots of nieces and nephews now. Avram, Toba, Max and Hymie all had babies---and there were even two babies named Joseph for Papa. Mama had been so pleased. But now Tillie was having a baby, and, of course, that was extra special because, well, Tillie was extra special.

93

Gussie lit the fire, took out some leftover bread from dinner for breakfast, and called out, "Frieda! Sam! Get up! The baby is coming."

After breakfast, Gussie, Frieda, and Sam cleaned up the kitchen and swept the apartment.

"Can we go now? Please?" Frieda was anxious to go to Tillie and Aaron's and wait for the new baby to arrive. Sam was less interested, but would do whatever his sisters wanted.

"I think everything's in order. Get your shoes on, and let's go!" Gussie said.

They walked out of the building together, Gussie holding Sam's right hand, Frieda his left, and they walked the few blocks to where Tillie and Aaron lived.

"Don't go upstairs," Gussie warned. "Tillie doesn't need a bunch of young ones watching."

Gussie herself started up the stairs.

"How come you get to go?" Sam whined.

"Because I am the oldest, and Mama put me in charge."

Sam and Frieda pouted and sat on the bottom step.

"Bossy!" Frieda yelled up at her.

Gussie didn't care. She wanted to go see Tillie. She hadn't gotten to see her other nieces and nephews born, but Tillie would let her in. She was sure of it.

As she reached the third floor where Tillie and Aaron lived, Gussie heard an awful wail. She swallowed hard. Was Tillie okay? It brought back memories of when Papa died and she'd heard the awful crying from inside their apartment. What if Tillie died? Gussie suddenly forgot about the baby and was in a panic. She ran into the apartment.

"Is Tillie all right? Mama?" she called out to her mother. Aaron was sitting in the front room, his head in his hands, but she knew better than to talk to him right now.

Mama, who was sweating and red all over, came out of the backroom and said sternly, "What are you doing here? Where are your sister and brother?"

"They're downstairs, Mama. I wanted to come help."

"Gussie, go back downstairs. Tillie doesn't need your help. The baby will be here in a few hours. I will come get you then."

But Gussie ran to the back room and looked at Tillie, who wasn't making a sound at that moment, but who was also all sweaty and red. She had her knees up on the bed, spread open, with a sheet over them,

94

and her hair was all wet and matted. When she noticed Gussie, she turned and said, "Gussie, don't worry. It's just the baby coming. It hurts, but I will be fine."

But then Tillie turned her head and tightened her face. "Another one, Mama. It's coming again." And Tillie started to breathe heavily and then called out in pain again.

Gussie turned away and quickly left the apartment. She was never going to have a baby. Not if it looked like that.

It was five more hours until Mama finally came downstairs. Gussie, Frieda and Sam had been back and forth a few times. The hours had crept by. Toba and the brothers and their wives had come by at times, stayed a while, and left. Now it was just the three younger children waiting. Mama came downstairs, looking exhausted but very excited.

"You have a new nephew!" She exclaimed. "A beautiful baby boy."

"What's his name?" "Can we see him?" "Is Tillie okay?" They all loudly asked their questions all at once.

Mama chuckled. "Tillie is fine, very tired but very happy, as is Aaron. Yes, you can see him, but just one at a time. And we won't know his name until the bris. In eight days."

Sam had forgotten about that rule, but Gussie and Frieda knew. The name would be a secret until the bris. But Gussie hoped it would be another Joseph.

Toba stood over the stove, watching the food that was cooking. Tillie stood in the kitchen by Mama, squeezing her hand and digging her face into her shoulder. Gussie held Tillie's other hand, but peeked around the corner into the front room of Tillie's apartment. Their big brother Avram was holding the tiny baby on a pillow while the mohel said prayers over the baby. Tillie was not allowed to look or be in the room. But all the brothers were in there, including little Sam. Frieda was in the kitchen with them, holding her hands over her ears so she wouldn't hear the baby cry.

Gussie just wanted to hear the baby's name.

Finally, the mohel said the name in the blessing----"Lezer ben Aharon." Lezer? Gussie looked at Tillie.

"Who's Lezer?" Gussie asked.

"Aaron's father, silly. What did you think? We're going to call him Leo." Tillie said. Gussie felt stupid. Of course, Aaron would name his first child for his father.

The women heard everyone yell out, "Mazel tov!" and knew the worst was over. The baby had stopped crying. The mohel must have given him a drop of wine. Hymie looked into the kitchen and gestured to Tillie that all was okay. She could come back and take the baby now. Tillie wiped her eyes, sighed, and went to retrieve little Leo. Just eight days old and now an official Jewish boy with a Hebrew name and everything. Gussie was happy, though she was disappointed that the baby's name wasn't Joseph. But maybe it was okay. Hymie's Joseph and Abe's Joseph were always a reminder of what was missing from their lives. She pushed away the thought and went inside to the backroom to sit with Tillie while she nursed her son. Leo Bernstein. Another little boy in the family.

CHAPTER 15

Fortunately, it was finally March, and the gray, grimy snow was starting to melt. Isadore's feet were not as cold as they had been just a few weeks ago as he'd trudged through the streets on his way to Brooklyn. The winter months had been unforgiving. So much snow and ice. Many times he'd been unable to get to Brooklyn. His Sundays had felt endless. He'd spent some with Srul, but at times they'd been like sandpaper against each other, both rubbing each other raw. The long silences were excruciating, and Isadore often wished he'd just stayed home.

The jar hidden under his bed was more empty than full, the empty spaces reminding him how far he still was from seeing his family. The winter had cost him money. Boots. A warmer coat. Gloves. Money he didn't want to spend. Luckily, his cousin Abe was bigger than he was, even though he was a year younger, and Abe had given Isadore some of his old clothes, though most had to be saved for his own brothers.

As he got off the trolley just a few blocks from the Gustav's house, Isadore smiled softly and felt his shoulders relax. Finally a day of fun and relaxation with people he cared about and who cared about him. He hadn't seen them in weeks. He walked up the stairs to their apartment, kicked the mud and slush off his shoes, and untied them and took them off and placed them to the left of the door. As he was about to knock on the door, a loud voice echoed through the closed door. Uncle Gustav was upset and yelling at someone; a girl was crying. Who was it? Aunt Hennie was also upset, both now yelling and crying.

Isadore wasn't sure what to do. Should he knock anyway? Put his shoes back on and go away? He didn't want to interfere or embarrass anyone. He looked down at his shoes, sighed deeply, and picked them up. He sat at the top of the stairs and starting putting them back on again.

Just then he heard the outside door slam downstairs, and a minute later Abe was walking slowly up the stairs, head down.

"Abe? What's wrong? What's going on?"

"Uch, you don't want to know."

Isadore waited. He didn't want to pry, but he could feel his heart pound. Something was wrong.

"It's awful, just awful." Abe sat down next to him on the step, then stood up again. "Let's go downstairs. The younger ones are out there, and I am supposed to be watching them. I just came up to drop off the milk I got at the store."

Abe walked to his apartment door and knocked quietly.

"What? Who is it?" Gustav yelled.

"Just me, with the milk."

Gustav opened the door a crack and took the milk. Isadore stayed back, but could see Lilly in the background, wiping her eyes.

"All right, let's go downstairs."

Isadore followed Abe downstairs and out the door. The other cousins were all now outside, hanging around the front stoop. Although the younger ones were fooling around, Rebecca and Sarah were whispering to each other, their heads tilted together. They didn't even look up to say hello.

Abe poked them and said, "I am going to go with Isadore for a while. I'll be back. You're in charge of the little ones."

Isadore and Abe walked down the street. When they were a safe distance away, Abe told Isadore what was happening.

"My parents and Lilly are having a huge fight. My father wants Lilly to get a job and move out. He says he just can't afford to take care of her and Billy anymore. That she's an adult and she needs to grow up."

Isadore didn't know what to say. How could Lilly afford a place of her own? She was a girl, she had no husband. What kind of job would pay enough for her to take care of herself and Billy? Plus what would she do with Billy while she worked?

"How can she do that, Abe?"

"She can't. Not really. My mother doesn't agree with my father, so they're fighting with each other. It's been terrible."

"But what happened? Why now?"

"It's been a tough winter. Not enough work for my father. Higher bills for coal. And higher food bills. Billy's four now and eating more. And so is Rachel---she's not just a baby anymore."

"But Lilly's their child. Billy's their grandchild." Isadore was quite perplexed and troubled. He didn't know this side of his uncle.

"Well, you know, things haven't been great with Lilly ever since..."

Abe's voice dropped off. *Ever since what?*

"Ever since Lilly ran off with Billy's dad."

Ran off? Isadore didn't know anything about that.

"I thought she was married."

"Well, eventually she married Toscano." Toscano. *The father? The one who'd died?*

Abe looked at Isadore. "He wasn't Jewish. He was Italian. Not one of us. And she was only seventeen and married him despite my parents' objections. And without a rabbi. My parents didn't talk to her for years. They didn't even accept Billy as their grandson---until Toscano died."

Isadore understood. His parents wouldn't be happy either if he married someone who wasn't Jewish. But how could they not accept their own grandson? Isadore thought things were different in America. With all the troubles Jews had, who were they to hate others for being different? He thought of his friends Gina and Rico and how much they'd helped him when he first arrived.

"So what's going to happen?"

Abe sighed heavily. "I don't know. They threw us all out so they could talk, but it sure doesn't sound like much talking is going on."

"Maybe I should go home. Let your family have some time?" Isadore asked reluctantly.

"No, it's fine. You're family. Let's turn back."

They turned around and started to walk back when they saw Lilly running down the street, dragging Billy with her. Her hair was flying loose, and Billy was yelling, "Stop, Mama, you're hurting my arm!"

Abe and Isadore stopped walking, watching as Lilly and Billy approached. She took one look at Abe and pushed him aside, shouting at him, "Get out of my way. Go live with your miserable father. You all can go to hell!"

Abe spun around and grabbed her arm, "Lilly! Where are you going? What happened?"

"I have to take Billy to the orphanage or else we both will be on the streets. Mama said I could stay if I go to school or get a job, but Papa insisted that Billy had to go. His own grandson!"

Isadore knew from his neighbors that many children who were not really orphans ended up in these homes when the parents were ill or unable to care for them or really destitute. He never thought it could happen in his family. But he didn't say a word.

Abe also was speechless and let go of Lilly's arm. They both stood and watched as she continued her way down the street, dragging Billy with her.

"I'd better go home, Abe. I'll see you all soon," Isadore said, kicking his shoes into the dirt near the sidewalk. Abe didn't argue, just hung his head and nodded.

Isadore walked towards the trolley to make the long trip back uptown. He looked forward to being alone in his quiet room.

Billy was soon in the orphanage, Lilly in school, and Isadore was back to visiting on Sundays. Even so, things had shifted. Gustav was around less often, and Hennie kept to herself when Isadore visited. Even some of his cousins acted as though a fog had settled over the family. Robbie was quieter than ever, and the three older sisters hovered together and near their mother. Abe, Jack, Morris, and Lizzie acted as if everything was the same. But it wasn't.

This Sunday, however, Isadore was with Srul, who was now pacing back and forth, back and forth. Isadore had not seen him so nervous since their days in Iasi when they would run from the police. Srul was never a calm person, but now his pacing was making Isadore absolutely crazy. They stood near the dock, looking over to Ellis Island. They'd been there since seven that morning.

"Stop it, will you?"

"What??"

"Stop the pacing. You're making me crazy!"

Srul looked at Isadore as if he was the one who was crazy.

"Are you kidding me, Izzy? My sisters are on that ship. I haven't seen them in almost five years. My sisters! I have every reason in the world to pace. If it bothers you, go away."

Isadore shuffled his feet. "You're right. Sorry. I'm excited also. I can't wait to see them and to hear their voices and to learn about the rest of the family."

Another hour passed. And then there was their ship, the Noordam, passing Lady Liberty, about to pull into the harbor. Izzy remembered back to his own arrival. Pulling into the harbor, then taking the boat out to Ellis Island, then waiting and waiting. His last glance of Malke. His last conversation with Hirsh. He felt a pang in his chest. Uch. Such good friends. He missed those days. The

Fusgeyer days. They were hard, and he'd been tired and cold or hot and tired most of the time. But he missed the friends, the sense of mission, the music, the traveling.

"We've got a long wait. They still have to go to Ellis Island to be processed. Remember how long that took?" said Isadore.

"Yeah, I do. But I'm not moving until we meet them."

Isadore smiled. He remembered how long it took, and he knew Srul. Srul liked to eat, and he'd be hungry. At least it was late May. It was warm out, the sun was shining, and the boats in the harbor were dancing and bouncing on the water. Isadore hadn't been back here since that day over a year and a half ago. October 1904. A lifetime ago. He thought of what his cousins Bertha and Bella had ahead of them. So much for them to learn, so much to forget.

They took the ferry out to Ellis Island and waited for several more hours. The sun, which had been so bright and strong when they'd arrived at the harbor that morning, was now sinking behind the hills in New Jersey to their west across the Hudson River. The last ferry back would leave in an hour. Srul slid down and sat on the ground, the first time since that morning. Isadore sat down beside him and closed his eyes. He started to doze off, seeing images of boats and horses jumbled before him.

He suddenly felt Srul move sharply. "Izzy? Look!"

Isadore stood up just in time to see Srul jump up and run towards two young women, dressed alike in long dark beige dresses— the color of coffee with milk added--- with black shoes and bonnets tied around their hair. Isadore stood back, giving Srul a chance to see and hug them first. He calculated in his head. Bertha was now twenty; she'd been about eighteen when he'd left. She looked much the same. The deep eyes, the serious expression. Bella was his age. She had changed quite a bit---had filled out from a skinny teenager to a good-looking young woman. She looked completely bewildered.

Isadore watched them embrace, a tug of emotion threatening to overcome him.

Srul turned around and called out, "Izzy, get over here! Say hello to your cousins."

Isadore shyly joined their circle.

"Well, you're still short, but you do look older." Bertha said, eyeing him studiously.

Bella took his hand, "My cousin. How I've missed you." He and Bella had grown up together, playing together. Until Bella had

101

reached the age where it was not considered proper for girls to play with boys, even cousins, she and Isadore had been constant playmates.

"We'd better catch the next ferry. We don't want to sleep out here all night!"

As they rode the ferry back to New York, Bertha and Bella told Srul and Isadore about the family. How big the little children were. How beautiful Betty was becoming. How his brother David was learning to be a hat maker so he'd have a trade when he got to New York. How their brother Berl was also learning a trade---painting like his father and Uncle Gustav. Even Bertha and Bella had trades---they were seamstresses and ready to get work in New York. Isadore smiled to himself knowingly. It's not what they expect, he thought.

Bertha handed him a letter from his mother. He walked a distance away to read it.

Dear son, she wrote. *"I already feel better knowing that you will have your dear cousins with you. They are not your mother, but they will look after you and Srul. Please help them also. Teach them English. Teach them about New York. Protect them. We think of you always. Someday soon we also will be with you in New York. Be good.*

Protect them and teach them and help them. He would do his best. He knew that.

Gussie could not believe it. It was already June, and she was only a week away from the big day. The day she had waited for since Mrs. Wilson had announced it in January. The big class trip uptown to the museum and the park and the zoo. She had done everything she could to be sure she could go. She had done all her school work, done well on all her tests. She'd kept up with all her chores, helped Frieda with her homework, helped Mama with cooking, cleaning, and laundry. She'd been so good. She couldn't wait to see all the trees and open space---people said the park was like being in the country. She'd never been to the country, only read about it in her books and seen some pictures. Imagine being somewhere surrounded by trees and grass! And to see the animals in the zoo? Gussie didn't like many people, it was true. She was shy and awkward with most of them. But animals she loved! Not the dirty pigeons, but she loved all the dogs and cats that roamed the streets.

"Mama, don't forget. My big trip uptown with school is in just a week! Do you think maybe we could get some new shoes?"

Mama was washing the dishes from dinner. She stopped and wiped her hands on the dish towel. Gussie heard her take a deep breath.

"Oy, Gitele." Mama hardly ever called her that any more. It had been her baby name for Gussie, her Yiddish name. When Gussie started school, the teachers said she needed a more American name. Hannah Gittel wasn't American enough. So Hymie had suggested Gussie. But when Mama was feeling sentimental, she'd call her Gitele again.

"What, Mama?"

Mama put down the dish towel and took Gussie's hand. "We need to talk. You're a big girl now, almost eleven. You need to understand a few things."

Gussie felt her stomach rumble and growl.

"I don't have money for new shoes." Mama's eyes were tearing. Was that it? Gussie could wear her old shoes. Now she felt ashamed for even asking for new ones.

"In fact, Gussie, we need more money for food. The sewing work I am doing is not bringing in enough money. So I am going to go to work at the factory where Hymie works, making clothes. Just for a little bit. I am hoping we can find a lodger to help with the rent. But for the next month or two, I need to go to work."

Gussie felt her heart sink a little. Poor Mama. Gussie's eyes filled with tears also, watching Mama wipe hers away.

"I'm sorry, Mama. I don't need new shoes."

"It's not just that, Gitele. I need you home to care for Sam when I go to work. He's too little to be left alone, and Tillie is busy with her baby right now and can't take care of him either. I need you to be home with him. Just until I can figure out how to work at home and get enough money that way."

Gussie's tears stopped as she registered in her head what this meant.

"You mean....I can't go to school anymore? I can't even go on the trip?"

Mama couldn't even look at her. Gussie gulped back her tears.

"But I worked so hard, Mama, I worked so hard. Can't Frieda stay with Sam? Just that one day?"

Mama shook her head. "Frieda's still too young. You are so much more grown up."

"It's not fair, Mama. It's not fair at all. I don't want to be more grown up. Please? Just that one day?"

"Maybe I can get Tillie and Frieda to help that one day. Maybe. Now go do your school work."

Why do her school work if she couldn't go to school? She walked into the front room where Frieda and Sam were sitting. They had overheard the conversation, and they knew she was upset.

Gussie sat staring at Sam, feeling angry with him though she knew it wasn't his fault. She felt a large, hot tear drop onto her arm. It wasn't fair.

Although Gussie didn't go to school for the next two weeks, Mama did ask Tillie to help with Sam so that Gussie could go with her class to the museum. Mrs. Wilson at first said Gussie couldn't go since she'd missed so much school, but then she relented after seeing how much Gussie wanted to go.

"You've worked hard all year. You deserve to go," she told Gussie the day before the trip when Gussie showed up to school for the first time in two weeks.

So the next day Gussie woke up especially early, did all her chores, and dressed for school. Tillie showed up with Leo just in time for Gussie to walk with Frieda to school.

"Thank you, Tillie. I'll never forget this, and I'll do anything you ask for the rest of my life," Gussie exclaimed as she gave Tillie a hug.

Tillie laughed. "The rest of your life? That's a long, long time. Just go and have fun. You can come watch Leo one evening so Aaron and I can get a little time alone. How's that?"

Gussie smiled and said, "That would be just fine!" Then she rushed out the door.

The trip uptown had taken forever, and Mrs. Wilson had barked at them over and over to stay together, hold hands, and be quiet. But Gussie was spellbound by everything she saw: the tall buildings and wide streets filled with elegantly dressed men and women, striding along on the sidewalks. The horses pulling carriages filled with more people in fancy hats and beautiful clothes. The store windows filled with clothes or books or food. Everything seemed so shiny and new, not dingy like the stores in her own neighborhood.

When they got uptown to the museum at 79th Street, the class lined up and walked quietly with Mrs. Wilson watching every step they took. She warned them again to stay together, hold hands, be quiet, and pay attention. She counted them as they entered the museum. Thirty-four students.

Then they walked into the hallways and rooms of the museum, lined with photographs of animals and people from all over the world and some artifacts as well---old broken bowls and spoons, knives, and bones and stones and shells of all kinds. Gussie placed her nose against the glass to get closer.

"Miss Brotman, get your nose off that case!"

Gussie jumped back, remembering where she was. She wished she could touch the things in the cases. Or at least stay a bit longer and study them. But no, they had to keep walking, keep moving forward, or Mrs. Wilson would call out, "Pay attention, keep moving."

After an hour, they had circled back to the entry to the museum. Mrs. Wilson counted them once again. All thirty-four were still there.

She sighed and called out, "We will now leave the museum. Stay in your lines, hold hands, and be quiet. We are going to walk into the park for some free time and lunch before heading back downtown."

As they walked into Central Park, the children could no longer stay as quiet. Like Gussie, many of them had never seen so many trees and colorful flowers or so much open space. Acres and acres of green grass and huge boulders jutting out of the ground.

"Children, stop what you are doing now! We are going to go sit over there near those boulders and eat out lunches. Then you can have some free time, but you must stay close together where I can see you. No running or jumping. Any misbehavior and we will leave right away."

Gussie didn't want to run or jump or even eat her meager lunch. A hard-boiled egg and a dry roll. No, she wanted to look at the trees and the flowers, the blue sky above. She wanted to lie on the soft green grass and breathe in the aroma of the all the plants around her. She just wanted to capture everything she could see and hear and smell because she knew she wouldn't be getting up this way again for a long, long time, if ever.

CHAPTER 16

Isadore stared at the calendar on the wall in the store. It was another new year. 1907. He'd been in New York now for over two years. His Rosenfeld cousins told him that his English was perfect---that he didn't even have an accent. The money in the jar was slowly rising up, and he knew that he was making progress towards bringing his family to New York. His father could come, and then together they would make money to bring the others.

His life had changed since Bertha and Bella had arrived. Although Srul was shy and hadn't made a lot of friends, Bertha and Bella, especially Bella, were outgoing and social. Their English was still not as good as Isadore's, but it was good enough. And they both worked at dress shops where they met a lot of other young men and women. As a result, Isadore also now knew more people who lived up in East Harlem. Sometimes they would all go to Central Park together on Sundays and have a picnic and spend the day together.

Of course, that was during the summer. Now that it was winter, their visits to the park had stopped. But Isadore was not feeling as lonely as he had just a year ago.

He still went to Brooklyn as often as he could, even though he now had friends and family uptown. Sometimes Abe, Sarah, and Rebecca would come uptown on Sundays instead. They liked to get away from their own home and away from all the younger siblings every now and then.

Sarah was working as a sales clerk in a department store in midtown, and Abe was working at the Brooklyn Navy Yard as an office boy and thinking of someday joining the Navy and seeing the world. Isadore chuckled to himself: he had traveled across the world to get to America and avoid the military, and his American-born cousin was thinking of joining the military in order to get out of America and see the world.

Lilly, meanwhile, had taken Billy out of the orphanage after he'd been there for six months. They had moved not far from Isadore in East Harlem, and Lilly was going to nursing school part-time while also working and caring for Billy. Sometimes Isadore or one of the cousins even helped care for the little boy. But Isadore hadn't seen Lilly very much. She was too busy, and from what he heard from his other cousins, Billy was a handful. His time in the orphanage had left him angry with his mother and with the world. Lilly was having a lot of trouble handling him on her own.

Just then Srul ran into the store, out of breath.

"Izzy, I can't stay. I have to get to work." He stopped to catch his breath.

"What's wrong? Are Bella and Bertha okay?"

"Yes, yes, yes." Srul smiled. Then he laughed.

"Yes, everything is great. Everything is wonderful. Berl! Berl is on the boat! He will be here in just a few weeks. Berl!"

"Wonderful!! He's on his way? He's on his way here?"

Isadore ran out behind the counter and hugged Srul. They jumped up and down, hugging, laughing, even crying a bit. Their family was slowly but surely coming to America. Soon Srul would have three of his siblings with him.

"I've got to run to work before I get fired. But we should all celebrate later. Come up to our apartment for dinner after work, okay?"

"Yes, yes, of course! I'll bring something to share. Mazel tov! Such good news!"

Srul rushed back out the door, and Isadore leaned against the wall. He was both excited and envious. Srul had proven that it is worth the wait. Eventually his family would leave Iasi and come to New York. It gave him hope.

CHAPTER 17

The skies were gray and threatening, but the air was getting warmer. It was March, and spring was around the corner. Gussie took the rags out of the wash bucket and continued to scrub the kitchen floors. Mama had left to go to work, Frieda had gone to school, and once again she was home with Sam. She'd missed so much school this year. Mama needed her at home to help with Sam and to help with the household chores. Sam was six now, but still not old enough to go to school. Not until next year. He was sitting in the front room, bouncing a ball against the wall, over and over again.

"Sam, stop that! You're giving me a headache."

"Sorry, Gussie, but I'm so bored. When will you be done?"

"Well, if you came and helped me, I'd be done sooner."

"I can't wash floors. I'm a boy, and I'm only six."

"Well, then just be quiet and wait if you aren't going to help."

Gussie went back to her scrubbing. She actually liked to clean; it made her feel like she was worth something. Watching Sam was both boring and tiring. He wanted to run and climb and pick up dirty things, and she just wasn't interested in chasing after him or watching every step he took. Sure, he was sweet, and she loved him, but he was a burden.

But it was better than going to the sweatshops. Moshe from down on Attorney Street had dropped out of school completely to work in the shop. And Berel was only thirteen and working at the Triangle factory a little uptown. Gussie knew Tillie also had gone to work in the shops when she was only a little older than Gussie was now. Lots of her classmates missed school because they had to work at home or work at the factories. Gussie was not alone, but it didn't make her any happier about it.

Things were tough at home. Mama didn't make a lot of money from sewing at home, not enough to feed three children and herself, so some weeks she would go to the sweatshop and Gussie would stay home. They had also taken in a boarder, Mr. Friedman. He was a tailor and had only been in the country for six years or so; he came from Galicia, like Mama and Papa. He was tall, skinny, and his hair was always too long and greasy looking. He didn't smell great either. His eyes were kind, and he was nice enough, and Mama liked having a man sleeping in the kitchen by the front door. It made her feel more secure at night. He was younger than Mama, about ten years younger. He usually came home after they'd gone to sleep, and he got up before they all were up and ready to eat, so they didn't see him very much.

The extra money did help. Mama was able to work at home more, and some days Gussie still got to go to school. Gussie still had dreams of going back to school every day. She dreamed that someday she would get to go back to the museum and the park.

But Mr. Friedman was one more person for Gussie to clean up after. And do laundry for. Mama had agreed to do his laundry and provide food in exchange for his rent.

Oy, the laundry. It was hanging out to dry in the back. Gussie peered out the window.

"Sam, I've got to run into the back and take in the wash. It looks like rain. Come with me."

Sam dragged himself up, and they went outside to take down the clothes. At least it was an activity, he thought.

"Thanks, Sam. See? You can be helpful even if you are a boy and only six years old."

CHAPTER 18

Isadore stepped carefully into the chilly ocean water, being careful to stay close to the edge and not going too far. Around him, children were splashing and making noise, happy to be cooling off in the waves, happy not to be in school. The summer air was hot, and the smells of cooked meat and fried dough filled the air. It was the Fourth of July, and Mr. Greenberg had closed the store and given him the day off. He and his cousins Berl, Srul, Bertha, and Bella had taken the long train ride all the way from uptown to Coney Island where his other cousins, Abe, Sarah, Rebecca, Jack, Robbie, and Morris had met them. Lizzie and Rachel, whom they all called Ray now, were too little to come without their parents. But there he was with ten cousins. Ten! He couldn't believe his luck.

Today was America's birthday. Aunt Hennie had packed enough food for all the cousins, and Gustav had given Sarah some money to buy everyone ice cream. Isadore watched Morris, Jack, and Robbie racing into and out of the waves, laughing, pushing each other, and diving into the water. Isadore wanted to join them, but he'd never learned to swim. Abe had promised to teach him, but so far they'd not had a chance. He'd borrowed one of Abe's swimming costumes, but the top straps were always slipping down, and the bottoms hung on him like those loose bags of potatoes he saw at Mr. Greenberg's store. He was afraid if he went in the water, the whole costume would slip right off of him!

"Izzy, you want another sandwich?" Abe called out to him from the beach behind him.

Aunt Hennie had made meatloaf sandwiches. Isadore's mouth watered, thinking again of the taste. "Really? There are some left?"

Abe approached him, "Yeah, Bertha and Bella didn't like them. They said they tasted funny. Such snobs."

"Aw, Abe, there's not snobs. They're just Romanian. They aren't used to sandwiches like that. It's an American food. We don't have sandwiches like that in Iasi."

"I suppose. But they need to try new things. They need to learn to be more American. You did."

Isadore shrugged. He knew that not everyone learned English as quickly as he did. And he'd had no choice but to adapt. He didn't have

110

sisters and brothers to live with, to link him to the past. Srul and Berl and Bertha and Bella could speak to one another without learning English. And maybe they just found it harder to adjust. Everyone was different.

He tried to explain it to Abe, saying, "They're trying. It's not easy. You've always lived here. You didn't have to leave your parents and sail for two weeks across the ocean. You've always been able to speak English and Yiddish. Our cousins? They have a lot to learn. I'm just lucky, I guess. I learned more quickly."

Isadore gobbled down the sandwich and reached into the water to wash his hands and face. The salt water stung a bit where he had shaved, but it felt good on his hot face and sweaty, sticky hands.

"Hey, Bertha, Bella---you want to take a walk?" He called to them in Yiddish.

Srul and Berl were engaged in some quiet conversation by themselves off in the distance. The other boys were still in the water, and Abe dove in to join them. Sarah and Rebecca had been cleaning up from lunch and were talking to each other in English, which Bella and Bertha still struggled to understand.

Bella and Bertha got up to walk with him. The crowds of people surrounding them made it difficult to walk a straight line along the beach. As they weaved around all the people standing, walking, and sitting on the beach, Isadore was amazed by the scene. So many people at leisure, enjoying the hot sand and bright sunshine. This American birthday was a good thing.

"Are you enjoying the beach, girls?"

"It's okay. It's so hot. The sand? It's hot. And it sticks to everything." Bertha rubbed some sand off her shoes as she spoke.

Bella and Bertha were wearing the same long, heavy brown cotton dresses they wore to work. And large hats. No wonder they were hot. Sarah and Rebecca at least had lighter dresses to wear to the beach.

"Oh, Bertha, it's okay. It's better than being uptown in that apartment with no air," Bella responded.

Isadore shook his head. Would they rather be in Iasi?

"How's the English coming along?" he asked them.

"Not bad. Not bad. We understand it when they talk slowly."

"But not when they talk fast, like Sarah and Rebecca or the boys!"

Isadore couldn't help but feel for Bella and Bertha, but he also felt a bit impatient with them. They were having a hard time moving forward, but they needed to work harder to get there.

"Maybe you should go to night school. It will help you learn English faster."

The sisters looked at each other and shrugged. "Maybe. We're so tired at night."

Isadore decided to change the subject. "Any news from home?"

"They're getting closer to coming. Papa's not feeling well, and Mama wants to get him here as soon as possible. Her last letter said he's just not right in the head these days, very forgetful. She's worried."

"When will they come?" Isadore understood their concern.

Bella said, "Maybe in the fall. Before the New Year, we hope."

"And all the children will come with them. Our whole family will be together for the first time since Srul left over five years ago," Bertha added.

"Imagine that," Isadore exclaimed. "The whole family!"

It wasn't his parents, his brother, or his sister. But it was the next best thing. Isadore loved his American cousins, but the Romanian cousins had been part of his life forever. They were perhaps not as much fun, but they were as close to having his parents and David and Betty here as he could imagine. His Brooklyn cousins had never seen Iasi. They hadn't known him as a little boy. They'd never met Mama and Papa. But Aunt Perla and Uncle Yankel did. He couldn't believe it. A few more months, and they would be here.

When would it be his turn? Would the jar under his bed ever be full?

CHAPTER 19

"Mazel tov!"

Once again, the family was gathered at Tillie and Aaron's apartment. But now they lived in Brooklyn. They'd moved a few months before, and Aaron and Tillie had opened a grocery store. Gussie was angry that they had moved. Now she hardly got to see Tillie. She was busy with the store and with Leo. And Brooklyn was far. She could no longer walk a few blocks to visit her sister.

Now there was another baby, another boy, another bris. But this time the baby was named Joseph---Joseph Bernstein. Now it was Tillie's turn to name the baby for her father.

For the moment, Gussie was happy. Everyone was happy. Another little Joseph. Now there were three---Abe's Joseph, Hymie's Joseph, and Tillie's Joseph. Papa would be so proud. He deserved to be. All his children wanted to honor him, to name a boy for him. To remember him.

But as they walked home, Gussie felt a certain heaviness inside. It was almost September, and school would start. Finally Sam was old enough to go to school. He'd be seven, really almost a year late, but at least he was finally going. Gussie hoped she'd finally be able to get caught up at school. She'd missed so much at the end of the year.

"Mama," she said as they started to cross the bridge back to their neighborhood, "school starts in a few weeks. I'd like to go, if I can, even if I have go back to fifth grade again."

Mama sighed and said, "I don't know about school. You're going to be twelve. You can read and write and do numbers. You don't need school any more. Tillie didn't go to school after she learned to read and write, and she is doing just fine. Many of your classmates are working in the factories. You need to help also. You know we need more money."

How could Gussie explain? It wasn't that she needed to go to school. She wanted to go to school. Gussie liked working hard and learning. She wanted to know about the world; she wanted to read bigger and harder books. She wanted to understand all those big words in the Pledge of Allegiance. She wasn't finished learning.

But there was no arguing with Mama. She would do as she was told. She would do the cleaning, the cooking. She would get Sam ready for school. She would take in sewing and earn some money.

And Mama was right. She was growing up. Her body was changing. She no longer looked like a little girl. Her clothes were tight across her chest, and she could see that her breasts were starting to develop. Mama had told her that her monthlies might start soon also. Her skin was not as clear and smooth as it had once been, and her hair just didn't look as good as it used to look. Nothing felt right.

Frieda took her hand and tried to cheer her up, saying, "Gussie, stop moping. It's a happy day! We have a new nephew----a little Joseph. Here's a piece of cake I saved from the bris. You can have it!"

Frieda always was so cheerful. But Frieda still had another year to go to school. Gussie envied her.

"Sure, Frieda, sure. I'll have some cake, and then my skirt will be even tighter."

Frieda looked at her and shook her head. "Why do you have to make yourself unhappy? Try to be happy."

Gussie took the piece of cake from Frieda and turned, giving her sister a fake smile.

"See? I am trying to be happy."

CHAPTER 20

The Srulovici cousins sat in the dark front room of their apartment. Srul was beside himself with anxiety; Berl was sullen, sitting silently in a corner, staring at the floor. Bertha and Bella were taking turns crying. First one would cry and be comforted by the other; then the other would start crying. They'd both cry, and then one would comfort the other again. Isadore didn't know what to do for them. Their parents and younger siblings had been detained at Ellis Island.

Then he had a thought.

"Srul, I'm going to Brooklyn. Uncle Gustav might be able to help. He's been here the longest and knows a lot of people."

Srul looked over at him. Bertha and Bella stopped weeping, and even Berl looked up from the floor.

"Yes, good idea."

Isadore grabbed his coat and left their apartment. It was bitter cold---the end of December, 1907. As he walked to the train, he wished he had gloves. At least his head was covered. He pulled his coat tighter and ran to the train.

When he got to Brooklyn, Isadore explained what was going on, and Gustav and Isadore immediately hopped on a train back to Manhattan.

"Oy, my poor sister Perla. She must be ready to have a fit. To travel across the ocean with three young children and then get stuck at Ellis Island."

Uncle Gustav shook his head and pulled at his graying mustache. Isadore knew that Gustav had troubles of his own. Lilly had sent her son Billy to another home, a Catholic one this time. She had no money and was too poor to support herself, let alone a young child, and she had no one to care for him after school when she was at work. She'd moved back home again.

The train rattled on. Isadore had his own anxious thoughts. What if his aunt and uncle had to return to Romania? What would Srul, Berl, and their sisters do? Would they go back also? And would this discourage his own family from coming? He was getting closer and closer to saving enough for a ticket and had sent some of the money back home. He had hopes that maybe his father would come the following year. But if Perla and Yankel were sent home, his mother might refuse to leave.

Finally, Isadore and Gustav got to Battery Park. They stood in the line for the ferry to Ellis Island. The wind off the water was bitter cold, tearing at Isadore's skin and his coat, forcing him to remove his hat so it wouldn't blow away. He shivered. Uncle Gustav put his arm around him, warming him up a bit.

The ferry finally came back, and they hopped on with all the others once those arriving from Ellis Island had disembarked. The ride over the water was even more uncomfortable than it had been standing at the water's edge. Isadore blew into his hands, stomped his feet, and then pulled his hat on his head, holding it as far over his ears as he could.

Once they got to Ellis Island, Isadore ran to keep up with Gustav's wide strides. He wished his own legs were as long as his uncle's. Gustav opened the door to the building and spoke to some officers standing inside. Isadore couldn't hear much, but he saw them point towards a door down the hall.

"Isadore, you stay here. We don't need to make a scene. I'll be right back."

Isadore sat down on a bench, just grateful to be inside away from the cold. He leaned his head back against the wall and waited.

After thirty minutes, he looked up and wondered what had happened to his uncle. He stood up and looked around. Nothing. He started to pace, thinking of Srul and the others. Finally, he heard Gustav's voice, saying, "Thank you," and looked up. He was walking back towards Isadore. But his head was down, and Isadore couldn't see his face. His heart leapt up in his chest. This couldn't be good news.

He walked towards his uncle.

"So? What is it?"

Gustav grimaced.

"Not good. It's Yankel. Some problem with his eyes."

Isadore swallowed hard. He knew that eye disease was one of the biggest reasons immigrants were denied entry.

"Oh, no."

"Well, it's not that disease. Nothing contagious, so that's good. Just some scars in his eyes or something. He can't see well. They're afraid he won't be able to work."

"But he has four grown children living here. Can't they help?"

"Yes, but he's not supposed to be a burden on the country. Plus there's more."

Gustav shook his head and sighed.

"What? Tell me!"

"He's not right in the head, Izzy. That's what they say. Forgetful, senile, they said."

Isadore remembered that Bertha and Bella had said that their father was not himself. Now Isadore shook his own head and sighed.

"What's going to happen?"

"There will be a hearing. I made sure of that. I requested a hearing. I have permission to come, and I'll bring my friend Saul along. He's a landsman, also from Iasi, and he's made a lot of money here. Together we will try to stop them from deporting Yankel and the family."

"When's the hearing? Can I come also?"

"In two days. No, you're already missing work this morning. You go back, tell the others what is happening. Tell them the hearing will be on December 30, two days from now. Maybe it will be a happy New Year for 1908."

As they hopped off the ferry, Isadore hugged his uncle and ran to get the uptown train. He felt hopeful, knowing Uncle Gustav would be there. He would tell his cousins not to worry too much. But he also was worried.

Isadore couldn't go downtown the day of the hearing; Mr. Greenberg was not happy that he'd missed work already that week, leaving Mr. Greenberg in charge of the store alone. But he couldn't think of anything else the whole day. He made at least a few mistakes in shelving some products and was distracted when customers came into help. But it was almost closing time, and he'd still heard nothing from his cousins.

As he swept the floor for the hundredth time that day, mostly out of nerves, not need, he heard the door swing open. There were his four Romanian cousins. He couldn't read their expressions. What had happened?

"So?"

117

Srul spoke slowly and seriously.

"We don't know yet, but Uncle Gustav says it looks promising. The officer at the hearing was kind, and he told them that he was making a recommendation that my father could be admitted if something called a bond was posted. Uncle Gustav said that it means putting up some money to show that my family won't be dependent on the government and end up in a poorhouse. Also, we have to appear and show that we're all working."

"How much money is the bond? Who has the money?"

"Uncle Gustav said he does and his friend Saul does also. I guess they don't lose the money unless my family ends up in trouble. But it's a lot of money. Thousands."

Isadore was impressed. Uncle Gustav had that much money despite having all those mouths to feed in his own house.

"Well, that's great news, right? When will we know if the bond will work?"

Berl joined in, "Not for a few more days. It's going to take a bit to get the bonds issued, I guess. Then we appear. And then we wait for the decision."

Isadore wondered how the little children, especially Leah, the youngest, were holding up. Ellis Island was not a fun place to be stuck, but he supposed it was better than it had been on that ship across the ocean.

"OK, so we wait. We've waited this long, we can wait another few days."

His cousins nodded. They seemed confident now that it would all be okay. Uncle Gustav had seen the family at the hearing, and although their father was frail and confused, everyone else was holding up well.

"I just hope the US government is not like in Romania," Bertha said. "Who'd ever trust what they say?"

True, true, Isadore thought. A government is never to be trusted. But he kept that thought to himself.

Three days later, his aunt and uncle and his three younger cousins were released from Ellis Island and allowed to enter the US. Isadore would get to see them that night at his cousin's apartment once he was off from work. The hours moved slowly all day as he waited for the store to close.

Once he'd locked it up, he ran all the way up to his cousins' apartment. It would be very crowded now---with nine people living in two rooms. Soon they would have to find a bigger place, but for now they would all stay close. Isadore ran up the stairs and banged loudly on the door.

Bella opened the door, her eyes sparkling with tears and joy. "They're here! They're here!"

Isadore pushed her gently aside and looked around for his aunt. Perla looked just like his mother; she was the closest thing in the world to his mother. And there she was! She looked more than just three years older than when he'd last seen her. The anxiety, the burden of taking care of her husband as well as her children, the ride across the Atlantic, and the stress of the hearing had taken its toll. She was tired, but excited to see him. He hugged her tightly.

"Ah, my sweet nephew. How your family aches for you. I only wish I could have brought them along."

Isadore nodded in agreement. "Soon they will be here, Aunt Perla. I promise you. Soon."

Isadore knew that Perla would be lonely. A sickly husband, a foreign country, a foreign language, and so many children. But he also knew that she, like his mother and his uncle Gustav, was tough and strong and would do everything to survive in this new land.

He turned around, saw his little cousin Leah, now almost eight years old, and lifted her and twirled her around. "How big you've grown since I last saw you? You were only four then---do you even remember me?"

"A little. You look familiar." Then she whispered in his ear, "But I don't remember Srul at all."

Sure, she'd been just a toddler when he'd left. How odd it must be not to know your own brother.

Pincus, now almost ten, remembered Isadore well and came to shake his hand. And Rebecca, a sixteen year old now, hardly looked like the young girl he'd known in Iasi. As for his uncle, Isadore felt his heart break a little. He sat in a corner, smiling at the crowd, but with a foggy look in his eyes. Isadore went to say hello, and Yankel looked a bit quizzical.

"Uncle Yankel, it's me. Isadore. Ghitla's son. Goldschlager?"

"Sure, sure, sure. How are you? How is your mother?"

Obviously, Yankel was very confused. Maybe it was the trip. Maybe he'd be better after he settled in. Maybe.

119

Uncle Yankel never had that chance to settle in. He only got weaker and weaker, physically and mentally. He couldn't work and complained all the time that his stomach hurt.

The two youngest children were starting to adjust and learning to speak English and read it as well in school. Leah, in particular, was a fast learner and enjoying the challenges of her new school, her new friends, her new country. Rebecca was having a harder time. She'd left a boyfriend back in Iasi, someone she'd hoped to marry. Leaving at sixteen is very hard. Isadore knew that. He was hoping that soon she would move on and cheer up. It had only been a few months.

Aunt Perla was being strong, as expected. She was struggling to learn English, but at least was trying. She and her older daughters were all working as seamstresses, making beautiful clothing. But Yankel? He was lost. She had to keep her eye on him.

And then one morning in April he woke up, crying out in pain, holding his sides together, and sobbing. Perla knew that something was terribly wrong. She took him to the hospital where they discovered he'd broken his ribs. But she'd no idea how. He'd been in bed.

The doctors admitted him to the hospital, seeing how frail he was and how awful his color was. It didn't take many days before it became clear that Yankel was never coming home. He died a week after he'd been admitted. Cancer, the doctors said. Cancer in his ribs and in his lungs.

The family was in shock. After all they'd been through----the separation, the ocean voyages, the detainment, the hearing---to have it all end like this. For this they had come to America? For their father to die?

Of course, he would have died in Iasi also, but there was no consoling the children. Partly they blamed America. Maybe if he hadn't been detained? Maybe that got him sick? Maybe he got cancer from someone on Ellis Island?

Isadore knew better than to reason with them. They were grieving and the best he could do was to listen as they sat shiva after burying their father.

CHAPTER 21

Gussie sensed something was different with Mama. She was just, well, a little bit happier. Mama was always looking at the bright side of things, but this was different. She even hummed to herself and smiled.

Maybe someone was pregnant in the family again. There had been more babies. Max and his Sophie now had a little girl, Rosalie, just born a few months ago in June. Avram's wife Beatie was pregnant, but they had four children already. Mama couldn't be too excited about a fifth, could she? Maybe. Maybe David's Annie was finally pregnant? Or Toba or Tillie?

Maybe Mama was just happy that her children were growing up, that she had so many grandchildren, that she had friends and was adjusted to life in America.

Unlike Mama, Gussie herself rarely felt happy. When she wasn't working in the house and taking care of Sam and cooking and cleaning, she was doing piece work for a sweatshop, making belts for women's dresses. She missed school and being with other people her age. Aside from Frieda, she had no real girlfriends any more. She hoped that maybe she could go back to school at some point, though she didn't know how she could. Mama needed her help, and so she had no choice.

Then one Sunday morning Mama called them into the front room that morning after breakfast.

"Children, I have something to tell you. Something very exciting."

"What, Mama, what?" Sam was jumping up and down. "Are we going to Coney Island?"

"No, silly boy. But maybe we will when it reopens in the spring. No, it's even more exciting."

"Tell us, Mama. Don't tease," Frieda whined.

"Well, you all know Mr. Hershkowitz, right? Our good friend and neighbor?"

Gussie felt her tummy flip. Uh oh. Mr. Hershkowitz. The Hungarian man who lived in the next building on Ridge Street; his wife Fanny had died a few years ago. Fanny had been a good friend after Papa died, cooking meals and bringing them over.

"Sure, Mama, his daughter Annie is my friend. She's just a year or so younger." Frieda was being stupid. Didn't she know what was coming?

"Well, Mr. Hershkowitz has asked me to marry him. And we will all be living together."

Frieda looked at Sam, and Sam looked at Frieda. Gussie stared at the floor, thinking, *Mr. Hershkowitz is no match for Mama. He's a shoemaker and smells like leather and oil. His hands are always stained from shoe polish. Plus he has nine children living with him---from Morris, who is already 28 to Annie, who is ten. What was Mama going to do with all those children?*

And who needed a man anyway? Mama had her children. As far as Gussie could tell, men were just annoying. They stared at her when she walked on the streets, sometimes whistling or whispering as she passed. She knew she was pretty. Her body was developing in all kinds of ways---taller, fuller. She knew men liked all those curves and bumps, even if she didn't like their attention. But she had to admit. It did feel good. She liked that they thought she was pretty. She just wished they wouldn't stare and whistle and whisper.

"Are they moving in here? There are an awful lot of them, you know," Gussie muttered under her breath, not wanting to get Mama upset with her.

"No, no, of course not. We'll move into his place. He has four whole rooms. And the best part? I won't have to go to work anymore. Mr. Hershkowitz has a good business, making shoes, and he will support us along with his older children, many of whom are working. Some are working as tailors, some as shop girls, all making a decent living. Isn't that wonderful?"

Gussie had to admit that the idea of Mama staying home again sounded good. Maybe she could go back to school? Maybe she would have more time to read, to be with friends, to take the train to other parts of the city. Or maybe she could get a job in a factory and start earning money herself.

But the thought of living with those nine Hershkowitz brothers and sisters made her queasy. All those older boys. Some of them already looked at her in ways she didn't like.

"Mama, can I go back to school?" Gussie asked Mama hopefully.

"I don't know, Gussie. You're thirteen now, and you've already missed a whole year of school. I'll probably need you home to help me with the household. After all, there will be a lot of cooking and laundry to do."

Gussie felt her eyes sting with tears and her face flush bright red. She put her hands to her hips and exclaimed, "Then I am not going. I am not going to clean up and care for all those Hershkowitz brats."

"Gussie! How dare you! This will be your new father and your new brothers and sisters." Mama was angry. She hardly ever sounded angry, but now she did.

Gussie ran from the room, her face hot and red, tears streaking down her cheeks. She didn't want to hurt Mama's feelings, but she knew she did not want to move in with the Hershkowitz family. More children to wash and clean for? Those sons with their dirty looks and private jokes?

And Mr. Hershkowitz would not be her father. She didn't need him. She had Papa. Sure, Papa had been gone for over seven years now, and his face and his voice were just shadows in her head. But he was her Papa, and no one was going to replace him. Maybe for Frieda, who barely remembered Papa, and for Sam, who never knew Papa at all. But not for Gussie.

If she was too old for school and old enough to work, then she was also old enough to make up her own mind.

That afternoon Gussie took the trolley over the bridge to Brooklyn all by herself; she'd gone many times with Mama, but never alone. But now Mama had sent her alone to talk to Tillie. Mama thought Tillie would talk some sense into her. Gussie smirked to herself as the trolley reached the other side of the bridge. Tillie was never going to change her mind. She got off the trolley and walked towards Tillie and Aaron's store in Brooklyn.

When she arrived, Tillie hugged her and squeezed her.

"Gussie, what are you doing here? What a surprise!"

Gussie hesitated for a minute. Should she wait a while, not rush right in? But she couldn't wait. She had to ask Tillie for help right away.

"Tillie, you have to help me. You know Mama is marrying the shoemaker, right?"

"Yes, of course, she told me on Sunday when I visited."

"She wants me to live with them, but I hate them. I can't live there. You understand, don't you? I don't want a new family. I don't want to live with them. There will be no privacy, and no one will care about me. I'll just be the stepsister no one likes."

Gussie thought back to some of those fairy tales with evil stepsisters and stepmothers. Cinderella? She would not be Cinderella.

"Let's talk, Gussie, but first sit down, slow down, and have some cookies and some milk."

Tillie made the best cookies. Soft and buttery and so, so sweet. Gussie gobbled down three or four and drank half a glass of milk. Owning a grocery store must be wonderful. You always have plenty of food.

Tillie stared into her coffee cup and then looked up.

"So, Gussie, I have an idea for you. But you really have to think about it carefully. There is no pressure, and I haven't talked to Mama. You're almost thirteen, but you're still Mama's child. She gets to decide. But here's my idea."

Tillie took another cookie.

"What if you lived with Aaron and me here in Brooklyn? We could use the help with the store and with Leo and Joe. We are very busy, and you know how to care for little boys after taking care of Sam all this time. You could sleep in the kitchen. We wouldn't charge rent, of course, since you'd be helping us. And you're family. What do you think?"

Gussie couldn't believe it. Tillie was not going to argue with her at all. In fact, she'd just solved all her problems. She could live with Tillie! What could be better? What could make her happier than to live with her big sister, the one she'd loved with all her heart forever, the one who could make her laugh when no one else in the world could?

"Yes, yes, yes! I'd love that! Oh, Tillie, I would love it!! Are you sure Aaron will agree?"

"Of course, I'll have to talk to him first. But he's sure to agree. He works all the time in the store, so he'd be happy to have me there to help more. I can do that if you're watching Leo and Joe."

Gussie jumped out of the chair, cookie crumbs tumbling to the floor. She was so excited that she didn't even notice that she'd made the floor dirty. She put her arms around Tillie's neck and hugged her.

"You're the best sister ever, Tillie. I'll never be able to thank you enough."

"Well, let's see what Mama says. Remember. It's her decision. Not yours. Not mine."

"Will you talk to her for me? Please?"

"Yes, I will.

The following week Tillie came with Leo and Joe to Ridge Street on Sunday, her one day away from the store. Aaron stayed back to work on the books.

Gussie hadn't said a word to Mama. She'd been quietly keeping the secret. But she'd been happier, humming as she did her chores. Mama knew that Gussie had gone to see Tillie, and she probably assumed that Tillie had talked some sense into her. But Gussie was determined to move to Brooklyn.

Mama was making some lunch for her grandsons. Leo was two, and Joe only a year old. They liked her chicken soup with the noodles. Leo could eat the chicken in it and the vegetables, and if she mashed it up, Joe would have some also. Mama was always excited to see her grandchildren.

Finally, just before noon, Tillie arrived, holding Leo's hand and carrying Joe as she walked down Ridge Street. Gussie had been waiting on the stoop, and she jumped up and lifted Joe from Tillie's tired arms. She would show Tillie how good she was with little boys.

Gussie whispered to Tillie, "I haven't said a word. I'm leaving it to you."

Tillie laughed. "I'll do my best."

They walked up the many stairs to the apartment where Mama was waiting anxiously to hold her little grandsons.

"I wish Brooklyn was closer," Mama said, as she kissed little Joe on the head.

Gussie felt that twinge in her tummy. Would Brooklyn be too far away for Gussie as well?

Tillie took off the outer garments the boys were wearing. It was a brisk November day. Mama and Mr. Hershkowitz planned to be married in early December. There wasn't much time to persuade her.

"So, Mama, are you excited for the wedding?" Tillie asked as she settled the boys into their seats.

"Well, it's just going to be a simple ceremony in Phillip's apartment with his children and mine. Well, those who can be there. I know it is hard for you all with your own families and work."

Gussie knew the others were also a little sad that Mama was remarrying. All of them missed their father and worried that Mama

125

would forget him. But Tillie said she understood. She knew Mama was lonely and tired of being on her own. Phillip was a good man. Why shouldn't they share their lives and make each other a little less lonely? But Gussie wasn't convinced.

"I'll be here, Mama. You know that." Tillie said gently, putting her hand over Mama's.

Mama smiled. Tillie was always her most reasonable child. Her first daughter. The little girl she'd dragged across the ocean when she was not even ten years old. How well she had adjusted to America, speaking English like an American, always cheerful, always helping others. Mama was so proud of Tillie.

After the boys had finished their soup, Tillie asked Gussie to take them into the front room and read to them. She gave Gussie a knowing look, and Gussie nodded. Then she picked up Joe and said, "Come in here, Leo. I have one of Sam's favorite books for you."

But Gussie stayed close enough to the kitchen so that she could still hear most of what Mama and Tillie were saying.

"Mama, let's talk about Gussie." She heard Tillie say. Gussie swallowed hard and again felt her stomach jump a bit.

She couldn't hear what Mama said, but then she heard Tillie say, "I'd like Gussie to come live with me. Aaron needs my help in the store, and Leo and Joe are a handful. Plus it's very early, but I am pregnant again. Don't tell anyone yet, but another baby will be here in 1909. I know you want Gussie with you, but she's thirteen and ready to work. Let her work for me. You don't need one more person in the Hershkowitz apartment. You'll have Frieda and Sam and all those Hershkowitz sons and daughters."

Gussie heard a crash as something fell on the floor, but she couldn't see what had happened. It was very quiet for a few minutes. Had Mama fainted? Was she too upset to talk? Then she heard Mama sobbing.

"Let her live in Brooklyn? My little Gitele? Yes, she's thirteen, but I need her with me. She's my American daughter. She's my helper."

Gussie wanted to rush in and stop Mama from crying. Then she heard Tillie talking quietly, saying, "Mama, she loves you, and she needs you also. But right now this is not good for her. She'll be happier in Brooklyn, and I'll be happier having her there. I promise that I will make sure she comes every week to see you, whether I can get here or not."

126

Mama wiped her tears. "Oh, Tillie, what would your father say to see his little girls separated? His two little American red head girls? What will Frieda do without her best friend? And Sam will be heart-broken."

"Just think about it, Mama. That's all I ask. Just think about it."

Mama shook her head. "I don't know, Tillie. I don't know."

Gussie peeked out of the corner of the other room and looked at Tillie, then at Mama. She saw the tears on Mama's cheeks, and her heart sank. But she didn't say a word. She took the book and went back to read to her little nephews. She would have to wait and see.

The next several days were very uncomfortable in their apartment. Mama didn't say a word about her conversation with Tillie, and Gussie didn't dare bring it up herself. They both just pretended it hadn't happened, but Gussie was anxiously awaiting a decision. Then finally Mama pulled Gussie into her room one morning and talked to her.

"Gussie, do you really want to live with Tillie?"

"Yes, I do. I really do."

"Won't you miss us? We will miss you."

Gussie burst into tears.

"Of course, Mama, of course, I will. But I can't move in to the Hershkowitz house. They're not my family. I don't want to be their little sister who cleans and cooks. I'd rather cook and clean for my real sister and my nephews. And Brooklyn is so nice. It's cleaner and quieter than here. But I'll miss you, Mama."

Gussie couldn't stop sobbing. Mama knew then that this was not a rash decision. That Gussie really knew what she wanted. And Mama couldn't stop her or change her mind.

"Then, you can live with Tillie. I've spoken to Philip, and he thinks it's for the best. And your brothers and sisters also believe that it is a good idea for everyone. But you must come home every week, every single week. Do you understand?"

"Of course, Mama, of course, I will. Any time you need me and more. I will be here."

They hugged for several minutes until Mama pulled away. "Then you'd better start packing your things. The wedding is just two days away, and you'll need to take your things with you that night. No point in dragging them down the street to Phillip's house only to move them again."

What did Gussie have to move? A few skirts and shirtwaists, her shoes, a winter coat, some under clothes. Her brush and her other personal items. One small suitcase would do it. And she could return it to Mama at her first visit.

"Thank you, Mama. Thank you so much."

Frieda had been happy at first about the marriage since it meant that she could stay in school for a few more years, maybe even go to high school. But when she heard that Mama had agreed to let Gussie move to Brooklyn and live with Tillie and Aaron, she was furious.

"It's not fair," she said to Mama with Gussie standing right there. "Why does she get to leave us?"

She turned to Gussie and spat out, "You can't leave me! With just Sam and all those Hershkowitz brothers and sisters. Why would you do this to me?"

And then she ran from the room before Mama or Gussie could answer.

Frieda hadn't talked to Gussie since. Sam hadn't seemed too upset. He was looking forward to having some brothers and a father in the home. He said he was tired of being the only boy in the house.

Although Gussie was disturbed that Frieda was so angry, she couldn't stop humming. Soon she would be free! She could live like an adult. She wouldn't be Mama's little girl helper any more. She was excited and so happy. But she knew there was no going back. She would never be her Mama's little girl any more. And Frieda might never forgive her.

But she was going to Brooklyn! Hurrah!

CHAPTER 22

The first months in Brooklyn were wonderful. Sure, Gussie was working just as hard as ever. Taking care of Leo and Joe was not easy. Two boys in diapers, both walking and running and getting in trouble kept her going all day long.

But she loved being in Tillie's house, and she loved Brooklyn. Tillie and Aaron were not her parents, and though Tillie made sure she ate and stayed out of trouble, Gussie had more freedom than she'd ever had before. When Tillie and Aaron closed the store each night and the boys went to sleep, Gussie could do as she pleased. Once the kitchen was cleaned, the room was hers and hers alone. She could read or sleep or just daydream if she wanted. And there was a toilet in the building down the hall---no more going out to the disgusting outhouse to take care of her business.

And Brooklyn was cleaner and quieter than life around Ridge Street. There were still lots of people, noisy trolleys, and crowded buildings, but somehow things seemed less dirty, less hectic. When she'd go to visit Mama, Frieda, and Sam on Sundays, she'd be surprised by all the noise from the people rushing through the streets and the smells of garbage, human sweat, and horse manure everywhere.

Of course, she missed Mama and Frieda and even Sam. But they were really not that far---just across the Williamsburg Bridge. It only took about a half an hour to walk across and get to Ridge Street from 100 Broadway where they were living in Brooklyn. A visit once a week was not enough, and she cried a little every time she left.

But she wasn't sorry about moving to Brooklyn, not one bit. Those Hershkowitz kids were just as obnoxious as she thought, and Mr. Hershkowitz wouldn't even look at her. He was annoyed that Gussie had upset her mother as well as insulted him. So it wasn't exactly comfortable for Gussie to be in his house. Frieda wasn't as angry any more, but Frieda had become close to her little Hershkowitz stepsister, Annie. Sam was as happy as could be to have so many big brothers and a stepfather. Gussie just couldn't understand it. But if Sam and Frieda and Mama were happy and if she was happy, then there was no reason to question it at all.

During the winter months, when the weather was comfortable enough, she walked around the neighborhood or went to the park. Once the days got longer and the temperatures warmer, she thought she'd be able to go out in the evenings as well. She didn't know many people, but there were some girls on the street who were friendly to her when they saw her. And there were some nice looking boys as well. She still thought boys were fairly annoying and gross, but she didn't mind when the handsome ones would smile at her as she walked past them. Maybe she'd actually make some friends her own age; at thirteen she shouldn't always be with just little children and married people.

But now that spring was here, Gussie found herself busier than ever. There was another new baby. Aaron and Tillie had named him Harry. Gussie stared into the drawer where little Harry was sleeping. Then she looked at her hands. They were so raw and tender that it hurt to hold anything hot or cold. She'd been soaking the diapers in hot soapy water for so long, wringing them out, dumping the water, heating more water, refilling it. She'd never known how much work was involved with diapers. Sure, Joe was still wearing diapers, but he didn't need so many in a day.

Harry seemed to need a new diaper ten times a day. Gussie looked at the wrinkled little newborn, just a week old, and hoped he'd stay asleep for more than ten minutes at a time. She didn't have to care for him much yet---Tillie had to nurse him, and he slept in their room so he didn't wake Gussie that often. But when Tillie went down to check on the store, Gussie had to watch the sleeping baby plus Joe and Leo. What was she going to do once all three of them were with her all day long? She'd gotten used to caring for two boys, but three---including a baby? She'd never have time for herself.

Even at this point, her evenings were no longer her own. After Joe and Leo went to sleep, she had to clean up the kitchen, do the laundry, and bathe the baby so Tillie could get some rest before her own long sleepless night. Aaron was no help. He'd just sit at the table and work on papers or go to the store. Anything to get some peace from the baby's non-stop wailing.

Just as she thought that, Harry started stirring, scrunching up his red, wrinkled face, and jerking his arms and legs into the air. Uch. More wailing to start. Tillie was napping in the other room, and Leo and Joe had finally gone to sleep in the back room. Aaron was out somewhere.

"Don't wake up, don't wake up, don't wake up," Gussie muttered quietly to the baby. He wasn't even nice-looking, but then no babies were at this age. He'd only been asleep for twenty-three minutes. Maybe he'd fall back to sleep. Gussie gently moved the drawer Tillie was using as his bed, trying to rock him back to sleep.

She looked at the pile of diapers---ten wet diapers that she needed to hang on the line after she took down the ten she'd washed yesterday and hung to dry. But they needed one more rinse. As she turned to heat the water again on the stove, Harry started to whimper quietly.

"Oh, no, here we go." His whimpering turned to short, piercing cries, and then finally to full wailing.

"Oh, Harry, your poor mama." Gussie lifted the baby on to her shoulder and looked at his face.

"Harry, you are lucky I'm just your aunt. I might hang you on the line with the diapers if you were mine."

Gussie wrapped his blanket around him gently and walked him back to Tillie, who had awakened after Harry's wailing began.

"Here he is, Tillie."

"Thanks. What time is it? Did he sleep an hour even?"

"Hardly half an hour, I'm afraid."

Tillie took Harry from Gussie's hands and looked at his little scrunched up face.

"How are you, beautiful boy? Are you hungry already?"

Gussie didn't understand how Tillie could be so happy to see that little noisemaker, that little diaper stinker, but maybe she would someday. For now she was glad she could hand him off to Tillie and return to the diapers in the kitchen. As she started to walk back to do that, Leo called, "Mama!"

"Can you go to him, Gussie? I have to tend to Harry."

"Sure." Gussie trudged to the back room. "What's the matter, Leo?"

"The baby woke me up." Leo was not happy, and now that he was three, he could let everyone know how he felt. "I don't like Harry. He cries too much."

"Well, put your head down and go back to sleep before you wake up Joe." Joe was asleep right next to Leo in the bed. Leo sat up and looked at him.

"He's asleep."

"Let's keep it that way. Go to sleep." Gussie walked out of the room, and Leo started to whine.

"Leo Bernstein, you'd better listen to me. No whining. Go to sleep before I have to tell your father."

Leo put his head back down.

Gussie went back to the diapers, wondering if she'd ever get to read a book or take an evening walk again.

CHAPTER 23

Isadore looked at the clock. It was almost six. Closing time was just another thirty-four minutes away. He tapped his fingers on the store counter, backwards and forwards, backwards and forwards.

"Stop it, Isadore. You're making me dizzy. You've been doing that all day.

Isadore shrugged his shoulders. And sighed. Mr. Greenberg sighed back at him and shook his head. How much longer could he work in this store? He tried to think of something to make the last half hour pass.

It was Friday. Tonight he would have Shabbos dinner with his Romanian cousins. It was just a short walk from the store, and he always was happy to have a real home-cooked meal, Romanian style, prepared by Aunt Perla and her daughters.

The first time he'd gone to for Shabbos dinner there after Perla and Yankel had arrived and he'd seen the candles and challah and heard the chanting of the Kiddush and the Motzee, he had been surprised to find himself in tears. The smells, the sounds, the sight of the bright flames on the candles brought him right back to his mother's table at home. He didn't have to believe in religion or God to feel that tug, that emotional tie to the traditions of home.

Finally, the big hand on the clock covered the twelve.

"Good-bye, Mr. Greenberg. Good Shabbos. See you tomorrow."

Mr. Greenberg checked the clock. "You can go."

Isadore strolled up to his cousins' apartment. It was overflowing. Eight of them in just three rooms. Srul was twenty-six already and a seasoned American, having been in the country for seven years; Berl was working in a butcher shop while waiting to get a job as a hat maker. Bertha and Bella continued to work as dressmakers, and Rebecca---now called Ray---was working alongside Bella in a factory making children's dresses. Imagine that---some people would actually buy ready-made dresses for their children! Pincus and Leah were, of course, still too young to work and were in school, learning English faster than their older siblings or their mother.

"Hello, everyone. Good Shabbos."

Pincus and Leah ran up to greet him. The others said hello, but didn't rise from their seats. It had been a long week for them all. The hours they kept were longer than his. Bertha and Bella and Rebecca worked in poorly lit shops, huddled virtually atop each other and the other dressmakers. Only a few minutes of break time all day to use the toilet and eat their lunches. The foreman scolded them if they even stopped to rest their hands. By nightfall when work ended, their eyes stung and their hands were cramped from sewing all day. No wonder they barely acknowledged him when he walked into the room.

Over dinner, his cousins reminisced about Iasi---the music, the horses, the sights he hadn't seen for five years. He pictured his parents and David and Betty. He imagined being in his bed with David, kicking each other under the blanket, with Betty just a few feet away in the other bed.

Would they even know him when they finally saw him? He was so different---still short and skinny, but his hair was starting to thin and his whiskers were darker and all over his face now, not just over his lip like when he'd left home. His arms and chest were hairier also. But besides his body, he himself had changed. He was freer in his speech, more willing to be outspoken. He felt comfortable and safe in America, and it had allowed him to be someone who had his own ideas and a view of the world.

After working all day Saturday, Isadore slept until nine on Sunday. He would have slept longer, but the couple above him were arguing again. When was he ever going to get more space? He'd lived in this small room for five years. Sure, he loved his neighbors Rico and Gina and had watched their beautiful children grow from babies to school children. The location was perfect, the rent reasonable. But he would be twenty-one in August. When would he have his own toilet and sink, not one in an outhouse shared with thirty other people?

He pulled himself out of bed, pulled on his trousers, and went to stand in the hallway to wait his turn for the toilet. Rico was coming out.

"Hey, good morning, Isadore."

"Rico, good morning to you."

"You going to Brooklyn today?"

"What else? It's Sunday, isn't it?

Isadore sighed. He loved his Brooklyn cousins, he really did. But the schlep out to Brooklyn was long. It felt longer all the time. His life felt old. Work Monday, Tuesday, Wednesday, Thursday, Friday. Dinner with the Srulovici cousins. Work Saturday. Sunday Brooklyn with the Rosenfeld cousins. Then it started all over again.

The rear door to the building opened, and out came the couple who'd been arguing ten minutes earlier. Now they were all smiles, holding hands. When would he find a woman to marry? He wasn't a child any more.

He thought about Malke more and more these days. Where was she? How was she? Had she married already? He had no idea. He'd never heard from her. She had no idea how to find him, and he had no idea how to find her. The one girl he'd ever really been close to, and she'd disappeared into the American landscape somewhere far away. Whenever he saw a woman with red hair, he'd turn quickly. Could it be Malke? But it never was.

He needed a change. He needed something new to shake up his life a bit.

As these thoughts jumped around in his head, he opened the door to his tiny apartment. He opened the door. His room felt damp from being closed all night during the summer heat. He sighed and pulled out the jar to place this week's savings into it. One more dollar. He spilled the money out and counted it, as he did each week. Slowly he piled each dollar onto another, counting slowly.

"Thirty-seven, thirty-eight, thirty-nine, forty. Forty? Forty?"

He'd reached the magic number! He had enough to buy one ticket from Hamburg to New York. He jumped up and counted the dollar again. Yes! Forty dollars. He would not be alone for too much longer.

The next day Isadore bought a ticket for the SS La Touraine, sailing from Hamburg on July 31, 1909. And he sent a telegram to his father in Iasi, letting him know that a ticket would be waiting for him in Hamburg.

July 31? His father would be leaving in thirty days. He would be in New York in about fifty days if all went well. Isadore could hardly believe it. His father would be here to celebrate his twenty-first birthday with him. Everything would change---everything would be better.

The next fifty days were Isadore's longest days in America. He'd been counting every single minute. The days at the store dragged more slowly, knowing that he wanted them to rush along and be over.

Many nights he couldn't sleep, he was so anxious with anticipation about seeing his father. It was over five years. A quarter of his life. How could fifty days feel like fifty years?

He did some things to get ready. For one, he'd found a new apartment up on East 147th Street---just one room with a kitchen, but bigger than what he'd been living in since 1904. They'd be further from his cousins and further from Mr. Greenberg's store, but the rent was cheaper that far uptown. There was room for two men to sleep and for a table where they could sit and eat. It would be fine until his mother and brother and sister arrived.

He moved in on August 1, dipping into his savings a little to pay the first month's rent, but soon his father would be helping to pay those expenses. It was hard to say goodbye to Rico and Gina and their children. They'd been such good neighbors, but he knew he'd see them and all the other people from the neighborhood at Mr. Greenberg's store.

Now he stood, waiting at the welcome post outside the big building on Ellis Island. It was a hot summer day, and the cool breeze off the water felt lovely. He thought back to the frigid winter day he'd gone with Uncle Gustav to see why Perla and Yankel were being detained. His heart skipped a beat. What if they detained his father? He thought he'd explode with anger if that happened. He paced frantically. He'd been there for three hours already and seen people come and go, greeting each other with tremendous hugs and tears. When would his turn finally come?

He kept his eyes on the door. He didn't want to miss his father's face when he saw him for the first time. He was even afraid to blink. And then behind the door he thought he saw a small man, no taller than he was, with a wide hat. Could it be? The man was so short that the people in front of him were blocking Isadore's view of his face.

The door opened, two large men came through, then a small boy. And then---there he was! Moritz Goldschlager himself! The theater lamplighter from Iasi. His own father in front of him. Isadore raced up and threw his arms around his father, who turned and embraced him tightly. Isadore wasn't alone any more.

136

PART IV New York and Brooklyn 1909-1911

CHAPTER 24

Although Isadore was himself still quite small in stature for a man, he had grown enough over the five years he'd been in America that he was now an inch or so taller than his father. As they took the train uptown to the rooms they would share, Isadore chuckled. How odd to be taller than his father!

His father must have been thinking the same way. "My son, you have grown several inches! And you have whiskers! How much time we've lost."

"Don't be sad, Papa. We have time now. We're going to have every night together, and every day that we are not working we'll spend together. It'll be better than ever."

His father smiled sweetly at him. "Oh, Izzy, you're such an optimist. Always looking forward, not backwards, ever since you were a little boy. Always wondering what will come next."

Isadore remembered how many times he'd thought to himself, "Keep moving, look ahead. Don't dwell on what has been."

Isadore brought his father to Mr. Greenberg's store the next morning and introduced the two men. They chatted quickly in Yiddish, and Mr. Greenberg invited Papa to stay with Isadore in the store. What a relief! He'd worried about leaving his father alone that first day, and now he'd get to spend the day with him.

As customers streamed in and out of the store, Isadore introduced them all to his father. "Mrs. Baker, this is my father Moritz," he'd say in English, and his father would nod and smile. Or to Mrs. Rinaldi, "Buon giorno, signore. Questa e mi padre." And to others, he'd introduce his father in Yiddish, and then his father would respond in kind, relieved to know that he could speak to some people in New York.

His father was fascinated by everything he saw, and Isadore loved showing off his Italian and English, and even the little bit of French he'd learned. His father was so proud of him---Isadore could see it in his smile and in the way his eyes twinkled whenever Isadore would explain something to him or translate what someone else was saying.

On the first Sunday, Isadore took his father all over the city. They even splurged and went to the Yiddish theater downtown, a treat that Isadore had denied himself for the last five years. Isadore sat and watched his father's face light up---here was proof that America would not be so different. People spoke Yiddish, people sang the same songs. There was theater—Yiddish theater. Perhaps his father could even get a job lighting the lamps here as he had done for so many years in Iasi.

And, of course, they visited the relatives. The second night after Moritz arrived, Aunt Perla invited him and Isadore to dinner. The visit began on a sad note. Moritz knew that Yankel had died, but he hadn't yet had a chance to express his condolences.

Aunt Perla shook her head and said wistfully, "He never recovered, Moritz, from the horror of that pogrom. He was never himself again. And moving to America---that ride over the ocean, the shock of the new place. It was too much."

"So maybe it's for the best," his father said.

"No, no. I'd never say that. But we're doing pretty well, the children and me. The older ones are working, and my little ones, Pincus and Leah, they're taking to America so well. Especially Leah---she's so smart and doing so well at school. When you hear her speak English---well, it's like she was born here!"

"What work are your boys doing? And your girls, too?"

"Yes, even the girls are working. All three are working in a dressmaking factory and becoming wonderful seamstresses. They make all our clothes also. Srul has been working as a paper hanger, thanks to my brother Gustav, who got him started in the trade. And Berl is now a butcher. So we have money coming in. Of course, we all miss Yankel. But we're doing pretty well."

Isadore knew better. All of the Srulovici cousins had a streak of sadness to them, except perhaps little Leah, who was only nine and, as her mother said, adjusting beautifully to school and to life in

America. She had the advantage of being a child, and although she missed her father, she'd really never known him to be fully healthy. But all the others seemed unable to shake the loss and still had trouble learning English and fitting into their new home, even though it had now been many years for some of them and over a year for all of them. Isadore didn't know whether their sadness came from what had happened to their father back in Iasi or from the loss they'd suffered once they came to America.

Isadore's older cousins sat and talked to his father, asking lots of questions about the old country and about people they'd known there. Bella and Bertha yawned a bit, explaining that they had to get up very early to get to work. Their long hours were draining them; there was so little time for joy in their lives.

When it was time to go, Moritz hugged each child and thanked Perla for dinner. As he and Isadore walked back uptown to their apartment, he said, "They seem so sad, Izzy. Why are they so sad? There is so much to look forward to, so much to be grateful for. Sure, life is hard. Losing your father is hard. I lost mine and my mother before I was even a schoolboy. But you move on, you live your life as best you can. You cling to all the good things, and you let them carry you forward."

Moritz sighed deeply. Isadore looked at the little man who was his father. How wise and strong he was. And how perceptive. Just a few hours with the Srulovici cousins, and his father knew right away that something was just not right.

A few weeks later was Isadore's 21st birthday, and his uncle Gustav wanted everyone to come to Brooklyn and celebrate. And by everyone he meant all of the Srulovici cousins, all of the Rosenfeld cousins, and, of course, Isadore and his father. They were to be the guests of honor---the new arrival and the birthday boy, or really, the birthday man. They were to meet at Prospect Park since there were far too many of them to fit into the Rosenfeld apartment. Gustav had even invited Zusi, but no one was sure she would come. She was living in the Bronx---a long distance away from Brooklyn.

Moritz enjoyed his first trip over the bridge to Brooklyn with great enthusiasm. "Such a wide river, such a huge bridge. How do they build such a big bridge?"

Isadore smiled, remembering his first day in New York, standing under the Williamsburg Bridge, being in awe of the wide river and the towering stone bridges. Now he took them for granted. Seeing them through his father's eyes made them magical once again.

As they walked from Grand Army Plaza into Prospect Park, Isadore and his father talked about the beautiful parks in Iasi. Isadore hadn't given much thought these last few years to his hometown; he'd missed the family and a few friends, but he'd not really ever thought about the city itself.

Listening to his father make comparisons between the old city and his new one, Isadore felt a twinge of homesickness, but then quickly squelched that feeling, saying, "New York City is the greatest city in the world, Papa. Iasi is a small town in comparison. Here anyone can be anything, and it doesn't matter if you are Jewish, Irish, Italian, Chinese---you can live here and work here and do as you please."

Of course, Isadore knew things weren't really that easy. Even in New York, people were mistreated, overworked, underpaid. People lived in squalid conditions. There was a lot of name-calling and worse. Even here there were those who hated Jews and the other recent arrivals from Italy or China or elsewhere. They used words like kike, wop, chink to humiliate those who were different from them. But at least here the government didn't encourage and promote such behavior. At least here you could move up and improve yourself if you were lucky and determined enough.

"Izzy, Izzy, here we are! Over here!!"

Isadore looked up and saw Morris and Jack, his cousins, running towards him. They charged right up to him, screaming, "Happy birthday! Happy birthday!" Isadore grabbed them both before they ran right over him, laughing out loud. Jack was now fourteen, Morris was eleven.

"Meet your uncle, Moritz Goldschlager, boys. This is my father."

"How do you do, sir?" Jack said politely in English. Moritz tipped his hat and answered in Yiddish that he was happy to meet them. Jack and Morris both knew enough Yiddish to respond politely, and then they ran back to where the rest of the crowd was gathered.

And what a crowd it was! Nine Rosenfeld siblings, seven Srulovici siblings, plus the parents. Gustav and Hennie had not seen Moritz in over twenty years. They'd all been in their twenties then, young adults. Now they all had children who were almost as old as they'd been when they'd last seen each other.

Gustav and Moritz gave each other a big hug. What a scene that was. Gustav, the large, bear-like man with the wild white hair and long mustache, could almost swallow his petite little brother-in-law. Moritz grabbed onto his hat for fear it would be blown away before the hug had ended. Then they both stared at each other, laughing and crying. And then laughing again.

"It is you, it is you! So many years, so many children. Ach, life is so fast. Here I am with my nine children, and you've never met most of them," Gustav exclaimed.

Then he gathered his children from Lillie, the oldest at twenty-five who had been a toddler when Moritz last saw her, to Ray, born just five years before, here in New York. He introduced them all to Moritz, who said, "Whew, you and Hennie certainly have a large and beautiful family! America must agree with you."

"Of course, of course. Hennie, get our brother-in-law something to drink, something to eat."

After that, it had all been the usual noisy and laughter-filled Rosenfeld event. Even the Srulovici cousins loosened up a bit and smiled at their rambunctious American cousins. Leah fit right in, of course, playing with Lizzie. And Morris, Robbie, and Jack took Pincus off to play ball in the fields nearby. Isadore sat with his older cousins, and they asked him lots of questions about how his father was doing so far.

"So far, it's great. I love having him here. We're having so much fun."

Abe chimed in, "Well, it's only a week. I am sure he will drive you crazy soon enough!"

Sarah, Lilly, and Rebecca looked at Abe knowingly.

"What do you mean by that?" Isadore asked.

"Well, we love our father, we really do. But he can be a bit much after a while. We're not children any more. Time to be treated like adults, I'd say." Abe was getting closer to joining the Navy. He needed to get on with his life, be an adult.

The girls didn't have that freedom, of course.

Sarah said, "I just have to wait for someone to marry me so I can get out and be my own person."

At this, Bertha Srulovici grunted. "I'd give anything to have my father here to drive me crazy. You Americans are so spoiled." Bella and her brothers nodded in agreement.

141

Abe looked at them all with a bit of fierceness in his eyes, "I'm sorry. I didn't meant to be insensitive. I'd be devastated if something happened to my father. But we aren't spoiled. We just don't want to be treated like children any more. We want to be independent. Is that so wrong?"

After an awkward pause, Bella said calmly, "No, it's not wrong. But for us it is different. We need each other still. We aren't ready to be independent of each other."

Isadore caught the eyes of Srul and Berl and saw that both had winced a bit. They'd been here longer than their younger siblings. Perhaps they were more ready to be independent.

Isadore thought to himself, *Well, I've been more independent than any of you for a long time. I came here alone, I've lived alone. I have nothing to prove. And I am thrilled to have this time with my father.*

But he kept his thoughts to himself, and at just that moment Aunt Hennie called out, "It's time for the cake!"

It was a perfect day. The weather was clear and not too hot. The food was plentiful and delicious, as Aunt Hennie's food always was. And the birthday cake was better than any he'd ever had---from an Italian bakery right there in Brooklyn, filled with chocolate and vanilla cream. Isadore couldn't have been happier.

Walking back to get the trolley after the picnic in the park, Isadore and his father passed a girl with thick and dark red hair like Malke had. Isadore stopped and stared, thinking for a second that it might be Malke. The girl, who looked about the age of his cousin Rebecca, maybe fifteen, was pushing a baby in a carriage and holding the hand of a toddler while another little boy was chasing a ball next to her. She wasn't Malke, he realized, but she was quite beautiful. Except for the scowl on her face. He couldn't help but wonder why she looked so sad.

Isadore turned to his father and said, "You're right, Papa. We need to grab onto all the good things and not let the sad parts of life hold us down." Moritz placed his arm on his son's shoulder.

"Always remember that, my boy."

CHAPTER 25

Gussie brushed the snow off the steps outside their building with her hands. The boys were playing on the sidewalk in front of Aaron and Tillie's store, and she wanted a place to sit. She had Harry in the carriage, but he was getting quite big for it. He was almost eleven months old now. He wasn't quite walking, so she couldn't really let him toddle along with his brothers yet. Crawling on the icy and wet sidewalk would not be a good idea. He was sleeping at the moment, but once he woke up, she'd have to take him out and carry him around. He was a fussbudget---never content to sit and watch like Leo and Joe had been at his age. Much as Gussie loved him, Harry was a challenge. She hoped he stayed asleep for a while.

Leo and Joe ran back and forth, throwing snowballs at each other and yelling.

"Keep it down a bit, boys. You will scare the customers away from the store."

They ignored her and kept up their roughhousing. *When will they go to school?* Gussie thought to herself. Her days with them sometimes seemed endless. Leo and Joe were often bored, playing in the apartment with the few toys and balls that Tillie had collected over the years.

Gussie had her routines with them. Mostly they stayed near the store, but she loved to walk them to the park on nicer days where they could climb and run and even go on the swings. It was quite a distance—it took an hour, but it was worth the time and effort it took to get the boys there. Leo and Joe held on to the carriage while she pushed Harry in the carriage. Often they'd have to stop, and sometimes she'd end up carrying Joe part way there.

But once there, the park was a wonderful place for the boys to play. Walking through the huge arch at Grand Army Plaza gave Gussie the feeling that she was leaving the city behind with all its dirt and grime and entering a different world. The fields in the park were deep green in summer, and for as far as she could see, there was nothing but trees and grass and some pathways for walking. It reminded of her day in Central Park with her class years before. She had one favorite spot where the boys could run around without any concerns and play freely. There'd be other children there, and that would keep the boys entertained. They'd chase pigeons, throw balls, and collect sticks and rocks.

Plus, Gussie got a chance to talk to some of the mothers who came there. At first she'd been shy. After all, she was not really a mother, and these women were much older. But a few women, after seeing her there day after day, started to talk to her, and soon she realized that they didn't care that she was only fourteen. They'd talk about the children or the weather or their husbands or their friends or sometimes politics. Gussie listened, not adding much since what did she have to say? But it was fun to listen to them. They'd ask her about Tillie and Aaron and why she was living with them and not her mother, but no one really seemed surprised by her answers.

There was also a zoo in the park, and although it was an even further walk, some days Gussie treated the boys to a trip to the zoo. Gussie herself loved the animals, and she loved watching Leo and Joe and even Harry gaze with wonder at the monkeys or bears or birds that lived in the zoo.

Some days Gussie took the boys to the library right next to the park or even to the museum. But usually the library since the museum really wasn't a safe space for three little boys with all the artwork and sculptures surrounding them. They all loved the library. The large building lined with pillars in front was so grand; it felt like such a special and important place. Gussie picked books to read to the boys while they sat quietly next to her, and then she'd pick two books to take home to read to them there. She'd also pick a book or two for herself. She didn't have much time to read, but when she could, she loved a good mystery or a romantic love story. She was so proud of her library card with her own name on it, Gussie Brotman.

And sometimes if she timed it right, she'd see other teenagers coming to the library to do their school work or to find a book for a paper for school. Erasmus Hall High School was just at the other end of the park, and many of the students came to the library after school. She would watch the girls whispering to each other, the boys showing off and sometimes slamming their books on the tables. She'd watch the boys tease the girls, and the girls pretend to be angry. None of them knew her, and why would they talk to her anyway? She was there with three children, not to have fun or make friends. Watching them made her a bit sad, but it also entertained her.

Then one day, while she was checking out the books she and the boys had selected, a tall, skinny boy with a funny hat and dark brown eyes stood behind her on the line and asked her, "Are those YOUR boys?"

"No, they're my nephews. I live with my sister and help her."

"Well, that makes sense. You seemed awfully young to have three children."

"I'm not THAT young. I am fourteen."

"I am sixteen. I go to Erasmus. I've never seen you before. Where do you go?"

Gussie looked down and was reluctant to answer.

"I go nowhere."

"What do you mean? Everyone goes to school."

"That's not true. You may go to school, but how smart can you be if you say something stupid like that?"

The boy laughed kindly. He shook his head and smiled at her.

"You're a spirited one, aren't you? I meant no offense."

"It's all right, no offense taken. I sure wish I did go to school. But I have to help my sister."

The boy stuck out his hand, saying, "My name is Sol, or Shlomo, as my grandmother calls me. I live on Eastern Parkway. What's your name? Do you live near here?"

Gussie shook his outstretched hand and was surprised to feel her body warm to his touch as if a small electric charge had gone through her.

"Gussie or sometimes Gittel, as my mother says. But mostly Gussie. I live on Broadway. It's quite a distance."

"Yes, that is quite a walk. You must get worn down, taking those three boys so far."

Gussie nodded, "It's a long walk, but it keeps the boys busy and entertained. And I get out of the house. Sitting at home can be very tiring also."

"Well, I think you should do something fun. Do you think we could maybe go for a soda sometime? Do you like egg creams? I know a good place to get them near here. Schiff's Deli."

Gussie grinned. "I guess that would be all right. But I don't know when. You see, I have the boys."

"They can come, also. Maybe we can meet next Monday here at the library?"

"Maybe. Maybe. Let me ask Tillie. My sister, that is. If I can, I will be here at 3:30. With or without the boys."

Sol tipped his silly cap and said, "See you, Red." He winked and walked away.

But the next Monday it was raining too hard, and Gussie couldn't take the boys out. She just stared out the window feeling so disappointed. She worried that Sol would be angry or forget her.

On the following Monday, however, the weather was fine, so she bundled up the boys and took them to the park and then rushed to the library as it approached 3:30. The boys dawdled, and she was afraid she'd miss Sol again.

But there he was, fooling around with a bunch of his friends standing in front of the library. Gussie hesitated. Would he remember her? Would he even talk to her? She decided not to say anything as she walked closer to the library steps.

"Hey, Red! Where are you going? I'm over here." She looked over and saw Sol waving at her. She couldn't help but smile. He walked towards her, and her heart started to race.

"Who's that, Aunt Gussie? What's he want?" Leo asked her.

"Never you mind, Leo Bernstein. Just hush up."

Sol tipped his hat. "Hi there. I missed you last week. I was afraid your sister had said no."

"No, she said it was fine. But it was raining."

"Hmm, I guess you don't have an umbrella?"

She thought he was serious, but then she realized he was just joking. "Not one big enough for me and three boys!"

"So do you want to get an egg cream?"

Gussie's mouth watered, thinking of the chocolatey taste of an egg cream and of sitting next to Sol while they sipped through their straws. But she had to be responsible.

"Well, it's going to get dark pretty soon. After all, it's winter time. Why don't we just walk a bit?"

As they walked, Gussie noticed that Sol was holding onto Joe's hand while Gussie pushed Harry in the carriage and held Leo's hand. How sweet he is, she thought. People stared---did they think that she and Sol were married and that the boys were their children? Gussie smiled at the thought.

Sol told Gussie about his school and his friends, about his older brother who was in the Navy and going to see the world, and about his grandmother who came from Poland before Sol was born. Gussie told him about her mother and about how her father had died and her mother had remarried. When they reached 100 Broadway, the boys raced into the Bernstein store, and Tillie peered out the window to see Gussie smiling at Sol.

Sol helped Gussie push the carriage up closer to the store and said, "I have to get home, but can I see you again?"

"Maybe next Monday, if the weather is good."

Sol smiled at her and said, "I'll be in front of the library."

Then he dashed off, saying, "See you next Monday!"

But when the next Monday came around, Joe had a bad cold, and they didn't go out. Now, a week later, there was so much snow that Gussie didn't think she could manage the boys and the carriage all the way to the library. She was sure that Sol would give up on her. After all, he had all those girls at his school. Why bother with a girl who was saddled with three little boys and who didn't even go to school? Gussie felt sick to her stomach. She jumped up from the stoop.

"Boys, we are going for a walk."

Leo and Joe fussed a bit, but when she said they were walking to the library, Leo piped up, "Can we see Sol again? He was nice."

"I don't know. Let's see if he's there."

As they walked along Washington Avenue about halfway to the park, Leo spotted Sol walking toward them.

"There he is!"

Gussie looked up and saw Sol smiling at her.

"Ha! I found you. Did you think you could just hide from me?"

"Now why would I do that?" Once again, Gussie hadn't realized at first that he was just kidding. Then she laughed.

"It's this darn snow. I almost didn't come, but..." She stopped herself.

"But? What? You missed me??" Sol said, with a smirk on his face.

"Don't you kid yourself. I needed to get some more books." She could tease back.

Sol said, "Well, in that case, should we keep walking towards the library?"

Gussie was trapped now. She really didn't want to keep fighting the snowy sidewalks with the carriage and the boys.

"No, I was going to turn back anyway. But feel free to tag along."

147

Sol laughed and took the carriage

"Let me push that. You watch Leo and Joe."

And so they did. This time Sol told her about a big test he'd had at school and how hard he'd studied and how he hoped he'd done well. His father would be upset if he did poorly.

"I do try. But it's not so easy for me. Words and numbers sometimes just jump on the page, and all I want to do is get up and run around and burn off some steam."

"I wouldn't even know. I can barely remember school." It had been over three years now since she had really been in school. "You're lucky, you know. To be able to go to school."

"I guess, but most days I'd rather be working. Making money instead of reading books."

Gussie shook her head and sighed.

Once they reached the Bernstein store, Gussie told the boys to go inside and warm up and she'd be right there. Sol still was holding on to the carriage. As she turned back to face him after she saw that Leo and Joe had entered the store, he put his hand on her arm gently.

"I like you, Gussie. You're different from the other girls. You may not be in school, but you're smart. And you say what you think. I wish you lived closer or went to my school. I like you."

"And I like you, Sol. You make me laugh, and no one makes me laugh much. But I live where I live. And I don't go to school."

"I know, I know. Do you think maybe one time Tillie will let you see me without the boys? Maybe we could really go get that soda and have some time alone?"

Gussie shivered. Was she cold, or was she nervous? She wasn't sure.

"Maybe on a Sunday. The store is closed, and usually Tillie has paperwork to do. But if you come here, maybe she will give me an hour to myself. If you can come by next Sunday, I will be here either with or without the boys."

Sol moved his hand from her arm to her cheek.

"Your cheeks are so red from the cold! You'd better get inside. I'll try and come next Sunday."

Then he removed his hand, touched her arm one more time, tipped his hat, and turned to walk back towards his home on Eastern Parkway.

Gussie put her hand where his hand had been and sighed. "So this is why girls like boys," she thought. She then turned to get Leo and Joe from Tillie to take them all upstairs and make their dinner.

CHAPTER 26

Winter was never Isadore's favorite season. It was dark too much of the time, and the cold made walking or even waiting for the trolleys or trains so painful. But this winter was harder than ever. Isadore was walking from Mr. Greenberg's store at 112th Street up to the room he now shared with his father on 147th Street, fighting the fierce wind that was barreling down Second Avenue. He should have been happy that his day at work was over, but he was not anxious to get home. He stopped every now and then to huddle next to a building, blow on his hands, and pull his coat and hat closer to his body.

Why was he delaying the walk? His father would be there when he got home, waiting for him. Isadore punched his own arm as he walked up Second Avenue. How could he not want to go home to his father? Just a few months ago he was beside himself with joy at the idea of his father living in New York, living with him. He had scoffed when his Rosenfeld cousins had suggested that he might grow tired of spending time with his own father. He had missed him so desperately for five years and worked so hard to get him here.

And now? Now he was half-wishing to live alone again. As much as he had often been lonely living alone in his small room at Rico and Gina's building, he'd grown used to having time to himself, away from the constant bustle at the store and all the neighbors coming in and out. He had time to read the paper, write letters home, and even just sit and relax.

What was wrong with him? Again, he smacked his own arm, as if to punish himself for his thoughts. It's not that his father was doing anything wrong. And they weren't fighting or arguing. And having someone else to share the expenses of food and rent certainly meant that they could save more money and get his mother, brother, and sister here sooner. And yet...

Isadore looked up and saw that he had made it to 147th Street. Their building was half-way up the block. He looked up and saw the light in the window and knew that his father was there. He shivered, tightened his coat, and hustled the remaining steps to the building, then climbed up to the third floor where their room was.

He opened the door and saw his father, hunched over the steam pipe rubbing his hands together. The room never really got warm enough. Isadore took off his hat and his gloves, but kept his coat on.

"Papa, how was your day?"

Moritz shrugged his shoulders. "It was not too bad. Mr. Seligman gave me a scarf to wear while I was making deliveries."

Mr. Seligman owned a clothing factory---a sweatshop, really---downtown, and Moritz worked sometimes in the shop, but more often making deliveries and also peddling the clothes in the Lower East Side along Delancey Street. He'd had no luck finding a job in the theater like the job he'd had back in Iasi, and Isadore knew that his father was disappointed. He missed the music and the excitement of theater work. But Isadore, as much as he understood, thought his father should be more willing to do whatever was necessary. After all, working at Mr. Greenberg's store for over five years was not exactly exciting either.

"What's for dinner, Papa? Shall we boil some meat and potatoes and have a stew?" Isadore went to light the stove that sat in the corner of the room next to the sink. They had no toilet---that was outside in the outhouse---but at least they had their own stove. Isadore had carried some fresh meat and a few potatoes home from Mr. Greenberg's store.

"Sure, sure. Whatever you like." Moritz went to sit on one of the two beds in the room, their only furniture aside from two stiff wooden chairs and a small table that they used to prepare and eat their food and write any letters. Isadore sighed, his father sighed, and a heavy silence hung over them.

Another long night, Isadore thought. He knew his father was lonely. Moritz missed his wife and his other two children, but mostly he missed his city, his home. He missed the life he'd had. Sure, being a Jew in Iasi was terrible in many ways, but it was what he'd known. He complained that New York was so noisy and dirty, that people were rude, that no one knew him wherever he went. So many of his sentences started with, "At home..." or "In Iasi."

What had happened to that man who just six months ago had told him to hold on to the good things in life? Isadore both felt sorry for him and exasperated by him. He also had been lonely when he'd arrived, and he had not had a son or a parent for company. But his father was older, not a young man as he'd been when he'd arrived. Adjusting was harder.

The smell of the meat and the potatoes began to permeate the room, and Isadore felt himself relax a bit, his shoulders dropping from where they'd been tightly raised near his ears. His father was resting, his eyes closed. Dinner would be ready before too long, and then they could eat and go to sleep.

Having warmed up sufficiently, Isadore took off his coat. He looked at the newspaper he'd brought home. The women who worked at the Triangle Shirtwaist Factory downtown were picketing and on strike, demanding that the owners not lock them inside the building during work hours. Today there had been some violence on the picket line, and several women had been injured. Isadore's heart beat faster. *What was wrong with this world? How could anyone hit a woman? And how could they treat them like animals, locking them inside the building?* He clenched his fists. Something had to change in this world.

He heard the water boiling rapidly in the pot and touched his father on the shoulder.

"Papa, the food is ready. Do you want to eat?"

"Sure, sure. Why not?"

Isadore poured some of the stew into two bowls and gave one to his father, one to himself, and took two spoons off the shelf as well.

"It's good, very good. You've become quite the cook. Your mother will be so surprised."

"Thanks, I am glad you like it."

His father smiled, but then started to cough. He'd been coughing on and off for a week or so now.

"Maybe you should see someone about that cough?"

"Nah, it's just a cold. It's winter. People get colds."

Isadore nodded. He went back to eating the stew, the meat nicely softened and the potatoes, soft enough to cut with his spoon. Next time he would add an onion and a carrot. But he had to be careful about what he spent, even though Mr. Greenberg was always very generous and often gave Isadore food that he could no longer sell as fresh or at least gave him a discount below his regular prices.

After a while there was a knock on the door. Isadore walked over and opened it. Nathan Blum, the building superintendent who lived on the first floor, was standing there.

"Hi, Mr. Goldschlager, how are you? I don't want to disturb you, but I thought you'd want this letter that came today."

A letter! That always brought a smile to his father's face. And his own.

"Yes, yes, thank you. How kind of you to bring it upstairs to us."

"Well, I know how it is to get a letter from the old country." He handed Isadore the letter, smiled, and turned around.

Isadore tore open the letter and sat down at the table with his father. The letter was dated January 22, a few weeks ago, and was written by his mother Ghitla.

My dearest Moritz and Isadore, I hope you are well. All is fine here. David is working hard and becoming an excellent hat maker. His work gets many compliments, and he is in much demand. Betty is doing well at school, but at thirteen she knows that this would be her last year.

We are very grateful for the money you are sending, but we hope you also have put aside some there as well. We think that between your savings and ours we now have enough to send Betty this spring. Since she is not earning money here, we think it is better for her to go first. I will stay with David since he is earning good money. We think perhaps by next fall he and I will be able to come together to New York.

Let me know if this plan is agreeable to you. If so, we should arrange for a ticket for Betty perhaps in April or May? Because of the delays in the mail, we need to make decisions soon.

We send you our love and hope you are both well.

Your wife and mother.

It was so like his mother to be so understated and blasé about such big decisions. Isadore had to smile. His father made him read the letter over two more times.

"Well, your mother knows best. If she thinks it's best for Betty to come first, then that is what will be. I thought David would come first; after all, how long can he avoid being drafted into the army? I would have liked them all to come together, but there is not enough money quite yet for three tickets. But Betty is not yet fourteen---so young to travel alone, a young girl on those trains and that ship. Oy. I cannot imagine. You know, Izzy, she isn't a little girl any more. She has become a beautiful young woman. The boys on that ship? I don't want to think about it."

Isadore thought of the Betty he knew---an eight-year-old girl when he left home, still playing with her dolls and losing her milk teeth. Now she was a teenager. Would he even recognize her? Would they be like strangers to each other? She'd barely written any letters in the five years he'd been away. Maybe she was still mad at him for leaving.

"Let's not worry about it now. We can worry later. For now, let's finish our stew and open the bottle of schnapps. Let's drink to the thought that by next fall all five of us will be reunited, here in New York. Think of that!"

With that, Moritz laughed and nodded his head. For the first time in weeks, Isadore saw his father with a real smile on his face, tears forming in the corners of his eyes. They clinked their glasses together and said, "L'chaim!" Isadore added, "To the Goldschlagers, reunited again in 1910."

They swallowed their schnapps and held each other's hands, both of them forgetting for a moment the cold, the ice, and the darkness that loomed outside.

CHAPTER 27

Gussie and Sol sat on the stools in Weiss's Deli on Eastern Parkway, finally alone for more than just a few minutes. Tillie had decided to take the boys to see Mama on Sunday and given Gussie the whole day to herself. Mama would understand, she said, if Gussie skipped just this one Sunday.

Sol looked over at her and said, "A penny for your thoughts? You're awfully quiet?"

"Oh, I just was wondering when the egg cream would get here."

Just then the soda jerk turned and slid the glass down the counter. Sol stuck out his hand and caught it before it slid all the way down. He took two straws out of the glass canister that held the straws and handed one to Gussie.

"Mind if we share? They're pretty big for one person."

Gussie knew that Sol didn't have much money, nor did she. One egg cream would be just enough. She took her straw and stuck it in the thick, creamy liquid.

"Race you to the bottom?" she said as she started to sip on the straw.

Sol laughed and stuck his straw in. As they both sipped up the sweet, chocolaty drink, their foreheads bumped. Gussie looked into Sol's eyes and smiled, the straw slipping from her lips.

"Better be careful, Red! I'm going to win the race to the bottom."

This time Gussie laughed as she watched Sol slurp the egg cream down as fast as he could.

"Should we go to the museum? Or walk to the zoo? Or in the park?" he asked as he wiped his mouth.

It was already early March, and although it was still a bit cold outside, there wasn't any snow or ice, and the sun was shining brightly. Gussie thought a walk through the park would be best. Maybe another time they'd go to the museum. Today she wanted to be alone with Sol, not standing near other people, studying art or watching animals in the zoo.

"Let's walk in the park," she suggested.

And so they'd tightened their coats and hats and pulled on their gloves and headed down Eastern Parkway to Grand Army Plaza and walked into Prospect Park. As they strolled along, Sol took her hand.

"It's nice not to have to push the carriage or hold onto Leo and Joe," Gussie said.

"Yes, much nicer to hold your hand," Sol said as he swung their joined hands back and forth.

After walking through and chatting quietly for an hour, Gussie suggested they turn back.

"You will walk me home, won't you?" she said.

"Of course, I know my manners. I wouldn't let you walk home by yourself."

Gussie turned to smile at him and as she did, Sol let go of her hand and circled his arms around her. He leaned his head towards hers and kissed her gently on the lips. Gussie felt a warm stirring below as her lips lingered on his for a second, longer kiss.

"Oh, Sol. That was nice," she said as she felt her face full of heat. She pulled back a bit, not wanting to seem too eager. A girl had to be careful.

Sol took her hand again, saying, "Well, we've a long walk back. We'd better start before it gets too dark."

Tillie called out to Gussie, "Time to wake up, sleepyhead. I have to go down to the store soon, and the boys are up, waiting for you." Gussie pulled her blanket over her head, "A few more minutes, Tillie." Gussie wanted to spend a few more minutes, daydreaming about Sol.

Tillie walked over to her and pulled the blanket down. "I can't wait. Aaron has opened the store, and I need to be there to help when the morning customers arrive."

Gussie groaned and sat up on the bed, reaching her feet out from the blanket and rubbing her eyes. "I'm up. I'm up."

She pulled on her dress and a sweater and hugged her arms around herself. There was coffee on the stove and some bread and jam on the table. She poured herself some coffee, spread some jam on the bread, and sat on the chair, watching Leo and Joe play on the floor. Tillie had brought some empty boxes upstairs from the store, and the boys were building a tower. Then they would knock it down, laughing at the loud noise and the mess it made.

Tillie came in, carrying Harry on her hip, and handed him to Gussie. He was almost eleven months old now, sitting up and starting to crawl, so she had to watch him carefully. He'd stick anything in his mouth. He reached for her coffee cup.

"No, Harry. Hot!" He frowned and pouted at her.

"Bye, boys. Bye, Sister. I'll be downstairs." Tillie shut the door behind her.

Gussie looked around. What would they do today? She put Harry on the floor and walked over to the window. There were children and high school students walking to school on the street below as well as men and some women rushing off to work. How she wished she could join them.

She opened the window a crack and felt cool air rush through. But it wasn't cold, and the sun was shining. The air had that aroma of spring---a lushness that smelled more like grass and flowers than like the smell of coal burning. Even though there was not much grass yet and only a few flowers starting to bud on the trees, the ground was softer and warmer than it had been just a few weeks ago. And the days were longer. It was staying light until almost six o'clock now.

Today would be a good day to go to the park and then meet up with Sol at the library. She hadn't seen him in over two weeks. But how he'd helped to make the long winter pass. She was excited to think about being able to spend the warmer and longer days with him. More walks in the park, more gentle kisses.

Suddenly she heard crying and turned from her daydreams to see that the tower of boxes had fallen on Harry. Leo and Joe looked awfully guilty while Harry sat crying.

"Oh, boys, what happened?"

"He knocked it down. He did it." Joe stood with his arms folded.

Gussie picked up Harry and kissed his head. "You're fine. Nothing to cry about."

"Leo and Joe, let's get dressed. We are going to go to the park today and then the library."

"Goodie!" said Leo. "Can we see Sol?"

"Maybe. Maybe."

The walk to the park had been long, but easier than usual because the wind was light and the temperature much more comfortable than it had been in winter. Gussie could wear just a light jacket, and the boys didn't need their scarves or boots. Soon Harry would be walking, and maybe it would be even easier to get to the park.

They'd arrived after lunch and had played for two hours, chasing the pigeons, building with rocks and sticks, and climbing on the hills, racing each other up and down. Harry was getting tired and in his carriage, sucking his thumb to comfort himself into his nap. It was time to walk to the library and find Sol.

"Let's go, boys. Library time."

Leo and Joe raced to her, and they strolled along to the library. On the steps Gussie saw a bunch of boys and girls gathered, and in the middle was Sol, laughing and smiling. Gussie had to smile herself.

Leo ran ahead. "Hi, Sol!" he shouted.

Sol looked up and waved to Leo, then waved to Gussie. He turned back to his friends to say something and then walked towards Leo and scooped him up.

"Hey, fellow. How are you?

"Good, Sol. Where've you been? I haven't seen you in a while."

"Busy. You know. I have school and work."

Leo shrugged and wriggled out of Sol's arms, back to the ground.

"Hey, Red. How you doing today?"

"Fine. Just fine. Nice to feel that winter may be over."

Sol took Harry's carriage away from her and started to push it.

"So I have a question for you."

Gussie felt her heart beat louder. They were too young to marry, but was he proposing?

Sol turned to her.

"There's a social at our school next Saturday night. Nothing fancy. Just a group of us getting together in the school to talk and maybe dance. Will you go with me?"

Gussie's stomach flipped and clenched. A dance? What would she wear? And she couldn't dance. And she didn't know his friends. They all went to high school. She would feel stupid. And out of place.

"I don't know. I have to ask Tillie. I don't know." She blushed and looked down at her shoes. Her ugly shoes. The other girls would have nicer shoes. And nicer clothes. And would be smarter and more interesting. What did Sol see in her anyway?

"I know. You have to ask Tillie." Sol sounded a little annoyed and disappointed. He kicked a pebble that was lying on the sidewalk in front of him and, like Gussie, looked down at the ground.

"Let's walk back and ask Tillie now," Sol suggested.

"No, I don't want to make a scene with you there if she says no. I'll ask her later. We can meet on Monday next week, and I'll let you know."

"I don't know, Gussie. You don't even sound like you want to go." He rarely called her by her name. "What if I want to ask someone else? By Monday it'll be too late."

Gussie felt herself gasp a bit and hoped he hadn't heard.

"Ask anyone you want then. I'll just say no now and make it easy."

Gussie grabbed the carriage back from Sol and called to Leo and Joe, "Let's go home, boys. Sol is too busy for us today."

"Come on, Gussie, don't be mad. I didn't mean it. Please."

"I don't want to go anyway. I don't know your friends, and they don't know me."

"But how will you ever know them if you don't meet them and spend time with them?"

"I won't, I guess. Who needs them?"

Gussie turned quickly so he wouldn't see the tears forming in her eyes and yelled one more time to Leo and Joe to come with her. She pushed the carriage away from the library, her eyes stinging, and did not look back at Sol once.

Sol stood there, threw his hat on the ground, and crouched down. He shook his head. Then he stood up and ran back to the library steps where his friends were gathered.

Gussie said nothing to Tillie about her conversation with Sol. She didn't even know what it meant. Would they see each other anymore? Was it over? Had she ruined it? She tried to tell herself it didn't matter, but when she went to bed at night, her tears flowed.

On Sunday they went to see Mama and Frieda and Sam in New York, crossing the bridge and walking along to Ridge Street. The Hershkowitz gang would be there, and for once Gussie was glad. Mama always knew when something was wrong, but with all those Hershkowitz people around, maybe she wouldn't notice or at least she wouldn't ask.

But Mama was smarter than that. She said to Gussie, "Come with me. I need to pick up something on Delancey Street for dinner."

Once outside, Mama said, "So how's your young man? Everything all right?"

"Yes, Mama. Everything's fine." Gussie bit her lip, knowing she had lied.

"Really? Then why the sad face today? You've been smiling since December, but today you look sad."

Gussie said nothing, trying to think of what to say.

"Gussie? I'm your mama. You can tell me." Mama took her hand as they walked.

Gussie struggled to keep her tears from coming.

"Oh, Mama, we had a fight."

Gussie told Mama everything that had happened and everything they'd said.

Mama listened and hugged Gussie. Then she said, "Gussie, you did nothing wrong. Do you want to go to the social?"

"No. I don't. I will be embarrassed and uncomfortable."

Mama sighed. If only she hadn't had to take Gussie out of school. This was her fault.

"Well, maybe you'll have fun. You won't know if you don't try."

"But I can't dance. And I have no clothes." Gussie wiped her eyes.

"You don't have to dance, and your clothes are fine. These are Brooklyn girls just like you. They aren't rich girls either."

"I don't want to go." Gussie was insistent.

"Then you have to tell Sol why. If you leave it like this, he won't understand. If he's truly the right boy for you, then he will. And if he doesn't, then he's not the right boy. If it's meant to be, it will be."

Maybe Mama was right. Sol was a good person. Maybe he would understand.

"I'll think about it, Mama. Maybe I'll go talk to him tomorrow."

Mama knew that meant that Gussie would. She hugged Gussie again and said, "Let's go back now."

"But we didn't buy anything for dinner."

"I remember now that I already have what I need."

Gussie smiled at her mother. "Oh, Mama."

The following day Gussie once again headed to the library, but this time alone. She had begged Tillie for just a few hours off so she could talk to Sol without the boys around. Tillie agreed, saying they could stay in the store with her. But just this once.

Gussie sat by the library steps, waiting for school to get out and for Sol and his friends to arrive. Her stomach was in knots. She watched people walking by on the street and going up and down the library steps, holding her breath and then remembering to breathe.

Finally she heard the familiar sounds of the young people chatting and laughing down the street and saw a group of them approaching the library. She sat quietly, waiting to see if Sol was with them. Then she heard his laugh. Why was she so sad if he was laughing?

She turned around and saw his face. He looked at her, shocked.

"Gussie? What are you doing here?" She wasn't sure he was at all happy to see her.

"I need to talk to you. Alone."

His friends made funny sounds, mocking Sol. Sol blushed and shook his head.

"Stop it, guys. Not funny." He looked at Gussie and said, "Come on. Let's talk."

They walked several yards away from the steps.

"What do you want to talk about?" Sol said, looking at her quizzically.

"I want to explain. I want to tell you why I said what I said."

Sol waited, standing with his hand on his hip.

"I don't want to go to the social."

"Well, that was obvious." Sol snorted.

"But not because I don't like you. I just am nervous that your friends won't like me. That I will be embarrassed. And I can't dance."

Sol looked at her, rubbing his chin.

"I understand that you are shy. I do. But I need my friends. I wanted them to know you. We can't always be by ourselves or with your boys. We have to have other people."

Gussie nodded her head. Sol was a sociable person. He was always with his friends, always laughing and talking. She knew it was a big part of his life, a big part of who he was.

"I understand also. I can try. I can give the social a try."

Sol shook his head and stared at his feet. What had she said wrong now?

"I'm sorry, Gussie. I really am. But I thought we were done. I thought it was over. I asked Pauline from my school. She said yes, so I have to go to the social with her."

Gussie's stomach was churning violently. She didn't know what to do or what to say.

"Well, I guess that we *are* done now. It *is* over now."

"It doesn't have to be. I don't like Pauline like I like you. It's one social. Then we can see each other again. There will be another social

161

at the end of the school year. You can come with me and my friends to Coney Island in the summer. We can still try."

Gussie shook her head. "No, Sol. I don't think so. It won't work. I like you, but you have your friends and school, and I have the boys. Our lives are different, and I can't be like Pauline and the other girls in high school. I won't have time in the summer for Coney Island. And I have nothing to talk about to your friends. They won't want to hear about Leo and Joe and Harry, and I won't want to hear about school and socials and whatever else you all are always laughing and chattering about."

"I guess maybe you're right, Gussie. I'm sorry. I really liked you. You're special. Someday I hope you know that."

Sol leaned over and took her face in his hands like he had that first time he'd walked her home.

"I will miss you. Some guy someday will be a lucky man. I am sorry it won't be me."

Gussie wanted to grab his hand, kiss his lips, sob into his shoulder. But what was done was done. Time to move on. She simply moved his hand away and said, "Goodbye, Sol. Have fun with Pauline."

She pulled away and turned her back on Sol and the group gathered at the library. She refused to cry; she knew it was the right thing. When she reached the corner to cross over to Grand Army Plaza, she turned back to look at the library. Sol had walked back over to his friends and was already blended into the crowd.

CHAPTER 28

March 26, 1910. Isadore looked at the calendar on Mr. Greenberg's wall over and over again. He couldn't believe his eyes. The date had finally arrived. Betty was going to be boarding the boat in Hamburg to sail to the US. Little Betty. Just thirteen years old, sailing all alone across the ocean. In ten days or so she might be here, depending on how rough the seas were.

Isadore remembered his own trip across the Atlantic almost six years ago. How sick everyone had been, rolling around below the deck where the air was rancid from spoiled food, urine, vomit, and worse. Where rats had been almost as numerous as the people or so it seemed. Where children slept curled up against each other to keep warm. Where Malke had been sick for the entire trip. How long ago it seemed. A lifetime. But here he was, and his father had made it, and all his Srulovici cousins. Betty would make it also. She'd been a tough little girl, and his father said she was just as strong as ever as a young woman.

Isadore closed his eyes tightly, imagining what Betty had looked like the last time he'd seen her, a young girl, curled up in bed holding her doll tightly and refusing to look him in the eye when he said goodbye. He remembered her large blue eyes, her blond curls, her round face. But she was a young woman now. Her hair might not be so blond or so curly. Maybe her face would be longer, her features more sharp and angular. How would he recognize her? Of course, his father would be there. He would recognize Betty, even if Isadore didn't.

Mr. Greenberg looked up from the newspaper he'd been reading. He chuckled and cleared his throat as he saw Isadore daydreaming.

"Ahem, Mr. Goldschlager. You've been staring at the wall all day."

"Sorry, Mr. Greenberg! Just thinking about my little sister, all alone on the ship."

"Ah, yes. It's hard to wait for them, isn't it? I remember waiting for my wife and my son to arrive twenty years ago. Every day felt like a year. Worrying about them on that ship. Ech. But Betty will be fine. If she's like you, she will be just fine."

Isadore smiled back at Mr. Greenberg, taking his comment as the compliment it was intended to be. He himself had only been two years older than Betty when he came all alone. Of course, he was a young man, not a young woman, but he'd known less about what to expect on the ship or in America than Betty knew now. He'd written to her and told her what to do and what not to do on the ship. Sleep next to a woman with children or a man with a family. Or with a large group of girls her age at the very least. Don't eat anyone's food. In fact, eat as little as possible. Keep your papers tucked inside your clothes at all times. Don't talk to any man at all. Not even if he looks friendly. Especially the crew.

Betty was smart. She'd be okay.

Mr. Green chuckled again, "There you go, back to dreaming. Go home, Izzy, tomorrow's your day off. Relax. Go see your cousins. Enjoy the spring air. And stop worrying!"

"But it isn't closing time yet? Are you sure?"

"Yes, yes, it's a Saturday in the spring. Everyone is in the park or walking along the piers or meeting friends. No one wants to buy groceries right now."

Isadore grabbed his jacket, waved goodbye to Mr. Greenberg, and ran out the store door, remembering at the last minute not to let it slam. Free! After six days straight of working, he was ready for a night and a day off.

Tomorrow he and his father had plans to go to Brooklyn to see the Rosenfeld cousins. He hadn't seen them in several weeks now. The winter weather had made it harder, and his father was so tired on Sundays that he rarely wanted to travel anywhere. He still had that nagging cough. Maybe the spring temperatures would help with that. Isadore was excited to see his Brooklyn family.

Abe wouldn't be there. Abe had finally done it---joined the Navy. Isadore wasn't sure how much of the world he was seeing, being stationed in Philadelphia. But at least he was in a different city, doing different things, and meeting different people. He hadn't been there very long, but Isadore looked forward to Abe's first leave so he could hear the stories about life in the Navy. Isadore couldn't imagine living on a ship, not after his own experience coming to America, but Abe hadn't ever been anywhere except New York, and now Isadore also better understood why a man his age would want to live away from his mother and father and siblings at least for a while. Abe had just turned twenty-one, so like Isadore he was a full grown man now.

Isadore thought about what he should do that night. He did not want to sit in the room with his father all night. Maybe he would go see if his cousins Berl and Srul were free or even Bertha or Bella. Someone under thirty he could spend a few hours with for a change. He'd better go home first, check on his father, and then he could return to 110th Street.

He sprinted up the blocks on Second Avenue to 147th Street and bounded up the stairs to the room he shared with his father.

"Papa? You here?"

His father opened the door, clearing his throat, and coughing gently.

"Hello, son. How are you? Shall we make some soup for dinner?"

"Oh, no, I forgot to bring home the chicken for soup. Mr. Greenberg let me out early, and I was so excited to get an extra hour of freedom that I just ran out of the store."

"It's all right. We will make do with the vegetables we have. We can throw in extra potatoes. Maybe a turnip."

"Sure, sure. I thought I might go see Perla and the cousins after we eat. Do you want to join me?"

"I think not. I am very tired. It was a hard day, schlepping schmattes around Delancey Street. But at least the snow has melted away now. It wasn't too cold. But you go. Go say hello to Perla and the kids for me. I will rest so I can go to Brooklyn tomorrow."

Isadore wasn't so sure his father should even go to Brooklyn the next day. He looked quite thin, and his skin looked almost yellowish.

"Papa, you should see the doctor. You don't look well."

"Isadore, we've discussed this. I am not going to a doctor. After Betty gets here, I will go if I still am coughing. But the weather is better, and I am sure I will feel better."

Isadore didn't understand why his father wouldn't go to a doctor. It did cost money, but not that much. Most doctors made allowances for poor immigrants like his father. But Isadore didn't like doctors either. They only delivered bad news, it seemed.

His father ended up not going to Brooklyn the next day, but Isadore went without him. He and his cousins decided to have a big celebration the Sunday after Betty arrived. They were hoping for good weather so that they could have a picnic in Central Park. His aunts

Perla and Hennie would prepare the food with their daughters, and Abe was hoping to get leave so he could meet his little cousin. It was going to be just grand.

When Isadore returned from Brooklyn, he shared the plans with his father, who was looking forward with great anticipation to Betty's arrival. The following week at work went very slowly for both of them. And then finally it was Friday. Isadore checked with the shipping line and learned that Betty's ship was due in New York harbor that Sunday, April 3. Two more days! He only had to get through Saturday at work, and then Sunday both he and his father could go downtown to meet Betty at Ellis Island.

The next day when Isadore got up for work in the morning, his father was still sleeping. Isadore tried to get him up to go to work, but Moritz couldn't drag himself out of bed.

"I will rest today. It's Saturday. I will feel better, and I have no work tomorrow."

Isadore was worried. Not only was he worried about his father's cough, which had kept him awake most of the night; he was now worried that his father would lose his job. The whole day at work Isadore was restless, more so than usual. He made more errors in adding up customer's bills than he had in all the years he had worked for Mr. Greenberg. He was anxious to get home and check on his father. The day dragged on and on.

Finally, he couldn't stand it anymore.

"Mr. Greenberg, I am very sorry. I'm having a terrible day."

"Too excited about your sister? She comes tomorrow, no?"

"Yes, yes, she does. But it's not just that. I am worried about my father. He's been ill. I need to go check on him. I know it's only four o'clock, but I can't stand here anymore."

Mr. Greenberg shrugged, "Then go. If you have to go, you go. Honor thy mother and thy father, right? Go. Take care of your father."

Isadore ran from the store, again forgetting to take the chicken, but not willing to waste time going back to get it. He had a bad feeling that was making his heart beat faster than it should. He felt scared, more scared than he had in a long, long time. More scared than he had when the Romanian guards had stopped them at the border. Or when the Iasi thugs had beaten his uncle Yankel and the other Jews. Or when he himself had been beaten. Certainly more scared than when he'd left home or when he'd arrived in New York.

166

He was sweating heavily by the time he reached 147th Street and had to stop to catch his breath before he could climb the stairs to their room. He unlocked the door, his hands shaking so hard he could barely fit the key in the keyhole. When he walked in, he saw his father still lying in the bed. He was covered in sweat. Was he breathing?

"Papa, papa. Wake up!" Isadore pushed his father's shoulder back and forth. His father just groaned.

"Papa! Talk to me!" At least he was breathing. Then Isadore saw the blood in his father's handkerchief and realized he had been coughing up blood.

"Papa!!" Isadore sat down and stood up. He walked and paced. What should he do? What should he do?

"I'll be back. I'm going to get help." He asked Mr. Blum to come up and stay while he ran to get his cousins. He ran back down to 110th Street to the Srulovici apartment and banged on their door.

"What is it?" Perla called out. "Who is banging?"

"It's me, Izzy, Aunt Perla. Please hurry. I need help."

Perla opened the door and saw Isadore standing there, drenched in sweat and white with fear.

"What's wrong?"

"My papa. He's really, really sick. I need to get him to the hospital, but I can't lift him or take him down the stairs by myself. I need someone to come with me."

"Berl is here. He will help. Berl!" she shouted, "Come quick. Go with Izzy. Uncle Moritz is very ill."

Berl and Isadore ran back to 147th Street, Isadore pumping as hard as he could to keep up with his taller and less tired cousin.

When Berl saw his uncle, he shivered. Memories of his own father's illness and death haunted him.

"We have to get him to the hospital as fast as we can. The closest is Harlem Hospital on 135th Street and Lenox Avenue. We can't carry him all the way there," Berl said with some urgency in his voice.

"We'll have to find a cab. Help me get my father down the stairs, and I will ask Mr. Blum to find us a cab."

Eventually, Isadore got his father down the stairs, and Berl and Isadore lifted Moritz into the horse-drawn cab. There was only room for two so Berl turned to go home.

"Please let us know what they say, Izzy. Come stay with us tonight."

Moritz woke up a bit as they rode crosstown and over the Harlem River to the hospital.

"I don't want to go to the hospital, Izzy. They will send me home. And then they will send Betty home."

Was that what this was about? He was afraid he'd be deported if he got sick? Isadore shook his head, tears dropping from his face mixing with the sweat already there. He felt chilled, his clothes were so wet from sweat. What foolishness. Why hadn't he pushed his father harder and sooner to go the doctor? Now what would happen?

Once inside the hospital the nurse listened to Moritz's chest and his heart. Isadore could see her consult with another nurse, shaking her head in the most discouraging way. Isadore sank into a chair near his father.

"Your father has to stay. The doctor will see him as soon as he can. You can wait or you can go home," the nurse said in a firm but compassionate manner.

Isadore waited. His father slept on and off, when his cough didn't wake him. Isadore's clothes started to dry, and the warmth of the hospital took the chill off his body. But not off his heart. He could feel it pounding and pounding. He didn't allow himself to think of what could happen. Betty was coming tomorrow. He would just have to see what the doctor said. Maybe there was a medicine for his father's cough.

Finally, the doctor arrived. Dr. Smith, an elderly man with a distinguished air and a bushy gray moustache, probably sixty years old. Isadore stood up and introduced himself.

"Hello, Mr. Goldschlager, so this is your father?"

Isadore nodded.

"How long has he been coughing like this?"

Isadore felt ashamed. Ashamed that his father was sick, ashamed that his father hadn't gone to a doctor, and mostly ashamed that he hadn't done a better job of taking care of his father. He stood with his head hanging.

"Well, he had a little cough most of the winter, but it's gotten much worse in the last few weeks. But he wouldn't see a doctor."

Dr. Smith examined Moritz, listening to his chest and heart as the nurse had and asking Moritz to cough into a cup. The spit looked pinkish. Isadore felt his heart racing again.

"Dr. Smith, what is it? Why is he so sick?"

The doctor turned around.

168

"I can't be sure, Mr. Goldschlager, but I think your father has tuberculosis. TB. Have you heard of it?".

Isadore knew from the newspapers that thousands of people all over the world had died from TB, maybe millions. He knew it was bad.

He nodded his head, afraid to look at his father or at the doctor.

"Can you help him?" he asked the doctor.

"There's not much we can do except make him comfortable and keep him cool and hydrated. Give him water, that is. Some people get better, some people don't." The doctor shrugged.

Isadore leaned over to whisper to his father.

"Papa, you have to get better. Betty is coming tomorrow. Tomorrow. She will want to see you. You have to get better."

Moritz turned his head and looked sadly at Isadore. "I'll try."

Dr. Smith put his hand on Isadore's shoulder.

"Let's see how he does. Don't give up hope."

Isadore followed the doctor out of the room.

"Doctor, I need to make arrangements for someone to meet my sister at Ellis Island tomorrow. Is it safe for me to leave for a while?"

Dr. Smith knew what he was asking.

"It should be. We never know. God does what He does, and doctors don't know everything. But you go do what you have to do."

God? Ha! thought Isadore. What kind of God would let a good man like his father get so sick right before his daughter was to arrive in America and just seven months after he himself had gotten here? I waited over five years for him to arrive, and now I may lose him so quickly? How could there be a God who would be so cruel and twisted?

Isadore took his father's hand.

"I will be back soon, Papa. You be strong, and I'll be right back."

Isadore got back as soon as he could. Aunt Perla had reassured him that she would be at the dock when Betty's ship arrived. She gave Isadore a sandwich to take back with him, which Isadore ate as he walked quickly back to the hospital.

He was exhausted, and he was heartbroken and angry. Mostly he was overwhelmed. How could this be happening? It wasn't fair. It just wasn't fair. When he got back to the hospital, his father was asleep. Isadore sank into the chair near his bed. At first his head was spinning, his heart racing. His thoughts jumped from memories of growing up in Iasi to worries about his sister. How was he going to

169

tell her that their father was sick, possibly dying? And his mother—how would he get word to her? How would she and David feel, being so far away and unable to help?

Despite all his upsetting thoughts, eventually his exhausted body took control over his mind, and he fell asleep. It was already almost midnight. Almost April 3, the day he'd been looking forward to since that night in January when his mother's letter had arrived. How happy they'd been that night.

When Isadore awoke, the sun was rising. His body ached from sleeping in the chair, and at first he wasn't sure where he was. Then he remembered. Rubbing his eyes and stretching, he stood up to check on his father. He was still breathing, loudly and unevenly. The nurse came and said they had given him something to make him more comfortable. At least he wasn't coughing like he had been.

For a minute, Isadore let himself believe that his father would get better. But the look on the nurse's face told him otherwise. He got up to find a toilet. He realized how awful he looked and how terrible he smelled. He needed a shave, and he needed a bath. He needed new clothes. And he was hungry.

How dare he think of his own body when his father was lying there dying? But he was hungry.

He didn't know anyone in this neighborhood or any place to go. He walked into the hallway and found the nurse.

"I have to get something to eat. I'll be back." The nurse nodded and smiled. She was awfully pretty, and in other circumstances, Isadore might have tried to flirt a bit. But not now. Not when he stank and looked awful and felt awful. Not with his father in there, struggling to breathe.

"Where are you going?" she asked.

"I guess back home. To get clean clothes and some food."

Once again Isadore walked crosstown, this time to 147th Street. First he used the toilet out back, and then he boiled some water in a large pot to give himself a quick sponge bath. He changed his clothes, made himself some coffee and some toast and eggs to get him through what he knew would be a long and hard day. He thought of Betty, pulling into New York Harbor within the next several hours, going through the lines at Ellis Island, expecting to see her papa there to greet her.

He swallowed hard, choking a bit on his food as well as his tears. Was this really happening? As he got ready to head back to the hospital, he saw the photograph his father had posed for soon after he'd arrived in New York. He looked so dapper and distinguished, dressed up in some clothes the photographer had had in his studio.

"How proud your mama will be when she sees what an American I have become," he had exclaimed proudly.

Isadore shook his head in disbelief. This was just seven months ago. Just seven months. His father had been so happy, homesick, but nevertheless happy to be here in America. Then winter came, his cough started, and the sadness had overcome his father.

He trudged back to the hospital, half rushing and half stalling. Not sure what he would find when he got there. He hoped his aunt and cousin were heading downtown to the Battery to meet Betty at Ellis Island.

When he got to the hospital, his father's nurse was standing in the room, listening to his chest once again. Her face looked grim.

"He's failing, I'm afraid. It won't be too much longer."

Isadore nodded. He knew. He sat once again in the chair and waited. He cried a bit, but mostly he just sat. Too numb to do much of anything. He wished he believed in God; he wished he could say some prayers and find them helpful. He wished more than anything his father would wake up at least one more time so he could tell him that he loved him, that he would take care of Betty and David and his mother, that they would all be safe. He wished he had a radio or phonograph so he could play some of the music that his father loved so much.

His father never woke up again. At 9:14 that evening, Dr. Smith came into the room and told Isadore that his father had passed away.

That last walk back crosstown was a long one. All the memories he had of his father came flooding into his head. Listening to music with him back in Iasi, and hearing his stories about the operas and musical performances at the theater. His father's kind demeanor, a man who never raised his voice, never lost his temper, even when Isadore argued with him or wrestled with David or teased Betty. He remembered saying goodbye to his father when he'd left Iasi, and he remembered embracing his father just seven months ago when he had arrived at Ellis Island. He remembered bringing his father to Brooklyn and showing him around New York. He also remembered with guilt and regret his own impatience with his father these last few months. Why hadn't he cherished those times instead of feeling trapped?

His father's words also rang in his ears. Let go of the bad, hold on to the good. How could he do that now? How would he tell his mother that her husband had died? And David and Betty? How could he be the strong one when all he wanted was to be comforted himself?

Betty! Isadore suddenly remembered that Betty had arrived that day. He walked a bit faster, heading towards 110th Street. Had Aunt Perla told Betty about Moritz? Or was she waiting to hear from Isadore about how he was doing? How would Betty handle the news?

And then Isadore's pace slowed again. He had decisions to make. He had to get his father buried. His father would want to be buried as soon as possible, as Jewish law required. But he had no plot. Where could he get a plot? He would have to talk to Uncle Gustav.

His uncle Yankel had been buried in a pauper's cemetery, but Moritz Goldschlager was going to have a proper burial in a proper cemetery. Isadore's head was spinning. How was he going to do all of this and take care of his sister? Not to mention his job. Tomorrow was supposed to be a work day. Now he'd have to miss at least a week of work in order to bury his father and sit shiva for another seven days. He hoped Mr. Greenberg understood. He couldn't lose his job now on top of everything else.

One step at a time, he told himself. One step at a time.

CHAPTER 29

Isadore reached 110th Street and stopped at the corner to catch his breath. He wasn't sure he had the strength to face his little sister for the first time since he'd walked out on her in the spring of 1904. How could he tell her that their father had died? She would hate him. Would she ever forgive him? He wasn't sure he would forgive himself.

He bit his lip and pushed himself to walk the rest of the way to his cousins' building and to climb the stairs. When he reached their door, he again stopped to take a deep breath before knocking gently. It was after ten o'clock at night. Some of his cousins might be sleeping.

Slowly the door opened, and his cousin Bertha stood there, staring at him.

"So? How is your father?"

Isadore just shook his head, looked at the floor.

"Oh, no! Oh, Izzy! Oh, no!" Bertha opened the door and grabbed Isadore by the arm, dragging him into the apartment. Behind her sat all his cousins except the little ones Pincus and Leah. Aunt Perla pushed herself up from the daybed where Berl usually slept and walked slowly towards her nephew.

"Isadore, tell me. Is my sister's husband gone?"

Isadore nodded his head, and Perla let out a wail like he hadn't heard in a long time.

"Oh, my sister, my poor sister. Why has God treated us so poorly? Two of us to be widows, alone in America. Oh, my God, my God."

Isadore felt his knees buckle beneath him, and his cousins Berl and Srul rushed over and led him to sit on their bed. He let out a cry, saying, "My cousins, now I know better the pain you must have felt when your own father died." Bella brought him some water to drink.

His aunt came over and said to him, "Isadore, have you torn your shirt?

Isadore shook his head. He'd forgotten that he was supposed to tear his clothing when something like this happened---the death of a parent or a child or a spouse or a sibling. Even though he no longer had faith in God, he still wanted to follow the traditions of his family. He opened his jacket and made a deep tear in the collar of his shirt. The sound of the cloth ripping echoed the ripping he felt in his heart.

Everyone was silent. Isadore looked around and saw Srul, Berl, Bertha, Bella, and Rebecca. And his aunt. But where was Betty? Had she gone to sleep with Pincus and Leah? Isadore hoped she had. He wasn't sure he could face her at this moment. The morning would be better.

"So is Betty sleeping with the little ones in the back?"

His cousins all looked either at their mother or the floor. No one made eye contact with him. Finally, Perla stopped her sniffling long enough and wiped her eyes.

"Oy, Izzy, such a bad day. I went to the boat and waited and waited. All the people came off, but no Betty. I waited and waited some more. Nothing. Finally I asked a man how I could find my niece. He pointed me to another person, another man, who checked his list and told me she was detained. I think that was the word. Like my Yankel. They were keeping her."

Aunt Perla started to cry again.

"Why?" Isadore screamed. "Why? Is she sick? Why?"

"I don't know. I was afraid to ask. But the man said to me---are you Moritz Goldschlager's wife? I said, no, I am his wife's sister. He said that's no good. She can only go with Moritz Goldschlager. I tried to tell him that my sister's husband was sick, but he didn't listen."

Isadore felt his stomach churn, and he suddenly vomited all over the floor. He had barely eaten all day, and he was feeling dizzy and sick all over. Now what could he do? He felt helpless, paralyzed. He couldn't even cry any more. His baby sister, just thirteen, alone in that awful place just like he had been when Aunt Zusi's husband had failed to meet him. He couldn't imagine what Betty must have been thinking. How she must hate him.

As Bella silently mopped the floor, Srul came and put his arm on his younger cousin's back. He spoke gently.

"I am going to Brooklyn. Only Uncle Gustav can help us. Berl, you go with Mama to the boat first thing in the morning, and we will meet you there. Mama's English isn't very good. When we explain that Uncle Moritz has passed away, they will let Betty go with Mama, I am sure. But I will get Uncle Gustav just in case. Plus we need to tell him anyway. Aunt Ghitla is his sister also."

174

Isadore protested, "Srul, let me go to Brooklyn. I need to talk to Uncle Gustav about a plot to bury my father."

"Izzy, you are a mourner. You need to stay here. For once let someone take care of you. You have done so much to take care of others. I've been here even longer than you have. I can get to Brooklyn, talk to Uncle Gustav about all these matters. Don't worry."

Isadore sat down. He was too weak, too drained to argue.

Then Bertha added, "You will do your father a greater honor by staying here and mourning him properly. And I will go past Mr. Greenberg's store in the morning and let him know why you won't be at work."

Before Isadore could say another word, Srul was out the door, on his way to Brooklyn.

In the morning, Isadore woke and found himself sleeping on the daybed. He sat up and took a minute to remember where he was and what had happened. Rebecca was standing near the stove, looking at him.

"Some coffee, cousin?" she asked.

"Yes, please." Isadore stood up and straightened his clothes, feeling the tear in his shirt as he did.

"Where are the others?" he asked.

"Bella and Bertha had to go to work. Pincus and Leah went to school. Mama and Berl went to the boat. Srul went to Brooklyn."

Rebecca was his quietest Srulovici cousin, eighteen years old and quite beautiful, but shy and not too sure of herself. She somehow was lost between her two older sisters and her baby sister Leah.

"What time is it, Rebecca?"

"A little past nine. Can I get you some breakfast?"

Isadore was hungry, but he hardly had any appetite for food. "Just coffee."

"You should eat. You will need your strength."

"All right then. Some bread and butter."

Isadore went back to the daybed and sat down, thinking about the day ahead. He couldn't do too much until Srul returned. He dreaded his reunion with Betty. He also felt sick at the thought of returning to the room he shared with his father. All the clothes, the photograph, the memories of seven months of living together there. He knew he'd had some frustrating and even lonely moments there, but now he would cherish those seven months forever. His eyes filled with tears again, and he wiped them with his sleeve. Rebecca called to him to come eat so he did. He needed his strength.

All day Isadore sat quietly in the apartment. Rebecca had gone to get more food and then was busy doing laundry, sewing, and reading. He thought over and over in his head about what he would say to Betty. And how he could tell his mother and brother David about his father. Every time he thought about it, he just gave up. Rebecca had made him some lunch, and they had sat in silence while they ate. Although usually Isadore would have found the silence awkward, he was grateful that Rebecca wasn't trying to make conversation with him. She seemed to understand his need for quiet thoughts.

But he was growing impatient now. It was almost three o'clock. What was happening with his sister? Where were Aunt Perla and Berl? And what was going on in Brooklyn? He stood up to look out the window at the street. He opened the window a crack and felt the April warmth in the air. Down below there was a daffodil or two budding up through the earth. Buds were starting to form on the trees. So much life beginning, and yet he felt only the life that had ended. He had to keep looking forward. He had to hold on to the good.

Then from the corner of his eye, he saw something move down the street and turned his head to look more carefully. There were his aunt and Berl. Behind them were Uncle Gustav and Srul. And behind them were Pincus and Leah, on their way home from school, he assumed, and holding Leah's hand was a pretty girl with large round eyes. Isadore squinted and blinked. It was Betty! Taller than Pincus and no longer a little girl like Leah, but definitely his sister Betty's eyes. Her face.

Isadore wanted to run right downstairs and embrace her. But he thought it wouldn't look right. Plus he didn't know what she yet knew. Had Aunt Perla told her, or was she waiting for Isadore to tell her? He looked once more at her face. She wasn't crying, but she wasn't smiling. He couldn't tell. He went back to sit down on the daybed, trying to count slowly to mark the remaining minutes until Betty came through the door.

"Rebecca, do you think your mother told Betty?"

"I don't know. She might have. Maybe she thought you should."

The key turned in the door. Isadore felt his heart bang against his chest with force. As the door opened, he stood up. Aunt Perla walked through the door first. He couldn't read her expression. Uncle

Gustav followed her. He walked over to Isadore and gave him a long and deep hug, whispering in his hear, "May his memory be for a blessing. He was a good man. I wish I'd known him longer." Isadore nodded.

As he pulled away from Gustav, he saw Betty standing in front of him.

"Is it true?" That was all she said. Her first words to him in almost six years.

Isadore put his hands on her slender shoulders, which were already shaking, and nodded his head.

Betty stretched her arms around his waist and sobbed into his chest. "Why? Why did he die?"

"I don't know. He wouldn't see a doctor. He was afraid they'd send him home. He was afraid they'd send you back. I tried, Betty, I tried." Isadore once again started to sob.

Uncle Gustav heard this and said firmly, "Izzy, it's not your fault. You're not to blame. If he wouldn't go to a doctor, well, then that was his fault."

Isadore could tell that Betty was in shock. She was still trying to understand what had happened. She was only thirteen. Would she blame him?

"Betty, I am so sorry. I know he wanted to be here to greet you. He wanted to be there yesterday to meet you at the boat. You must have been so scared."

Betty didn't answer. She just continued to hold on to Isadore's waist. He continued to let her, stroking her blonde, wavy hair. She was almost as tall as he was. Where was the eight-year-old girl he'd left behind five and a half years ago? He closed his eyes, shook his head, and sighed.

Finally, Betty pulled away and looked at his face. "You look the same, Izzy. Same nose, same eyes, same mouth. And you're hardly taller than you were when you left. A few more rough whiskers, but that's about it. You still look like my brother."

Isadore laughed, and it felt good to laugh. "I am still your brother. How I have missed you. You are even more beautiful than when I last saw you. And yes, your eyes and mouth and nose are pretty much the same, but you are no longer that little girl. You're a young woman. My heart breaks to think that Papa missed seeing you by just one day."

Betty's eyes filled once more with tears, and she turned to Aunt Perla for comfort. Isadore sat back down on the daybed. He and Betty would have plenty of time to catch up, to share stories, to mourn their father. But now he and Uncle Gustav had to talk about the burial. Fortunately, Uncle Gustav had been able to take care of the details. His father would be buried the next day at Washington Cemetery in Brooklyn. Gustav had purchased the plot and arranged the whole thing.

Isadore felt a tremendous weight lift from his shoulders. Betty was here, and she was safe. His father would be buried properly and with honor. He was surrounded by his cousins, his aunt, and his uncle. His father would want him to focus on Betty, on the future, on getting his mother and David here safely and as soon as possible. There would be plenty of time for grief, but he also needed to look forward.

The burial the next day was dignified and peaceful. All of the Rosenfeld cousins were there as were all of the Srulovici cousins. Aunt Perla insisted that Isadore and Betty sit shiva at her apartment, and Isadore agreed. Sitting in that one room with Betty would have been too hard for her and too hard for him also. Aunt Perla made sure the mirrors were covered, and she kept Betty and Isadore fed. There was a minyan three times a day so that Isadore could say kaddish. Srul, Berl, Pincus, and Isadore made four, and there were always enough neighbors around to bring the number of men to ten as needed. Isadore knew the prayers well enough, and though he didn't think God was listening, he knew it would make his father smile to know that he was following Jewish tradition. He would say kaddish for eleven months, just as required, to honor his father.

Over the seven days of shiva, Isadore and Betty spent hours talking. They talked about their father---memories from Iasi and memories from his short time in New York. Betty shared with him stories about his family from the years he'd been gone. Stories about David's girlfriends, stories about old friends from Iasi, stories about his mother and father. It was all bittersweet. But in many ways those seven days were a blessing. He and Betty became reacquainted after their long separation, and Isadore came to see her not as his pesky little sister, but as his friend. She was not quite an adult, but she was far more mature than his Rosenfeld cousins Morris and Robbie, who were just about her age.

There were two big issues that had not yet been confronted as the days of shiva were coming to an end. Where would Betty live? She couldn't stay with him in that dark and sad room he'd shared with his father. It would be too lonely for her and not right for him either. She needed to be with women. But he couldn't pay for that room himself. He'd have to go back to his old place, which was much smaller but also much cheaper.

But Aunt Perla wouldn't hear of it.

"You will both move in here with me. It's only for a few months until your mother arrives. Betty needs a mother. She may seem grown up, but she's not yet fourteen. She can't be living with just her big brother. And you? You must come also. When your father was here, it was fine for you both to live alone. Now you need company. Believe me, the months ahead will be hard. Ask my children. And they had each other. You will need your cousins, your sister. You will need me."

Aunt Perla, like Uncle Gustav and his mother, was a hard person to fight. She was tough and stubborn. She wouldn't take no for an answer.

"But you already have seven children here. Where will we all sleep in just two rooms?"

"We will sleep as we have been. The girls and I will sleep in the back room. We have two large mattresses there, one for me, Leah, and Rebecca. One for Bertha and Bella, who will now share with Betty. Pincus will move to the front room; he's too old to sleep with us anyway. You, Srul, Berl, and Pincus will sleep in the two daybeds in this room up front. You can share or take turns, some of you on the floor, some in the beds."

So that was settled. It was also settled that Betty would not go to school but would get a job. She had learned a lot about making hats from David back in Iasi, and Bella and Bertha thought that they could get her a job helping out in a millinery factory.

That left one large question: what if anything should they do about telling their mother and brother about Moritz? Should they write a letter? Send a telegram? Or just wait until they arrive? The last letter they'd received from Iasi indicated that Ghitla and David hoped to leave Iasi in the fall---by mid-October, arriving in November. That would mean waiting six months before letting them know about the death in their family. Was that right? Would a letter be too cold, a telegram even colder?

179

The family was split on that. Gustav said not to tell them, Perla thought it wrong not to let them know. His cousins had different ideas also. Even he and Betty disagreed. Betty thought they should know, he worried that their mother would die from shock or never want to leave Iasi. They decided to let it sink in and think about it again in a few weeks.

CHAPTER 30

It was Sunday, a hot, humid day in August. Another Sunday visiting her mother and family on Ridge Street. Gussie both loved and hated these days. She always loved to see her mother. Mama could see right to Gussie's heart; her hugs could take all the heaviness off of Gussie's shoulders. It never failed.

But visiting also meant dealing with Mr. Hershkowitz, her mother's husband, the shoemaker. He still didn't like Gussie much. And his older sons were still living there, all in their twenties. They still made Gussie feel unwelcome and uncomfortable. And they looked at her in ways that made her cringe.

On the other hand, it was always fun to be with Frieda. How she missed her little sister! Frieda had turned thirteen that spring, and she was so much more mature. Gussie could talk to Frieda now like a friend, not just a little sister. Frieda had listened to all her stories about Sol, the good and the bad, and Gussie knew that Frieda understood, even though she was almost two years younger than Gussie. Now that Frieda was becoming more womanly, the two sisters even looked more and more alike. People always said that Tillie, Gussie, and Frieda could be triplets they looked so much alike---with their brilliant red hair that curled naturally, their high cheekbones, and their dark brown eyes.

But Gussie also felt some tension when she was with Frieda at the Hershkowitz house. Frieda was very close to Annie Hershkowitz, the shoemaker's daughter. Annie was just a year older than Frieda, and the two girls shared a bed and went to school together. They had their secrets, their friends, their jokes together.

Gussie knew in her heart that Frieda was really her sister, not Annie's. Yet right now Annie and Frieda were whispering together across the room, working on something for school, and giggling. Were they laughing at Gussie? *No, of course, not,* Gussie thought. *Don't be ridiculous.* Gussie just couldn't help being jealous. Annie wasn't as pretty as Frieda or Gussie---she was dark, had a long nose, and rather close-set eyes. But she got to live with Frieda.

And she was also envious of Frieda. Why did Frieda get to go to school and have friends and have a stepsister who lived with her and played with her? Frieda didn't have to work and take care of three annoying little boys. She got to read and learn and spend time with girls her age. Mama had told Frieda she could stay in school, even graduate from high school. Much as Gussie loved Frieda, sometimes she just couldn't help resenting her. She stood up from her chair in the corner and left the apartment, going outside for some air. She couldn't sit and watch Frieda and Annie for one more second.

Annie's brother Ben was sitting outside on the stoop; he was just about Gussie's age and going to high school. Gussie didn't mind him much, though he was as homely as his sister Annie. Same long nose, same beady little eyes, same sallow complexion. But he was also a smart boy and not mean and rude like his older brothers.

"Hi, Ben," she said, sitting down on the step above where he was sitting.

"Hi, Gussie, what's new?"

"Nothing. What could be new in my life?"

Ben turned to look at her. "I wouldn't know. You don't talk much when you're here."

Gussie sighed. It was true. She hardly ever talked to the shoemaker's children. Just to Mama and Frieda and sometimes Sam. Or one of her brothers if one of them came around.

"Well, let's see. My older brother Max—his wife Sophie is pregnant again. She's having a baby in October. And you know that my other brother Hymie---his wife had a baby in May. Another boy. Named Manny. I sure hope Max has a girl. So many little boys. Oh, but Avram has lots of girls—three."

Ben looked a bit bored. Who could blame him? Was this all Gussie could think to talk about?

"Did you hear about the guy who tried to kill Mayor Gaynor?" Ben asked, trying to change the subject.

"No." Gussie felt so dumb. She rarely even saw, let alone read, a newspaper.

Ben then told her about the angry city worker who'd been fired that spring, a man named Gallagher, who had shot the mayor in the throat as he boarded a ship that was supposed to take him to Europe.

"Did he die?"

"No, he's in the hospital. They say he will live, but the bullet is stuck inside."

"Oh, how disgusting!"

Ben shrugged.

What else could they talk about?

Ben tried again.

"Did you hear about the airplane that crashed in New Jersey?"

"No, I didn't."

"Eight people were hurt!"

"I just don't see the paper much," Gussie explained, somewhat reluctantly.

"I like to read the paper. I like to know what's going on in the world."

Ben took out his handkerchief and blew his nose. Allergies, he said. Gussie had to smile a bit to herself. He wasn't very sophisticated or good-looking, but he was nice enough.

"So why are you sitting out here, Ben?"

"Oh, I am waiting for my friend, Murray. We're going to work on our algebra together."

"What's algebra?"

Ben looked at Gussie quizzically. "Don't they teach algebra in Brooklyn?"

"I'm not in school, remember?" Gussie was annoyed now. And embarrassed.

"Sorry, I forgot. Algebra is a kind of math. It's sort of fun. You get to solve problems, puzzles really."

It didn't sound like it could be fun to Gussie. Ben really was a strange one.

Just then a short, chubby boy in glasses turned the corner onto Ridge Street.

"There's Murray now. Want to sit with us and learn some algebra?"

Gussie laughed. "I don't think so. I think I'll just go for a walk."

Gussie called up to her mother in the apartment upstairs. The windows were open because of the heat.

"Mama! Mama!"

Mama stuck her head out the window. "What are you hollering about? You'll wake up the whole neighborhood!"

"Sorry. Just wanted to let you know that I'm going for a walk. Maybe over to Hymie's place?"

It was only a fifteen-minute walk uptown to Avenue C. Her older brother Hymie and his wife Sophie had moved out of the old neighborhood as their family grew; they now lived in the newer buildings where her oldest sister Toba and her family also lived. Also, Mama's sister Sarah and her husband Sam Goldfarb had recently moved there from New Jersey. There were a lot of Goldfarb children. Four boys and three girls.

Gussie barely knew the Goldfarbs since they'd moved to New York after she'd moved to Brooklyn. But the Goldfarbs were fun and had good stories to tell about living on the farm in New Jersey, the same town where Papa's brother Moses and all his children lived as well. Gussie hadn't met them, and she wondered what New Jersey was like. A farm sounded so different. Lots of land, no tall buildings. And chickens. And goats.

As she walked past all the buildings along Avenue C, Gussie saw up ahead that Hymie and Sophie were outside with the baby Manny and their older sons, Joseph and Saul, playing on the sidewalk. And a bunch of the Goldfarbs were sitting on the stoop right next door. Gussie wished in some ways she hadn't moved to Brooklyn. It would be nice to have more family around.

"Hey, look who's here! Our little sister from Brooklyn!" Hymie was happy to see her, and he usually could get her to laugh. Gussie realized she was almost as tall as Hymie now. She'd gotten taller, and he'd started to get a little bald. He was almost thirty now.

"Hi, Hymie, hi, Sophie." She turned and waved shyly at the Goldfarbs. "Hi, Aunt Sarah, Uncle Sam, everyone."

"So what's new, Gussie?" Oh, no, not that question again.

"Hmm, I heard the mayor got shot in the throat. And a plane crashed in New Jersey and people got hurt."

Hymie chuckled, "I didn't ask for a news flash. I asked how you are. What's new with you?"

Gussie seated herself on the stoop.

"Not much. I get up, I take care of Leo, Joe, and Harry, I eat, I go to bed."

Hymie smirked at her. "You need to have more fun, little sister. You need to get out, see people, find a fellow." He took a large drag on his cigar and blew the smoke away from her.

She coughed anyway. "That stinks, Hymie. So dirty."

"See? You don't know what fun is. Cigars are fun. A little schnapps is fun. Taking care of Tillie's kids is turning you into an old woman at fourteen."

"I'm almost fifteen."

"Going on fifty," he snorted.

Gussie felt tears welling up in her eyes.

"Hyman, leave the girl alone. What do you want from her?" Sophie jostled Hymie with her elbow.

Gussie responded firmly, "It's okay, Sophie. Don't pick on him. He's right. I am like an old woman."

Hymie put his arm around her, the stinky cigar still in his hand. "Dontcha worry, my girl. Some nice guy will come and rescue you someday. Just like in the fairy tales, right?"

It was Gussie's turn to snort. "Sure, Hymie, I am some princess. Waiting to be rescued."

After that the talk turned to other things---first, how the new baby was doing, was he sleeping, eating, and so on. Then the boys were all excited about the Dodgers' game against the Pittsburgh Pirates the day before---a game that was called a tie. Gussie didn't understand much about baseball, but the men and boys were quite excited by the fact that the game had been tied 8-8, each team also tied with thirteen hits, three walks, two errors. Whatever that all meant. Gussie sat and listened, just enjoying the chance to hear adults talk and to be in a different place with different people.

After a while, she realized she had to get back to Mama's for a bit before she headed back over the Williamsburg Bridge with Tillie and her little boys. She stood and hugged Hymie, said goodbye to everyone else, and walked back down Avenue C towards Ridge Street. The sun was starting to drop a bit behind the taller buildings, and the temperatures were also dropping a bit.

As she approached Mama's building, Frieda came running up to her.

"Where did you go? I hardly saw you. Now it will be another week."

"Well, you were busy with Annie, and so I went to see Hymie. Next time we can go together."

"Oh, pooh. All right. I wish you'd told me. I'd have gone with you, you know."

"It's fine. I had a good time."

Frieda pouted at Gussie. "Well, I missed you."

Gussie felt a warmth inside. "Sorry, sister. I miss you all the time." She hugged Frieda. She turned to shout up at the open window again.

"Tillie! We should go home before it's dark. We have to get the boys across the bridge."

Maybe Hymie was right. She was an old woman. She needed to have more fun.

CHAPTER 31

Betty was driving him crazy. Maybe it was the tight quarters. Sharing a daybed with Berl was not easy. They were men---too big for that narrow bed. Half the nights Isadore ended up on the floor. He was tired and longed for the quiet of his little room in Rico and Gina's building.

But how could he complain? Aunt Perla had taken them in, and Betty would have been lost without her. Without her cousins. Betty hated her job, and she missed Mama. Isadore found himself biting his tongue many times.

Perla had found an apartment in the building next door for Mama, Isadore, David, and Betty to live. It was only two small rooms. David and Isadore would sleep in the front room, Mama and Betty in the back. Now Betty was sweeping the floors in the new place while Isadore cleaned the kitchen floor and the oven. Mama and David were arriving tomorrow. Isadore knew the place had to be spotless for them.

Betty was muttering under her breath. He tried to ignore her.

"We are going to be in so much trouble," she whined.

Not this again.

"Mama is going to be so mad at you."

Me? Isadore thought.

"David probably won't talk to you at all."

He'd had enough of her nagging.

"Leave me alone, Betty. What's done is done."

"We should have told them. We should have sent a letter. It's been over six months." She clucked her tongue.

They'd had this fight at least once a week for the last six months. What was the point of having it again? Especially now when it was too late.

"It will be fine, Betty. Stop with the whining. Mama will understand."

"No, she won't."

"What if we'd told her, and she died of a heart attack? What if she'd refused to leave Iasi? What then?"

"She's not a weakling, you know. You wouldn't know. You haven't seen her since 1904. And David is a man now. He'd have helped her. You just think we're still children, don't you?"

Isadore shrugged and stuck his head into the oven, looking for a reason not to make eye contact with his sister. Betty stomped her feet and stormed off to the back room. Finally some quiet.

The next morning, Isadore once again found himself down at the harbor, waiting for a ship to arrive. *This will be the last time,* he thought. *Now everyone will be here. All my family.* He would not miss these hours spent staring out at the water, straining his eyes to watch for a ship to come over the horizon.

Betty was the pacing one this time. Nervously, she kept pulling her hair up and back, fixing her hat, adjusting her coat.

"It's cold," she said.

"Not too bad, really. It's just the breeze off the water that has a chill."

"How much longer?"

"I don't know. Ships don't run like trains. They come when they come."

"What's the name of the ship again?"

"Pennsylvania."

"What does that mean?"

"It's the name of the state next door to New York. Where Hirsh lives."

"Oh."

They'd been there for three hours already, and they were definitely getting on each other's nerves. Isadore decided it was time for some peace; he took out the newspaper he'd folded into his pocket.

Betty walked to a bench nearby and sat, resting her feet.

Finally, a ship loomed over the horizon. Isadore waited for it to get closer. He strained his eyes, trying to read the name on the ship. Was it the right one? Other people crowded near him, also trying to read the name on the ship.

He could see the P. *Maybe this was it?* He didn't call Betty. Let her sit a few more minutes.

Then someone called out, "Pennsylvania! There she is!"

Isadore whistled to Betty, waving his arms. "It's coming!"

She ran up to him. He then explained that the ship would drop off only the first class passengers and then move back to Ellis Island. He'd told her before, but he reminded her.

"I know, I know. More waiting."

Finally, after taking the ferry to Ellis Island and many more hours of waiting, Isadore and Betty spotted their mother walking out the door at Ellis Island. She looked old to Isadore, her hair gray now, the lines under her deep set eyes even deeper than he remembered. Her mouth was a tight line, her eyes staring straight ahead. And who was that tall and handsome man beside her? Could it be his little brother David?

"Mama! Mama! David!" Betty ran ahead of him, straight into their mother's arms. Mama squeezed her tight, still peering ahead, staring. Isadore knew what she was looking for. And it wasn't him.

He ran up to greet them.

"Mama, it's me---Isadore?"

"Yes, yes, my Izzy." She let go of Betty and pulled him to her. He wanted to cry, but the heaviness in his heart kept him from feeling that joy he'd felt when he seen his father at Ellis Island just a little over a year before.

David stood quietly, waiting his turn.

"David? Is it really you? How did you get to be so tall?"

The brothers hugged, Isadore only reaching to David's chin.

"Where's your hair gone, Izzy? America eating it all?"

"Uch, same old David." He punched him playfully on the arm.

Then the silence hung like lead between them all.

"So? Where's your father? Too busy working to come meet us?" Mama asked with an annoyed tone.

Betty looked at Isadore. Isadore kicked his shoe into the ground. Isadore and Betty hadn't quite figured out how they would tell their mother that Moritz had died. But once Ghitla asked the question, Betty couldn't keep the terrible secret any longer. She burst out, sobbing so deeply that it was hard to understand her words, "Mama, it was awful. He died the day my boat arrived in New York."

David looked at Isadore for confirmation. Isadore nodded and said, "It's true. He had tuberculosis, they say. He was very sick. I couldn't save him."

Again, Isadore felt weighted down with the guilt he felt for not taking better care of his father. His shoulders curled forward. David and Mama looked at each other. They said nothing. For a minute that seemed much longer, there was a dead silence.

"You're telling me he died last April? How could you not tell me?" Mama exclaimed. "He was my husband. I should have known." She dropped her bags to the ground; David held her so she wouldn't collapse.

David looked Isadore in the eye, stating with much agitation, "He was my father. I should have been saying kaddish all these months. How dare you not tell me? You had no right."

"It was Izzy's idea, Mama. I wanted to tell you," Betty interjected.

Isadore bit his lip and gave Betty the iciest stare he could muster. Then he said as calmly as he could, "I'm sorry, Mama, David. I didn't think you should learn from a telegram. I didn't want you to be alone with no family around. Betty's right. It was my decision."

Mama lifted her bags without saying a word.

"So where do I go now?"

"Let me take your bags, Mama."

But she wouldn't let him help her. If she hadn't needed Isadore to lead them back to East Harlem and to their new home, she probably would have preferred to leave him standing there alone.

But within a few days Mama and David were more upset than angry as their grief set in and the shock wore off. Isadore took them to Brooklyn to see where Moritz was buried, and Mama was consoled by her sister Perla and her brother Gustav. David joined Isadore every morning and every evening at the shul to say kaddish, and the two brothers found that the time spent there gave them a chance to share in their grief.

David adjusted quite easily to life in New York. He had no trouble finding a job. His skills as a hat maker made him a good catch for many millinery shops. And, of course, David had the advantage of having his whole family with him in New York when he arrived---his mother and siblings, his aunts and uncle, and all those cousins. Even the Rosenfeld cousins, who'd never met this new cousin before, wanted to be his friend. David was, after all, a pleasant young man with a sweet and easygoing manner.

Isadore had to admit that he was somewhat envious of his little brother. His little brother who now towered over him, tall and strong, with deep blue eyes. There was no question. David was the good-looking brother. Already there were young women paying attention to David, whether from the women's section at the shul or even on the streets. David seemed a bit oblivious, but Isadore knew that David would soon have young women keeping him company.

Mama's adjustment was harder, but she found great comfort being with her sister Perla and her brother Gustav. Mama had even managed to get her sister Zusi to meet with her. Isadore hadn't seen Zusi at all since those awkward first few days in New York when she barely spoke to him. She and Gustav had never been close, and Zusi hadn't even known about Moritz or Yankel's death. She'd never met Betty nor did she know David. It had been almost thirty years since Mama had seen Zusi, and the distance between them was just too large to bridge. She said it broke her heart, but her baby sister had become someone she didn't recognize at all.

But Perla and Gustav were a tremendous help to Mama and to her three children. Even though Gustav also had not seen Ghitla for almost thirty years, he had always stayed in touch, even before Isadore came to New York. Gustav invited Ghitla and her family to Brooklyn for their first American Thanksgiving. Ghitla and David had been overwhelmed by the food, the number of children, and the hectic trip to Brooklyn.

Although his mother and brother were too distracted to notice, Isadore spent that Thanksgiving observing that something was very wrong between Gustav and Hennie. Although the Rosenfeld cousins tried to pretend that everything was just fine, laughing and rough-housing as usual, Isadore noticed that Gustav was not his usual boisterous self. He spent much of the afternoon in silence, brooding, and not eating with his typical gusto. Hennie spent the whole time rushing around, which wasn't really unusual. What mother ever really sat down to eat during a family meal? But she barely made eye contact with Isadore, and the chill between Gustav and Hennie was palpable.

Not my business, Isadore thought to himself. They'll work it out. They have before, he assumed.

CHAPTER 32

It was a New Year. Isadore looked at the calendar on the wall in Mr. Greenberg's store. January 2, 1911. He was not sorry to see 1910 behind him. In America people made New Year resolutions, putting the old year behind them and looking forward. Isadore thought back over the past year.

It had been a hard year, no question about that. Losing his father had left him feeling empty, and although he now had his mother, brother, and sister with him, every morning and every evening when he and David went to the little shul to say kaddish, Isadore was haunted by memories of that awful day in April.

After nine months in America, Betty was speaking English as if she'd been born in America. But Mama and David were still learning the language, and he and Betty made them speak it at home as much as they could. David was doing better than their mother, mostly because he had to use some English at work. Perla and Ghitla would revert to Yiddish or Romanian when they were together, which was much of the time.

Despite the grief he so often felt about his father, Isadore also had a sense of peace. He had survived the long six years of working and waiting for his family to be here. He had made it in America, and he had accomplished the job he'd taken on when he'd left Iasi. His family, what was left of it, was here. He had his Srulovici cousins next door and his Rosenfeld cousins in Brooklyn. He could not yet think of his father without feeling somewhat guilty and terribly sad, but overall life was okay. The future looked promising.

Now it was time to think about that future. His family was here, and now he had to find his own way forward. What would it be? He didn't want to work in Mr. Greenberg's store any more. It was time to move on, find a new challenge, something that paid more, something that introduced him to more people.

It was also time to find a wife. He was twenty-two now. He wanted the comfort of a woman who loved him. He wanted children. He wanted his own family. It was time for him to create a path and a life of his own.

Over in Brooklyn on that January day, Gussie also was thinking of her father and of the future. Leo would be turning five soon, Joe four. In another two years they would both be in school, and little Harry would be three years old. What was to become of her? Was she going to live with her sister forever? Was she ever going to have her own life?

Sure, she was only fifteen, going on sixteen, but she had to start thinking about the future. In fact, she was already dreaming of the future. Having those few months with Sol in her life had shown her what it could be like to have someone care about her. She longed for some romance in her life, something that would take her out of this boring life of caring for her nephews and show her that life could be fun and exciting. When she took the boys to the library, she would always look for a love story to take home and read. She saw no escape from her sister's home except through the arms of some man who would rescue her.

But for now she was stuck, caring for the boys, living in her sister's front room, and watching time go by in Brooklyn. She'd heard Mama say that Avram was moving to Brooklyn soon and also her brother David. Although that probably meant caring for Avram's little ones in addition to Leo, Joe, and Harry, Gussie also had daydreams that Avram would introduce her to some Prince Charming who would whisk her away from her current world and into one much more romantic. At the very least it meant more people she'd know living closer by.

On cold winter days like this, she couldn't help but think of her father. In two weeks it would be exactly ten years ago that he'd died. She remembered sitting outside on Ridge Street in the frigid weather, thinking only about how cold she was. Little did she know that those were her last real minutes of innocence, of pure happiness.

Her father's face and voice had mostly faded from her memory. She had to work really hard to remember what he sounded like or even how all the features of his face were aligned. She could, however, conjure up the smell of coal and perspiration on his clothes and his skin and the feel of his hand around her little five year old body as she sat on his lap. She could remember his laugh more distinctly than his voice. Sometimes she truly wished she could step back ten years and find herself sitting on his lap again, hear him again call her his American daughter. The past felt so much sweeter than the present.

But maybe the future would be even sweeter. She would have to wait and see.

PART V Gussie and Isadore
1914-1916

CHAPTER 33

"Gussie, can you bring these boxes downstairs?"

Tillie was calling to her from the window above. Gussie had just carried a box of clothing down the stairs from the apartment above, her fifth trip already that day. What did Tillie want from her?

Aaron was packing up the store while Tillie packed up the apartment. After all those years on Broadway, Aaron had found a bigger store on a nicer street in Brooklyn. Pacific Street. Even the name conjured up better things, Gussie thought. The ocean far away in California. Why there was a street called Pacific in Brooklyn made no sense to her. Atlantic Avenue---that made sense. It ran to the ocean, the Atlantic Ocean. But Pacific? Who made up these names anyway?

Aaron and Tillie were excited about the move. Gussie had to admit she was as well. A change was most welcome. Although she'd grown accustomed to the Broadway neighborhood and the small apartment she shared with Tillie, Aaron, and their three boys, she liked the idea of a new place in a new neighborhood. Maybe she'd meet new people there. She'd still have no room of her own since she'd still have to sleep in the front room, but she would be closer to the park, closer to the library. There were more stores nearby.

And now at least Leo and Joe were in school. Once she walked them to school, she only had to care for five-year-old Harry, and even he'd be in school by next September. One boy was so much easier than three.

She would be a little further now, however, from her brother Avram's family. Her niece Ethel was now almost sixteen, just four

194

years younger than Gussie and old enough to be more a friend than just a niece. Even her younger sisters Sadie and Ruth were now mature enough to be good company. Of course, they were all in school so not around during the weekdays. But at least in the evenings Gussie had been able to visit her nieces. Now it would be harder, but still with the trolleys she could still get back to Maujer Street and visit them. And on the weekends they could all go to the park together.

Gussie trudged back upstairs to get more boxes. She had to admit that she was feeling quite hopeful about things to come. She looked around the new place. It was bigger and better lit than their old place, and she and Tillie had worked hard, scrubbing every surface until it shined. The front room here was bigger than back on Broadway, and her daybed was placed close to the window that looked out over Pacific Street. She stood in front of the window, watching the people coming and going. A group of teenage boys were walking down the street, hooting and hollering along the way. Teenage boys---so annoying, she thought. Loud and dirty and rude, most of them.

She was now nineteen. These boys were just that---boys. She was a woman now. Old enough for sure to be married. But the men she'd met so far? Either they were barely men---the ones her age were no better than those hooligans down on the street. Immature and awkward.

Or they were older and boring. Like the ones that her brother Avram dragged in to meet her. Men almost his age---almost forty years old! What would she do with a man that old? Sometimes they were widowers with young children. No way was she going to take care of another woman's children ever again. She wasn't going to be like Mama and marry some old man with a houseful of children.

Sometimes those men were lonely old souls who'd never married at all. They were born in the Old Country and barely spoke English. Or if they did, it sounded like a foreign language with their terrible accents. What was Avram thinking?

Tillie had better taste, but even so, Gussie had not yet met one man she could imagine kissing, let alone marrying. Gussie knew she was beautiful; everyone told her so. Any man her sister or her brother brought along was immediately taken with her. She probably could have snared any of them, if she wanted. But she didn't. She'd scowl at her sister or at Avram, as if to say, "What is wrong with you?" The men quickly realized that she wasn't interested and would make some

195

excuse to leave as soon as they'd finished their dinner or their coffee or whatever. And Gussie then breathed more easily.

Maybe the new apartment would bring men with more potential. Meanwhile, she had clothes to unpack as well as all the dishes and the pots and pans. Tillie was downstairs helping Aaron set up the new store, and soon she'd have to go get Leo and Joe at school. Fortunately Harry was playing quietly on the floor, emptying all the boxes and looking for some hidden treasures in each one.

Two weeks later, they were all more or less settled in to the new place. The boys were adjusting to their new school and their new teachers and classmates. Aaron was worried about the store---would new customers come? Had he made a mistake? But gradually more and more neighbors were stopping in to check out the new grocery store in the neighborhood.

"Hey, Gussie, did I tell you about the new neighbor I met?" Tillie asked her. She had brought some food up for Gussie to use for dinner that night. There were advantages to owning a grocery store---fresh meat and vegetables right downstairs.

"No, but I bet he's either blind or deaf and fifty years old," Gussie said with sarcasm

"It's not even a "he," smarty pants. She's a young woman. Sarah Klein. She's married, lives in Manhattan now, but her family recently moved a block or two away. Anyway, she seemed nice. Maybe her family is nice. Maybe she has a brother."

Gussie gave Tillie a look. "Don't count on it, Tillie."

"Well, you never know. She also has some younger sisters. A new friend would be nice also."

Gussie just nodded, looking over the potatoes Tillie had brought up from the store. Should she fry them or roast them? Mash them? So many choices.

"And I invited another neighbor for dinner on Friday. Will you make your special brisket? And some chicken soup? The weather's getting colder. It might be nice?"

"Yes, yes, of course. Who's this neighbor?"

"Mr. Markowitz. And his sister Esther. From a village not too far from Dzikow. You know, the village where I lived as a young girl."

"Yes, of course. The old country. How long have they been here?"

"Five years or so. I want to hear news about my old town. He seemed nice. Not married."

196

Gussie snorted. "Is he blind or deaf?"

Tillie now gave Gussie a look. "He's thirty-three, a tailor, very kind seeming."

Gussie shrugged. "Fine. I will make my best brisket and my best soup."

"Good girl. I'm going back to the store. Don't forget to get the boys. It's almost three."

"Have I ever forgotten them?"

Tillie smiled and left, and Gussie turned to Harry, "Got to go get your brothers now. Let's get your shoes and jacket on. It's getting colder out there."

Gussie found herself somewhat excited about meeting Mr. Markowitz when she started cooking on Friday. Thirty-three wasn't that old. He had a trade. Tillie thought he was nice. Maybe this was the one?

Her soup was simmering on the stove, and the aroma of the chicken and onions was filling the air all through the apartment, even seeping out into the hallways. The brisket was cooking, the meat getting more and more tender, the gravy around it getting darker and richer looking. In another half hour the guests would arrive.

Tillie and Aaron had just come up from the store, and the boys were being bathed and cleaned up for dinner. Gussie looked into the glass door on the cabinet and checked her hair. She took off the apron and made sure her dress looked clean, then put the apron back on so she wouldn't spill anything on the dress.

The table was set. Candlesticks were shined and held the Shabbos candles, ready to be lit before sunset. It was getting close to sunset.

"Tillie, you want me to light the candles?" It was usually Tillie's job; it was her home, after all.

"Yes, why don't you tonight? Joe is being ornery and not getting dressed, so go ahead."

Gussie took a long wooden match and lit it on the stove, then lit the two candles, saying the blessing quietly to herself, covering her eyes as she did. Before she opened them, she thought, "Please make this the one. Maybe this will be my knight in shining armor."

A few minutes later Tillie and the three boys came out to the front room, everyone looking clean and shiny like the candlesticks.

"Aaron's shaving. He'll be right out."

When a few minutes later there was a knock on the door, Gussie felt her stomach flutter a bit. Tillie opened the door and welcomed in her guests.

"Gussie and boys, this is Mr. Markowitz and his sister Esther."

"It's Yitzhak, or Irving they call me here."

Gussie smiled at Irving, but her heart sank. He looked older than thirty-three, but more to the point, he looked shabby. His clothes were worn, even torn in places. What kind of tailor could he be? His shoes were dull, even dusty, and he had flecks of white on the shoulders of his jacket. His shirt was wrinkled. She sighed. Maybe he would be so entertaining that she could forget his clothing? After all, a good wife could take care of that.

He wasn't bad looking. Tall enough with light brown hair and muddy colored eyes. His chin was rather short, but his mouth was nice, and his nose not too big. He did have a pleasant smile, and he did seem rather gentle.

His sister Esther looked like a female version of Irving. Same coloring, same mouth, same short chin, but on a woman it was less unattractive. She at least was clean looking and had on a well-pressed if dull colored dress. She seemed rather shy at first.

Aaron said Kiddush and the motzee over the challah, which Gussie had baked that morning, and then Gussie and Tillie served the soup.

"It's delicious soup!" Irving said. Esther nodded in agreement.

"Thank you, it's my mother's recipe from the old country," Gussie responded.

"Ah, yes, just like home. We lived in Radomysl nad Sanem. You know it?"

"No, I've never been there. I was born here," Gussie said proudly.

At that point Irving turned to Tillie and began speaking in Yiddish to her about the old country. Gussie tried to engage Esther in conversation, but she also was more interested in reminiscing about Galicia. Soon enough Gussie was happy to clear the soup dishes and be away from the table. Clearly there would be no magic tonight. No knight in shining armor. Mr. Markowitz was stuck in the past.

At least she knew her food was good. That made all her work worthwhile.

CHAPTER 34

Isadore stood outside the building on East 109th Street. It was an unseasonably warm February day. Although there were still a few patches of snow on the ground, the air had an almost spring-like feel to it. There was no wind blowing, and the sun was shining so brightly that Isadore took his hat off to feel the warmth of it on his head. Of course, with his increasingly balding head, it still was too cold to go bare-headed, but for a few minutes he wanted to feel the sun's rays directly, not through his cap. It was going to be a great day. He was wearing his best clothes, even his good shoes, which hurt his feet somewhat.

Finally, his mother, his sister, and his brother came out of the building and headed for Grand Central Terminal to catch the train to Newark, all the way in New Jersey. Grand Central deserved its name. It was truly grand. That huge open concourse in the center of the station with its star studded ceiling was perhaps the most beautiful building Isadore had seen since leaving Iasi. And all those people, rushing from one place to another, gave the place an almost other worldly feel. Although Isadore had walked through the terminal before, this was the first time that he'd been taking a train from there.

Isadore hadn't been to New Jersey before, even though he'd now been in the United States for more than ten years. He and his family waited impatiently, all dressed in their best, tapping their toes and pacing back and forth along the platform waiting for the train. Once it finally arrived they found a seat where they could sit facing each other, Mama and David on one side, he and Betty facing them. Isadore was fascinated by the scenery as they left New York and came out from underground in New Jersey, across the Hudson River. He was mesmerized, looking out the window of the train and seeing behind them the cluster of buildings that made up New York City.

New York City. It had been his home now for over ten years. Even his mother and siblings had been here now for almost five years. They all spoke English, and they rarely reverted to Yiddish any more. They rarely spoke about Iasi. They rarely spoke about the past at all.

The four of them, living crowded together in those two small rooms, had become very close over these five years. And now one of them was moving out. Isadore sighed as his heart beat quickened a bit.

The empty fields they passed along the way made him think of Romania and his trip through the countryside of Romania and Hungary as he walked with his fellow Fusgeyers so many years before. He wondered how Hirsh was---was he still in Philadelphia? If they stayed on the train for another hour or so past Newark, they'd come to Philadelphia. *Maybe someday I will do that,* Isadore thought, smiling to himself at the idea of showing up at Hirsh's door.

And that made him think of Malke. He thought of her often these days. *Had she married? Was she still out in Chicago or living on a farm like those they were passing in New Jersey?* He sighed deeply, wondering whether he would ever find love. He looked across the seat at his brother David. David was fidgeting a bit, looking anxious as could be. His brother, the groom. The newlywed to be.

"You nervous or something, brother?" Isadore asked, stepping lightly on David's foot, smudging his brightly shined dress shoes.

David gave him a look, half-smiling, half-smirking.

"Nervous? What's to be nervous about? Marrying a girl with five younger sisters and three younger brothers? And a father who makes hats better than I do? And a mother who protects them all like a lioness with her cubs? Why should I be nervous?"

Isadore laughed. As he'd predicted, David had made the girls' hearts beat faster wherever he went. He could have had his pick of the girls in New York, but he'd found a girl from New Jersey. He'd met her father Shlomo Weiss through the hat trade, and they had hit it off. Shlomo had invited David to meet his daughter Rebecca, or Becky, as everyone called her. And Becky had stolen his heart.

Becky was small and round and had a round face framed by dark, black hair. Her eyes were deep set and as dark as her hair. She was warm and sweet, and her face reflected those traits with a smile as broad as her face. When David had brought her back to New York to meet the family, even Mama had warmed to her. She hadn't been thrilled that David had met a girl from so far away, but how could she not like Becky? Her smile was so genuine, and her affection for David was so clear. And she had a twinkle in her eye. Most people would look at Isadore strangely when he told a joke or made a wisecrack, but Becky just laughed and understood his humor right away.

200

His sister remained skeptical of Becky, but Betty was now eighteen and still new to the idea of love. Betty had grown to be a stunning young woman. Her large, piercing blue eyes could either freeze you with a cold stare or set you on fire, if she wished it. She had young men hounding her all the time, but had no time for the ones in the neighborhood. She was holding out for someone with class, she said. She liked Becky, but she wasn't sure she was high class enough for her brother.

When they arrived at the Weiss home, Isadore again teased his little brother. The Weiss family lived in a house, not a tenement. It was more like their house in Iasi---small and attached to the houses on either side, but they had three rooms on two floors, a kitchen and living area on one floor where the three brothers slept and two small rooms upstairs where the parents and six sisters slept. Above those two floors were two more floors where another family lived. That family had a spare room, which David and Becky would rent after they married.

"So you going to live out here now in the country? Work for her father and be the big brother to all those sisters and brothers, like a little shepherd boy with his sheep?"

David gave him a dirty look. "Just for a while until I have a bit more money in the bank. Then we will move back to New York. Maybe set up my own hat shop." David looked off dreamily. Unlike Becky, he didn't always appreciate Isadore's sense of humor.

Isadore laughed, "You are such a romantic. Always the good boy in the family."

David wasn't sure whether to be insulted or flattered. He looked at Isadore quizzically.

"Ah, come on, David. You know how lucky you are. Becky is a real catch, a great girl. I envy you, I really do," Isadore said in a gentle tone.

And he did. Much as he was happy for his brother, he felt it was somewhat wrong that David, the younger brother, was getting married first. But Isadore had not yet found someone to marry. His cousins kept setting him up with their friends and cousins, but no one had made Isadore think of love. And if there was a girl who made his pulse race a bit, she'd just ignore him. After all, what could he offer them? He was short and balding, he lived with his mother even though he was twenty-six years old, and he didn't own a business or know a trade. Who'd want to marry him?

There was a loud clapping of hands by Becky's father, Shlomo.

"Attention, everyone, the rabbi is here. We can begin the ceremony soon."

Shlomo spoke with a Romanian accent. The Weiss family was originally also from Iasi. That's what had helped David make the connection with Shlomo and then with his daughter Becky. Shlomo had left Iasi back in 1899 and sent for his family just four years later. Becky had been thirteen when she'd arrived with her mother and siblings. Becky had enough memories of her childhood in Iasi that she and David had quickly found much to talk about. They were the same age and had found that they even knew some people in common, although Becky hadn't seen them for over ten years.

The marriage ceremony was short and simple. David signed a few documents, the rabbi said the seven blessings, there was Kiddush, a sip of wine, and a smash of a glass, wrapped safely in a napkin. Everyone shouted, "Mazel tov!" And then they ate. Betty and Mama sat stiffly in one corner, both a bit shy around so many new people. Isadore made small talk with Becky's sisters, but it was soon clear that they were not really interested in talking to him.

Etta, the second oldest after Becky, and Annette, the third daughter, both giggled at him when he told them what he did for a living.

"I drive a milk truck."

"Really? A milk truck? In New York City?"

"Yes, why is that strange?"

"A Jewish boy driving a truck? Isn't that a job for a goy?"

Isadore bristled. He'd heard this before, even from his own family. Learn a trade, his mother had said. Your brother can teach you hat making. Or you can learn to paint like Gustav and your cousin Srul.

But Isadore had no time or patience to learn a trade. He'd spent six years working for Mr. Greenberg by the time his mother and siblings had come to New York. He'd been twenty-two when they'd arrived. He couldn't go back and become an apprentice, wasting time earning less than he'd been making at Mr. Greenberg's store. He'd been actually excited when he'd told Mr. Greenberg he was thinking of looking for something new and Mr. Greenberg had introduced him to the driver who delivered milk and dairy products to his store for the United Dairy Company.

Soon after that, Isadore had gotten a job and was thrilled to be on his own, driving a horse-drawn truck all over the city---to Brooklyn, Queens, and the Bronx, not just in Manhattan. He loved the freedom he had, being alone in the truck, whistling, singing, and daydreaming, and he loved being with a horse again. It made him think of the better days in Iasi and of Malke. But now the dairy had switched to motorized trucks, and Isadore had learned to drive one of those. He missed his horse, but the new trucks were faster, and there was no smell of manure.

Sure, the days were long, and lugging the milk crates in and out of the truck was exhausting, but he was earning double the money and felt more independent than he had as the clerk in Mr. Greenberg's store. It was good, honest work, and he was no snob. His fellow drivers, mostly Irish or Italian, were good men, hardworking and quick-witted for the most part. He liked them, and they liked him.

But that wasn't good enough for the Weiss girls or for so many New York girls. Isadore wondered whether he would be living forever with his mother on 109th Street.

He looked up to see David and Becky, sitting by themselves, eating their wedding feast, and looking at each other with love. How lucky they were.

Two months later, the family gathered again. Once again they wore their best clothes, but this time there were no smiles, no laughter. The weather was playing a cruel trick on them that April morning. It was a gorgeous spring day. The temperature was in the low seventies, and the warm breeze was just enough to feel refreshing. Once again the sun was shining brightly, but this time Isadore did not remove his hat.

They were in Queens that April day, standing at Mt. Zion cemetery. His aunt Perla was leaning against her son Berl and her daughter Bertha, all of them moaning and crying. There was once again a rabbi, but no broken glass this time. Just a hole in the ground with a coffin, waiting to be covered with dirt. In that coffin was Isadore's cousin, born Srul Srulovici. Just thirty-one years old. His first cousin, and the cousin he'd known all his life. The one he'd followed around Iasi, the one he'd looked up to as a small child. The one who'd left for America first, setting the path for Isadore's own departure.

Srul had been sick since the winter and had been to a doctor, but no one knew how sick he was. Now they knew he'd had a tumor on his liver. He'd gotten weaker and weaker, more and more in pain. It had been terrible to see him waste away before their eyes. Isadore shook his head over and over. Why was life so unfair? How many times would his family be broken-hearted, losing a father, losing a child?

And this was not the first time he'd lost a cousin in recent years. He could barely bring himself to think of the other lost cousin. Little Robbie Rosenfeld. Always the quiet middle brother. The other Rosenfeld brothers were so much like their father Gustav---loud, outgoing, fun-loving. Robbie was different. He kept to himself, he read books, he played alone. He was his mother's favorite, but somewhat of an outcast with his brothers and father. Not that they didn't love him; they just didn't know what to make of him.

So when two years ago, Robbie, then just thirteen, had gone by himself to swim at Sheepshead Bay, no one thought it was strange. He'd told his mother he was meeting friends there, and she'd thought nothing of it. But he hadn't come home. Gustav had searched for him, visited all his friends' homes, but Robbie did not come home that night. No one knew where he was. None of his friends had been at Sheepshead Bay that Sunday.

Then the next day Gustav went to the police station where the police produced some clothing found at the beach. Gustav had nearly fainted when he recognized the clothes as those Robbie had been wearing the day before. Later some people who'd been at Sheepshead Bay that day told the police that they'd seen Robbie wade into the water, all alone, far from where anyone else was swimming. The family would never know or understand what had happened to Robbie.

Isadore looked up as the men in his family slowly walked up to the gravesite, each one turning the shovel on its back, scooping up some dirt, and tossing it onto Srul's coffin. Each one pausing, lost in his thoughts. Gustav hesitated the longest, sobbing loudly, not only for his nephew but for his son Robbie and all the babies he and Hennie had lost in their marriage.

And for their lost marriage as well. Losing Robbie had been too much for Hennie and Gustav to bear together. They'd somehow survived all those earlier losses and the struggles with Lizzie and her son Billy. But this was too much. Gustav blamed Hennie for babying

Robbie; Hennie blamed Gustav for ignoring Robbie. Finally Gustav had moved out, and now Hennie lived with her children on Pacific Street in Brooklyn. Gustav had moved to Manhattan, living as a lodger, right up the block from his sisters Perla and Ghitla on 110th Street. Although it was good to have him close by, coming for Shabbos dinners regularly and stopping by during the week, it was hard to see him look so defeated. Gustav missed his children terribly, but they blamed him for their mother's unhappiness and did not come by to see him.

It was Isadore's turn to pay his respects and say his goodbyes to his cousin. He lifted the shovel, turning it back up so that it would be harder to pick up the soil. He knew that Jewish tradition said that one should bury the dead slowly, not in a rush. Isadore looked down at his good shoes, worn just two months ago to celebrate his brother's wedding, now covered with dirt from the cemetery. He lifted the shovel and gently tipped the dirt into the hole, hearing the thud as it hit the wooden casket below. He shivered and felt himself choke down a gasp. He closed his eyes, feeling the tears drop below his lids.

He thought quietly to himself, *Goodbye, my cousin. Be at peace. Thank you for being there for me in Iasi and in New York. I will always remember our evenings alone together when I first got here, my first friend in America as well as my cousin. Be at peace.*

Isadore handed the shovel to his brother, the newlywed wearing what two months earlier had been his wedding suit and his wedding shoes. Clenching his fists, Isadore once again promised himself and his poor deceased father that he would look forward, not back, and make the best of what was to come.

CHAPTER 35

Isadore was exhausted. He'd been driving all night, as his job often required. He had to get up around midnight, dress, and take the train out to the warehouse in Brooklyn to get there by 2 am. The milk had to be at the customer's stores before opening, and so he had to load up his truck first, which took a while, then start driving his route to get to the stores, some opening at 5 am, others not until 7 am. That often meant doubling around on his route since some stores were still closed when he first passed through some neighborhoods. He had to unload the crates for each store, take back the empty crates, drive on to the next store, and do the same thing at each one. Then at the end he had to drive back to the warehouse in Brooklyn, unload all the empty crates, and check out. By then it would be around 9 am, and he'd then have to head back uptown to 109th Street, where his sister would be gone for work and his mother would be waiting with a hot breakfast. It often felt more like dinner to him since he'd been up for so long.

After his breakfast, he'd nap for a few hours, get up, read the paper, take a walk, and then have an early dinner with his mother and sister, take another nap, and start the day all over again. He was making pretty good money, supporting his mother. Combined with Betty's earnings, they were doing okay. And he still enjoyed the job---the time alone and the time with his fellow workers back at the warehouse. Sometimes he would hang around a bit later and go to breakfast with some of them.

There was some grumbling among the drivers and talk of demanding more money. But the boss wouldn't listen, and the workers had little power to change things one by one. Workers at other companies were forming unions. After the disastrous Triangle Factory fire years back where over a hundred workers, mostly young Jewish and Italian immigrant girls, were roasted to death behind locked doors in the factory, there was more and more pressure on companies to treat their workers better. Isadore and a few others were talking more and more about forming a union. But no one wanted to lose the job, so they were all talking quietly and secretly.

Today was one of those days that Isadore had joined his friends at work for a breakfast meeting at the diner down near the river where the warehouse was located in Red Bank. Tony and Mick were two of the most outspoken of the drivers; both had large families to feed, unlike Isadore who had only his mother and himself to feed since Betty earned enough to cover her own expenses. Tony knew a union guy from the Teamsters Union who would come and help them get organized.

"We're making what, $3 a day? How can we live on that? We need some outside help to get organized," Tony whispered across the table where they were eating their fried eggs and hash browns.

"I don't know. Can we trust an outsider?" Mick was a bit suspicious of those he didn't know.

"What do you think, Isadore? You're a smart guy, like most of your folks are. This union guy, I think he's a Jew also. Would you trust him?"

Isadore thought for a minute, taking a sip of the hot coffee.

"I don't know either. I'm all for unions. But will the other guys be scared off? We have to stick together for this to work."

Tony leaned forward, "Will you guys at least meet with this union guy? His name is Jacob. No harm in meeting with him, right?"

Mick hesitated, but Isadore said, "Okay, I will meet with him. But not here. Somewhere away from the warehouse. Maybe in the park? Or Manhattan?"

"Manhattan?? Who goes to Manhattan?" Mick laughed. They both thought Isadore was crazy to travel all the way from uptown. But what could he do? That's where his mother lived, his sister, his aunt and cousins, and now his uncle Gustav.

They paid for their breakfast and left the diner.

Tony shook Isadore's hand, saying, "I'll talk to Jacob. See you tomorrow. Or actually tonight."

Isadore walked back towards the train to go home. He wouldn't get there now until almost noon. He'd sleep on the train, get home for a quick bath, and then read the paper until dinner.

Reading the paper wasn't very relaxing. All the news was about the war in Europe. The stupid war. A bunch of egotistical leaders fighting over land and putting their young men to death over their private squabbles. At least the United States wasn't involved. Not yet at least. Rumors were spreading that President Wilson was starting to listen to those who wanted the US to help the British and their allies defeat the Germans, but most Americans still thought the whole thing was none of their business.

Isadore had no fond feelings for the Germans, but he certainly didn't love the Russians either. The whole continent was filled with anti-Semites. Why would he want to have his life or that of his brothers and cousins put at risk? He threw the paper down, disgusted with the reports of thousands of deaths on the brutal battlefields overseas. He hoped President Wilson continued to use his good sense and keep American soldiers off those battlefields.

He thought of his brother David, his cousins, Avram, Jack, and Morris Rosenfeld and Perla's sons Berl and Pincus. Abe had finished his time in the Navy and was now married and had a brand new baby boy, Max. He was probably safe from being drafted. But Jack was now in the Navy, and Pincus and Morris---they could be drafted if there was a war. They might be killed. Who knows? They might even draft men as old as he was if things got really bad.

The more Isadore thought about it all, the more agitated he became. How was he going to get any sleep before heading back to work again later tonight?

Another April in Brooklyn. Gussie was walking back from the school where Leo, Joe, and now Harry spent the day. Getting those three boys out of the house was a struggle each morning. Leo was now almost ten, Joe nine, and they more and more had minds of their own, arguing about the clothes Gussie told them to wear and with each other over almost anything. Those two boys could fight about the silliest things. Leo loved to dress well and be neat and well-groomed and found Joe a bit sloppy looking. Joe thought Leo was just too fussy and couldn't bother with combing his hair or shining his shoes.

And Harry was quiet as always, keeping mostly to himself. He was still very attached to Tillie and to Gussie. But he was only six, just starting school. He'd hollered plenty those first few weeks when Gussie left him at school, but now he grudgingly went along, not happy to be there, but willing to go without screeching.

Between nine and three while the boys were at school, Gussie now had more time to herself. Once she'd cleaned up the apartment and done the laundry, she could actually sit and read her romance novels or listen to the radio shows or take a long bath. What a luxury! She knew there was a war going on, but as long as it stayed "over there," what did she care? Mama was worried because Sam could end up in the war if the US got involved. But why in the world would America want to do that?

Gussie stopped into the store before she went upstairs to clean.

"What should I make you two for lunch? And anything special I can take up for dinner tonight?"

Tillie looked up from the cash register. The move to Pacific Street had been a good one. The store was busy, and Tillie was working harder than ever. Aaron was tired much of the time and crankier than usual, but otherwise all was going well.

"We have some nice ground beef---how about a meat loaf tonight and some roast potatoes?"

"Sounds good. You want some of the leftover chicken for lunch? I can warm it up and bring it down around noon."

"Nah, I don't think I can stop for a hot lunch. Too much to do. I will just grab some cheese and bread down here."

"All right, then I will head upstairs for now."

"Gussie, if things get really busy, I might need you to come help later. I need to place these orders, and someone needs to help with the cash register. Aaron's just not feeling great right now and can't deal with too many demanding customers."

"Fine, I will check back around lunch time."

There goes my nice, long bath, she thought, as she carried the ground beef and potatoes upstairs.

That same morning Isadore met with Jacob, the union organizer, in a park not that far from work. He found the man likeable if a bit full of himself. These fellows were a lot of talk, high-falutin talk, but most hadn't ever worked a real job. Jacob was a college man, but his father had been a factory worker when he'd first come to New York from Europe in the 1880s. Jacob talked a lot about collective action, working as a team, the power of the many. He sounded more like those Russian Bolsheviks than an American.

But he had some good ideas, and Isadore told Tony that he'd talk to Mick and the others. A union would be a good thing, or at least it might be.

Since it was just about noon, Isadore decided to stick around in Brooklyn, maybe go visit his cousin Abe and catch a nap at his house.

Abe had left the Navy shortly after his son Max was born and was now working as a salesman for a bread company that had its warehouse not too far from the dairy company where Isadore worked. Isadore walked by the bakery, the smell of fresh baked bread wafting through the windows above. He waited for the noon lunch whistle to blow, figuring Abe would walk out around then for a lunch break. Abe wasn't a driver like Isadore, but rather a salesman going from store to store, trying to convince new stores to order their bread from his company. He might just be at the warehouse itself this morning, picking up information on possible accounts.

As Isadore leaned against the building, turning his head to the warm sun, he closed his eyes. He was exhausted, though the talk with Morris had gotten him stirred up. He was just about dozing off when he felt someone lift his cap off his head.

"Hey, cut it out! That's my hat."

He turned to grab the thief's collar when he heard the familiar hearty laugh of his cousin Abe.

"Very funny, cousin. Very funny."

Abe clapped him on the back. "What are you doing here at this hour? Isn't it bedtime for you?"

"Yeah, yeah, I got held up with the guys from work so figured I'd see if you were around. I haven't seen you in a while."

Abe nodded.

"Life is good, but crazy. It's different being married. When I'm not working, I'm at home with Reva and the baby. We almost never get much sleep, though Reva's the one who mostly gets up with Max. I love my wife and I love my baby. But I do miss hanging out with my brothers and with you."

Isadore smiled at Abe. "Well, it's not just you. I haven't been around much either. Working these crazy hours and then trying to take care of my mother and Betty---who has time to have fun? I miss all of you also."

Abe sighed. "You know what? I've only a few stops to make, and then I am heading home myself. Want to walk along with me a bit and then we'll go back to my place?"

"Won't the baby be sleeping? I don't want to disturb him. But I do need to close my eyes for a few hours before I go back to work tonight."

"Well, you can nap at my place."

The two cousins, one large and taller, the other skinny and short, looked quite comical as they strolled along the street.

"How's your mother doing, Abe? It must be hard for you all with your parents apart like this."

"We're getting used to it. It's hardest on the girls, of course. But Morris and Jack are doing okay. They miss our father a lot, but we all know that things were so bad between our folks that it had to end. It's hard to believe how much they once loved each other. And then? All they did was fight over everything."

"You know what? Maybe I should go and visit your mother for a bit instead of bothering Reva and the baby. I know that Morris and Jack will be at work, but maybe I will stick around til they all get home. And I'm sure someone will be happy to make me dinner, right?"

"Of course! I haven't seen them this week yet either, so I'll go with you for a while before heading home."

They continued walking, Abe making a few stops along the way, and then they caught the trolley towards Pacific Street.

CHAPTER 36

As promised, Gussie came downstairs to the store after her lunch so she could help Tillie. For a while the store was busy, but by one o'clock, things had quieted down. She still had more than an hour before she had to go to pick up the boys at school. She'd love to go for a walk to the park. It was a beautiful April day. The flowers in the park were blooming, the grass turning greener and lush. But she'd promised to help in the store, so she stayed put.

She figured she might as well sit near the window where she could at least see the sun and watch the people on the street. She propped herself up on a large crate turned upside down and settled in for a bit. Tillie was in the back, doing the books, and Aaron was off somewhere, talking to a supplier or something.

She leaned her head against the window so she could better see the street. Down the street she saw a few older people, some nasty pigeons, a drunk old man leaning on the lamp post, and a few mothers with their younger children. There was a dog eating some garbage from the coffee shop down the block. The trolley had stopped down at the end of the street where it met Ralph Avenue, and two younger men had gotten off.

Gussie giggled. They were quite a pair. One was a little guy with a funny cap on his head, the other a rather heavy-set guy standing at least six inches above the other. They were talking intensely as they walked, but also smiling at each other.

They seem happy, Gussie thought. As they got closer, perhaps half a block away now, she thought the taller one looked familiar. Hadn't he lived on the street at one time? Maybe he'd come into the store with that Sarah Klein Tillie liked so much? She hadn't seen him in a long time, so maybe she was wrong. But he did look familiar.

Oh, maybe it was one of Sarah's brothers? There was one named Jack who looked like this fellow, but no, that wasn't Jack. And certainly not the younger one, Morris. Well, who knows.

By this time, the two men were just a few buildings down, and Gussie looked the other way, not wanting to be caught staring.

As Isadore and Abe walked down Pacific Street from the trolley, Isadore told Abe about the union guy, and Abe warned him to be careful.

"You know, the bosses don't like troublemakers. And they don't like unions."

"Me? A troublemaker? I'm an angel!" Isadore snorted. Abe laughed. Isadore wasn't a troublemaker, but he was no angel either. He had strong opinions and wasn't shy about expressing them.

"I should stop and get something to bring to your mother---maybe some fruit or something?"

"There's a nice grocery store right down the block---Bernstein's. Opened a little over a year ago. I've not been there since I got married last year, but my mother seems to like their produce."

"Perfect! I'll stop there."

As they got a bit closer, Isadore noticed the young woman sitting in the window. She was striking. The first thing he noticed was her thick, beautiful hair, the color of the horses in Iasi, a deep red color like roan, but with more gold in it. It reminded him of Malke, whose hair had been similar, but not quite as dark or as thick. But this girl had more than beautiful hair. Her eyes were a dark brown, and her face was stunning. Apple cheeks—those high cheek bones that only aristocrats had. Pure white skin. Isadore had never seen such a magnificent face.

"Wow. Who's she?" He stopped Abe a few yards before they reached the store.

"I don't know. Never saw her before. She must work there."

Then Abe cocked his head. "Wait. Maybe I did see her once. I think Sarah spoke to her. Her sister may be the one who owns the store. Bernstein."

"I've got to meet her. I've got to marry her!"

Abe laughed. "She might be awful, Izzy. She also might be married!"

"Shush. Take me into the store."

Abe and Isadore strolled into the store, and Gussie jumped up from the crate in the window.

"Can I help you?" she asked.

Isadore lifted his cap, and Gussie noticed that his hair was thinning. How old was he? He was awfully short---was he even as tall as she was?

213

"Hello, I am looking for some fruit to bring to my aunt who lives down the street. Perhaps you know her?"

"How would I know who your aunt is?" Gussie answered sharply.

But Isadore laughed instead of frowning back at her. "You're right. You wouldn't. Do you know my cousin Abe?" he asked, pointing to Abe.

"You look familiar. You have a brother Jack who looks like you?"

"Yep, that's my brother. Abe Rosenfeld, nice to meet you. My mother lives at 1914. This is my cousin Isadore. Isadore Goldschlager. He wants to marry you."

Gussie's eyes widened, and she turned pink. But not as red as Isadore did. He gave Abe a stern look and then turned to look at Gussie. Was she disgusted? Angry?

But Gussie just looked bewildered. Isadore said with as light a tone as he could manage, "I apologize for my cousin. He's an old married man with a baby, so he just likes to make trouble for others now since he can't make trouble himself."

Gussie had to laugh. *Who were these guys? Abe is certainly American. He has no accent at all. Isadore speaks English like an American also, but there is something about him that's different, almost exotic seeming.*

She decided to ask. "Where are you from?"

Isadore couldn't believe she was engaging him in conversation. "I live in Manhattan. Uptown."

"Were you born there? I was born in Manhattan. Downtown."

"No, no, I was born in Romania. Iasi. Ever hear of it?"

"No, never. Where's that?"

Isadore explained, saying that Abe's parents were also from there, but had come much earlier to America.

"I came by myself when I was sixteen years old. Been here for almost twelve years now."

Gussie did the math quickly in her head. He must be about 28. She'd be 21 in September. Not too old for her. Better than all those old men Tillie and her brothers kept finding.

"When did your parents come here?" she asked him.

"I came first, all alone. Then my father came five years later. But he died not long after. My mother, brother, and sister came after he died."

"I'm sorry. That must have been very hard. Coming all by yourself and then living alone. And losing your father. I know how hard that is. Mine died when I was five."

Gussie looked down. Thinking of Papa always made her sad.

"I'm sad for you as well. Not growing up with your father must have been also very hard."

Gussie nodded and looked into Isadore's eyes. He wasn't much taller than she was so his eyes were right at her level. They were dark, soft brown eyes, full of emotion. He wasn't handsome. He had a large hook-shaped nose. His complexion was somewhat dark, and he was certainly skinny. But there was something about him that appealed to her. She wasn't sure why.

"Let me get you that fruit. There are some berries from New Jersey, though it's still pretty early. In fact, most of the fruit right now isn't great. But we have some boxes of candy. I bet your aunt will like that. And your cousins."

"You're right. That's a much better idea."

Isadore paid for the candy. He thanked Gussie for her help.

"It was nice to meet you. What's your name, by the way? I should know since I'm going to marry you," he said with a smile, punching Abe in the arm as he said it.

Gussie laughed again, "Gussie. Or Gittel, but everyone calls me Gussie. Brotman."

"Not Bernstein?"

"No, that's my sister. Well, actually my brother-in-law Aaron. He's Aaron Bernstein, my sister is Tillie Bernstein. They own the store. But I live here also."

Why'd she tell him that? He hadn't asked.

"It was nice to meet you, Gussie Brotman. I hope to see you again." He tipped his hat, took the candy, and walked out of the store with Abe.

Gussie watched them continue walking down the block, stretching her neck to watch them go. Isadore was bouncing as he walked. What a funny little guy, she thought. And very polite.

And clean and neat---not like that Mr. Markowitz. This Isadore Goldschlager knew how to take care of himself.

Carrying the candy under his arm, Isadore was bouncing as he walked. He felt ten years younger. He turned to Abe and said, "I think I'm in love."

Abe once again took Isadore's cap off, this time saying as he patted Isadore on the head, "You've lost your mind, haven't you?"

From then on, Isadore made a point of visiting his Rosenfeld cousins at least once a week, always going into Bernstein's Grocery to pick up candy or, as the fruit season improved, some fruit for his aunt and cousins. Each time he and Gussie would have a brief conversation, though nothing too personal. Just small talk.

Tillie noticed that Gussie was always in a good mood after seeing this young Goldschlager man.

"So? You like this guy?"

"He's not bad. He's funny, and he's smart. And he seems kind. But he's awfully short. And he's a milk man. Not exactly my knight in shining armor, but he's nice. I like him fine."

"I think he's very sweet on you, you know. We never saw him before that day he came in with his cousin, and he's not from the neighborhood, so what's he doing here once a week?"

Gussie knew that Isadore was interested in her. And she was intrigued. But so far aside from his initial light-hearted declaration that he was going to marry her, there had been nothing more than pleasant chitchat during his weekly visits.

"Ask him to Shabbos dinner this week when you see him."

"Are you crazy? I am not going to be that forward!"

Tillie sighed. She understood. Gussie shouldn't scare him off.

Little did she know. Nothing would scare Isadore off. He just couldn't figure out what to do next. Ask Gussie to go to his aunt's house for dinner? Ask her to take a walk? With his work schedule, it was so hard to find any time that would work.

So Tillie decided to do something herself. The next time Isadore came to the store, she came out and greeted him. Gussie had left to get the boys from school, so Tillie had him alone.

"Hello, Mr. Goldschlager. Nice to see you again. My sister's not here right now."

Isadore looked crestfallen.

"Cheer up. She'll be back soon. But if you don't do something soon, she may not always be here when you want her to be."

Isadore looked at Tillie, the older version of the woman he loved, but the version that was so much more confident and outspoken.

"So what do you suggest, Mrs. Bernstein?"

"Please, call me Tillie. Gussie is a wonderful cook. Ask her what she likes to cook. Tell her what you like to eat. One thing will lead to another, and then you can tell her you'd like to try her cooking sometime, and then you will find yourself invited to dinner."

Isadore took Tillie's advice, and it worked. The next Friday he came for dinner. First he went to his cousin's house and cleaned up. He still had to go to work that night, but he napped in the afternoon so he could stay up later than his usual eight o'clock.

He arrived at Tillie's home at six pm, and Gussie met him at the door. Her face was flushed from the heat of the kitchen, and she had on her apron, but she looked like a princess. She smiled at him shyly and invited him in. Immediately Leo, Joe, and Harry came rushing into the room, curious about this man who'd been invited to dinner not by their mother but by their aunt. Leo had a hundred questions, and Isadore was more than happy to be interviewed by Gussie's young nephew.

Tillie was impressed by how well Isadore treated her sons and gave Gussie an approving nod. When Aaron came into the front room, he and Isadore shook hands and started discussing politics almost right away.

"He's smart," Tillie whispered.

"Yeah, wait til he finds out how stupid I am."

"You aren't stupid, Gussie, and you know it. Just because we didn't get to go to high school doesn't mean we are stupid. Besides, you think he went to high school? He came here at sixteen, you said, right? So don't think he's better than you."

The dinner went smoothly, and, of course, Isadore loved everything Gussie had cooked and ate every single morsel of food on his plate. He talked mostly to Aaron and the boys, but couldn't take his eyes off Gussie. Gussie was taken by his attention and felt flattered by it. But was it love? She didn't know.

After dinner, Tillie said to Gussie, "I'll do the dishes, and Aaron will put the boys to bed. Go talk to Isadore."

Now would be the hard part, Gussie thought. *What would they talk about? The war? The news? Books? What can I add to the conversation?*

But instead she and Isadore talked about other things. He told her about Iasi and why he'd left and about his family. He told her about the Fusgeyers and his trip to America. She told him about moving to Brooklyn and why she'd left her mother behind after she married the shoemaker. Isadore understood.

"I left home also for better things. At least you only left your mother across the river."

Then Gussie decided to be straightforward.

"You know, I'm not very book smart. I had to leave school when I was eleven to care for my little brother. And then for my nephews." Gussie remembered Sol and how she'd felt left behind and different from him and his high school friends.

"Who has time for books? I also never went to high school. I read the newspaper, and I speak three or four languages, but no one's ever going to call me professor."

Gussie laughed. She liked this Isadore.

"Smart isn't about school, Gussie, it's about how you think about things. And it's never too late to learn, if you want."

Then it was Isadore's turn to ask a hard question.

"Do you want children? I know you've been taking care of children since you were a child. Maybe you've had enough?"

"Of course, I want children. But not nine or ten like your cousins! Two would be nice. Maybe three."

Isadore smiled. Who wanted ten kids? Who could afford ten children?

"I like you, Gussie. Abe was right. From the first time I saw you, I knew I wanted to marry you. But you are young and beautiful and could have any man you want. So if I am wasting my time, please let me know now. I don't want to be a fool."

"I like you also. I like talking to you. But I'm not yet ready to marry you. We've only known each other two months. But keep coming to the store when you can, and we'll talk. And you can come to dinner any Friday night---any night—you want. Let's get to know each other a little better."

Isadore put his hand on hers. It was as smooth and soft as a baby's hand. His heart was racing. She didn't pull her hand away. In fact, she turned it and squeezed his back. He was so excited he thought he would have to run out the door.

And Gussie felt her stomach flip the way it had with Sol when he'd held her. Maybe this funny-looking and funny little man was just the man for her. Maybe he was her knight in shining armor, just showing up in a disguise.

CHAPTER 37

The summer was a glorious one. Even Gussie didn't mind the heat, as she and Isadore would meet before he went to work to walk together in Brooklyn. He always had stories about the men he worked with that made her laugh. And he talked about the union and how he was working to make things better for all of them. He was a good man. A hard worker.

And she told him stories about the boys and their antics. And about Hymie. And Frieda and Sam. She told him about the shoemaker and his children. Isadore always listened quietly. He knew that Gussie had had a lonely childhood, that she didn't have friends. She had told him about Sol and how her own insecurity had ended that relationship. He'd told her about Malke and how his immaturity had ended that one. He felt ready this time to be serious. He wanted to make this beautiful young woman happy in a way that she hadn't been since she lost her father.

After another few weeks of walking and talking, Isadore decided it was time for his mother to meet Gussie and vice versa.

"Gussie, would you be willing to come uptown on Sunday and meet my mother and my sister? Maybe my brother David as well with his wife Becky?"

Gussie felt her breath stop and reminded herself to take a breath. She had dreaded this moment.

"Yes, of course."

Isadore had yet to meet Gussie's mother either.

"But first, you should meet my mother." Anything to delay meeting Isadore's mother. Not that she had any particular reason to be nervous, but new people always made her uncomfortable.

"I'd love to meet your mother. And the shoemaker also. And, of course, Frieda and Sam. And Hymie and Max and David and Avram and Toba."

Gussie laughed. "Just hold on a second. One at a time! Let's meet at my mother's new place. And I can take you past Ridge Street also."

Mama had finally left Ridge Street and moved around the corner from Hymie near Avenue C a year ago. Even now there were nine "children" living with her mother and the shoemaker, even though some of those Hershkowitz sons were in their thirties. Ben, the son her age, was now in law school. His father was so proud. Gussie always knew that Ben was the special one.

Gussie and Isadore made a plan to meet that Sunday when Gussie made her regular visit with Tillie and the boys. She'd have to give Mama fair warning first. Mama knew about Isadore and had asked many questions. Gussie was sure she would approve.

When Sunday arrived, however, Gussie's stomach was as jumpy as a grasshopper, and she couldn't eat her breakfast. Tillie smiled knowingly, noticing that Gussie had been extra careful in how she'd pinned her hair back and rouged her cheeks that morning.

Once they'd crossed over to Manhattan, Gussie pushed them all to walk faster. She had no patience for the usual dawdling of Leo, Joe, and Harry.

"Just walk ahead, Gussie. We'll meet you there."

Gussie sped off, hoping to meet Isadore at the corner before he got to her mother's building. And there he was, standing at the corner, waiting for her.

He smiled as she approached. She took his hand, which sent a shiver up his arms, making goosebumps appear. His heart pounded. He wasn't nervous, but he could see that she was.

"So are you afraid I won't like your mother? Or are you afraid she won't like me?"

Gussie gave him a funny look. Did he know her so well?

"A little of both, I suppose. I want you both to like each other."

Isadore felt his heart slow a bit. She cared so much. What did he do to deserve such a gorgeous young woman?

They walked up the stairs to the Hershkowitz apartment, and Frieda was standing at the door.

My, oh, my, Isadore thought. *How can there be two such beauties?*

As they walked into the apartment, Gussie was relieved to see only Mama, Mr. Hershkowitz, and Sam inside. Maybe Mama'd had the good sense to send away the hordes of Hershkowitz children.

Mama turned from the sink where she was slicing vegetables for lunch, dried her hands on the dish towel, and walked over to meet Isadore.

"Mama, this is Isadore Goldschlager."

"Nice to meet you, Isadore. I've heard nice things about you from Gussie and Tillie."

"Thank you, Mrs. Hershkowitz. I am so pleased to meet you."

Gussie then introduced Isadore to Sam and Frieda and Mr. Hershkowitz. Isadore shook everyone's hands and was very gracious to them all, even the shoemaker. Perhaps Mr. Hershkowitz would like Isadore and finally forgive Gussie for not wanting to live with him and his children.

They all sat in the front room at the table where Mama had prepared a salad, some lox, some bagels, even some whitefish. *She really went all out to impress Isadore,* Gussie thought. Mr. Hershkowitz asked Isadore a lot of questions about his job, and Mama asked about his family. Isadore patiently answered all the questions, occasionally looking over to Gussie to see how she was doing. She nodded gently at him, letting him know she was fine. All was going well.

After lunch, Sam asked Isadore if he wanted to take a walk to meet Hymie and his family.

"Sam, let him be. Meeting all of you here is enough for one day."

Isadore chuckled. "It's fine. I'd like to meet Hymie and his family and also the Goldfarbs and Toba."

Gussie raised an eyebrow, but Sam rose from the table, and Isadore followed him.

"I guess he's not annoyed," Gussie pondered.

Once Isadore and Sam were out of the apartment, Mama turned to Gussie and said, "He's a fine young man. A real gentleman. I understand what you see in him."

Tillie nodded in agreement, as did Frieda.

"What do you think, Philip? You talked to him a lot," Mama asked the shoemaker.

"He's a mensch. Not a snob. A hard worker who cares about his fellow workers. He's a mensch."

Today Gussie couldn't even be annoyed at her stepfather. He even made eye contact with her as he said it.

"I'm so glad you like him. I like him, too," Gussie said, smiling at them all.

Frieda laughed, "Well, that's obvious from the way you two look at each other!"

When Sam and Isadore came back, Gussie told Tillie she wanted to walk with Isadore a bit so would meet her back in Brooklyn.

"Come," she said to Isadore, "I want to show you where I was born."

They walked over to Ridge Street.

"They really liked you, Isadore. I hope you liked them?"

"Your mother is a warm and loving person. How could I not like her? I could love her! Your sister was quiet, but she is beautiful and sweet. Your brother was very nice to take me to meet Hymie. The Goldfarbs and Toba we didn't see, but Hymie was friendly and very funny. And even the shoemaker was very pleasant, much to my surprise."

Gussie grabbed his arm and rested her head against his. "Thank you so much for coming."

Isadore turned to face her and held her face in his hands. He kissed her gently on the lips, and she wrapped her arms around him, kissing him back. As they pulled apart, he looked into her eyes.

"You know I love you, right?"

"Yes, yes, I do." She felt herself blushing, her cheeks hot, her ears burning. She wasn't quite ready to say she loved him. Instead she leaned in again, kissing him again, with more passion than before. Then she pulled back.

"We'd better go."

"Yes, but now it's your turn. Next Sunday? I will come to Brooklyn and take you back to meet my mother and my sister. Maybe David if he can come from the Bronx. All right?"

Gussie felt her stomach jump again, but she couldn't put him off any longer.

"Sure, sure. I will do it."

Isadore appeared bright and early on the following Sunday, and together they took the train back to Manhattan all the way up to East Harlem. Isadore was shocked when Gussie told him that she'd only been uptown once in all her life---on a class trip to Central Park and the Museum of Natural History. She was born in New York, but she'd seen far less of it than he had.

He recalled his first trip uptown with Uncle Gustav, how amazed he'd been by the size of the city, its energy, its crowds, its noise. Gussie was not as amazed; she was used to crowds and noise and the energy of New York. But she was completely surprised by how long the trip took and how far uptown the city extended.

"You do this every day to get to work and home again? My goodness!"

"Well, perhaps soon I will move to Brooklyn?" He looked at her inquiringly. She looked aside, knowing what he was asking.

"Let's see how today goes."

Isadore breathed deeply, feeling his heartbeat pick up. This week he was more nervous than last week. His mother wasn't as easy as Mrs. Hershkowitz, and his sister wasn't as easy as Frieda or Tillie. His Mama had asked a lot of questions about Gussie and her family, and she had more than once grunted in reaction to his answers.

"They came from Galicia? Hmmm."

"Her father delivered coal? Her mother's married to a shoemaker?"

Isadore had no idea why any of that triggered a grunt from his mother. After all, they were hardly aristocrats themselves. He drove a milk truck. His father had been a peddler in his short time in New York. Who were they to look down on others?

He took another deep breath, watching Gussie fidget as she also kept her thoughts to herself. He hoped this went well.

As they entered the apartment where he lived with his mother and sister, all was quiet. Where were they?

"Mama, Betty? Where are you?"

His mother came out from the backroom.

"I was busy folding the laundry. Betty went out to the store. She'll be back."

"Mama, this is Gussie Brotman."

"Hello, Mrs. Goldschlager. Nice to meet you," Gussie said as she extended her hand, and Ghitla took and shook it stiffly.

"Hello, Gussie. Nice to meet you also. How was the trip from Brooklyn?"

Gussie looked at this woman, Isadore's mother, and could see the resemblance. The deep set eyes, the strong features. Ghitla was a proud woman, she could tell. She held her head high and did not smile. Gussie felt her stomach tighten into a knot. This would be harder than she'd even imagined.

They stood there awkwardly, Isadore wondering what to do next. No one said anything.

"So where is Betty?" Isadore said, breaking the silence.

223

"I told you. She went to the store. To buy something for lunch."

Why is she being so difficult? Isadore was dismayed. Gussie was looking at the floor.

"Let's sit down."

Finally, Betty came in, holding a bag full of vegetables and cheese and bagels.

"Hello," she said. "I'm Betty."

Gussie said, "Hello, nice to meet you."

"Let me put these down. Want to help make lunch?" Betty asked.

Isadore was steaming. *Gussie was a guest. Why should she make lunch?*

But Gussie said, "Of course," and helped Betty empty the bag. They rinsed and cut the vegetables into a salad, put the cheese and bagels on plates, and everyone sat at the table. Once again there was a chilly silence in the room.

Finally, his mother spoke, "So you're a Galitzianer? Right?"

Gussie tried to answer as gently as she could.

"Actually, I am an American. I was born in New York. My parents came from Galicia though. You're right about that."

"Oh. So you were born here? You went to school here?"

"Well, I did. But I had to help my mother, so I stopped school at eleven."

Betty furrowed her eyebrows.

"Eleven? I was thirteen, Isadore and David were fifteen. Eleven is young."

Gussie wasn't sure whether Betty was expressing sympathy or disappointment.

Isadore felt that soon he would say something he'd regret, so he changed the subject.

"Gussie is wonderful with children. She's practically raised her three nephews since they were babies."

Gussie felt her face redden again. She wished he didn't feel he had to prove something about her.

"Well, I didn't raise them. I just helped my sister and brother-in-law."

There was another long silent pause.

"Anyone want coffee? Some fruit?" Ghitla asked.

"No, thank you." Gussie couldn't wait to leave. Neither could Isadore.

"Me neither," he said. "In fact, we should head back. It's a long ride to Brooklyn, and then I have to return here. Let's go, Gussie."

His mother rose from her seat, looking embarrassed.

"I'm sorry you have to leave so soon. Perhaps next time you can stay longer."

Gussie responded politely, and then she and Isadore said their goodbyes and left.

Once they were outside, Gussie couldn't hold back her tears.

"Well, I guess she doesn't like me."

"Like you? She doesn't even know you. She was just being rude."

"Why? What did I do wrong?"

"You didn't do anything wrong. She is just difficult sometimes. My mother has never quite gotten over the way my father died before she could see him again. She's just angry with everyone."

"But that can't be all. It must be about me, too?"

Isadore took her hand, and she pulled it away.

"What's wrong? Are you mad at me?"

"No, but I don't like that your mother doesn't like me. How can I be with someone whose family doesn't approve?"

Isadore stopped walking. Gussie looked at him.

"I think she's jealous of you. I think she doesn't want me to leave. David left. If I leave, there will be no man in the house for them. Really, it's not about you."

Gussie was not convinced. They rode the train silently downtown, and when they reached the end of the line where they had to get the trolley to Brooklyn, she said, "No need to take me the rest of the way. I know how to do this myself. You go home. You have to work tomorrow."

"No, that's not right. I want to be with you all the way."

"I need to be alone. Please. Let me be."

Isadore knew better than to push. He reached again for her hand, and again she pulled away.

"Will I see you this week? Can I come to Brooklyn before work like usual?"

Gussie looked at his eyes, so sad, almost teary, and felt terrible.

"Maybe a week apart will be good. Come next week, not this week."

"Fine. I am so sorry, Gussie. I love you. I don't care what my mother feels. I hope you know that."

Gussie nodded, but turned and walked away.

The next two weeks were excruciatingly long. For both of them. Gussie told Tillie about her lunch with Betty and Ghitla, and Tillie sympathized.

"But you don't have to live with her, Gussie. If you love Isadore, that's what matters. And he will move here to Brooklyn, so you will probably hardly ever see her."

"That might be true. But she's his mother. I can't start a marriage with a man whose family doesn't approve."

"She'll come around. Really, don't let this make you throw away something---someone---good."

Meanwhile, Isadore could barely talk to his mother, and they continued the same icy silence that had filled the apartment that Sunday. He did, however, talk to his cousin Abe and his brother David.

David said, "You know Mama. She isn't good at sharing. She misses Papa, and she doesn't want to lose you. She wasn't happy about Becky either at first. Even though she was from Iasi and her father was a hat maker. She thought Becky wasn't good enough for her son. Now she likes her just fine, and Becky ignores her occasional rudeness. If you love Gussie, fight for her, and ignore Mama."

Abe gave him similar advice, but with a different perspective.

"Marriage is hard, Izzy. It sure is nice if everyone loves each other, but even so, there are no guarantees. Look at my parents. Nine children together. They must have loved each other, but look at them now. So maybe your mother is concerned about your happiness. But only you can make a decision about who to marry. It's your life. This isn't Europe. No one is arranging your marriage. You have to do what you think is right for you."

Isadore, strengthened by what both Abe and David had said, approached his mother after a week of silence.

"We need to talk."

She looked up from her newspaper, shocked to hear his voice.

"About what?"

"About Gussie. You were awful to her, and I don't know why. But I don't care what you think. I love her, and I'm going to ask her to marry me. If she says no, I'll never forgive you. And if she says yes, I hope that you will be happy for us."

Ghitla didn't move. She sat quietly. Then she spoke slowly in a calm voice.

"I only want you to be happy, of course. I am concerned, but you know best. If Gussie is the one you want, I will be happy for you as long as you are happy with her."

Isadore sat down next to her. He knew this was hard for his mother, whose natural toughness had only been hardened further by her losses.

"Thank you. Let's try to move beyond this and start again."

He kissed her cheek, and she patted his hand. She didn't make eye contact, but Isadore knew that she was trying to be happy for him.

Now could he convince Gussie?

When they next met, Isadore told Gussie what his mother had said, what his brother and his cousin had said. Gussie told him what Tillie had said.

"So can you forgive my mother?"

"It's not about forgiveness, Isadore. It's about wanting to feel like part of your family, like you feel like part of mine. But now I realize I can't make that happen just because I want it. And maybe I don't need that in order to be happy with you. Let's give it some time. Let's be together like before, and see if we can be happy together."

"That's fair. I'll come and see you like before. And we'll see how we feel after the summer is over."

So they went back to walking and talking every week, and slowly Gussie let him into her heart again. She admired his persistence and his loyalty. He made her happy. She couldn't deny it.

Two months later Isadore wanted to know if Gussie was ready to marry him. This time when he brought up marriage, she took his hand. She nodded and said, "Yes, I will marry you."

He reached his arms around her and pulled her closer. He kissed her tenderly, and then he felt her kiss him back, not letting go. When she did let go, she put her head on his shoulder. She felt safe. And loved.

"I love you," he whispered. "I will always love you."

She kissed him again, "I love you also."

EPILOGUE

They were married on the twelfth of November, 1916, in the rabbi's office on Broome Street near where Gussie had grown up. They moved immediately into their own apartment in Brooklyn at 965 Herkimer Street. There was no honeymoon, just a Sunday some weeks later when all the cousins and brothers and sisters and children came by their apartment to wish the new couple the best.

And they lived happily ever after.

Or did they? Did they have a perfect marriage? There is no such thing. Anyone who's been married knows that. Gussie had her demons and dark times, and Isadore also had times he'd withdraw and prefer to be alone. He continued to work for the dairy throughout their marriage and was active in the union all through his career there. It was a hard life. They lived from paycheck to paycheck, sometimes happy, sometimes not.

But they stayed together, and they loved each other. Isadore kept Gussie from spending too much time in the past, and with him she felt she had in some ways found the world she'd known before her father had died. She felt safe again. And despite the hard times---the war, the Depression, their own personal struggles---Isadore kept looking forward, pushing ahead into the future.

They did have three children: first, Elaine, who had her mother's red hair and father's wit. Then Maurice, who was named for his grandfather Moritz.

And then finally, another little girl was born; they named her Florence for Gussie's sister Frieda, who had died after giving birth six years before. Florence also was blessed with red hair like that of her mother Gussie, her aunt Tillie, her sister Elaine, and her namesake, her aunt Frieda. She grew up to be my mother.

AFTERWORD AND ACKNOWLEDGEMENTS

As you now know, this book was about my grandparents, Gussie Brotman and Isadore Goldschlager. They were real people, and most of the people mentioned in the book were real---their parents, siblings, cousins. The dates are real, and some of the events are real, but I have changed some of the first names and most of the surnames.

Isadore really walked out of Iasi, Romania, when he was fifteen. He in fact came under his brother David's name. He worked in a grocery store, and he became a milkman. His father really died the day before his sister Betty arrived. And he really had two large sets of cousins, one family living in Manhattan, one in Brooklyn. Isadore's uncle Gustav really helped his brother-in-law Yankel get off of Ellis Island, and Yankel did die shortly thereafter.

Gussie's story also has fact-based incidents. Her father Joseph died when she was five years old, her mother married the shoemaker, and Gussie moved out to live with her sister Tillie in Brooklyn. Gussie left school and took care of her three nephews while Aaron and Tillie ran their grocery store. And her younger sister Frieda died after giving birth to a baby boy, who also died.

Most importantly, Gussie and Isadore did in fact meet on Pacific Street, a story handed down by my Aunt Elaine, who wrote only that Isadore was with his cousin when he saw Gussie sitting in the window of her sister's store.

All the rest is poetic license on my part. In fact, much of the book is from my imagination. All the dialogue and many of the characters, including Hirsh, Malke, Mr. Greenberg, Sylvie, and Sol, are pure fiction as are most of the incidents in the book.

My grandfather died before I was five so my memories of him are vague and limited, but I've used those memories and the stories I heard about him from my mother, my father, and my aunt Elaine to try and create a character who was as true to Isadore as I could.

But I never knew any of his relatives; I never met his siblings or any of his many cousins. Only years of genealogy research allowed me to discover the existence of all those relatives. I learned something about some of the cousins by searching for, meeting, and corresponding with some of their descendants.

Fortunately, I was lucky enough to know my grandmother Gussie for 23 years yet I never once asked her about her life. What did she remember? What was her childhood like? What was her marriage like? What was her father like, her mother? How I wish I had asked. Much of what I've written about her life is speculation. I hope I've done her justice. Despite all her sadness and insecurity, she was a wonderful grandmother, and her nine grandchildren adored her.

My mother and my aunt and my father all talked about my great-aunt Tillie, and I've done my best to convey what a wonderful woman she was and how important she was to my grandmother. Hyman's grandchildren gave me a sense of what he was like, and my mother's memories of her grandmothers helped me round out their personalities. Most of the rest of the Brotman and Goldschlager families I knew almost nothing about except their names, occupations, and dates from census reports and other records, so I've had to use my imagination.

There are many people I need to acknowledge for their help and inspiration in writing this book in addition to my grandparents.

First, I have to acknowledge all the support I have always received from my parents. My parents know that I have dreamed of writing a novel since I started to read. Their love of reading was the source of my own love of reading and of my dream of writing a book myself.

My cousin Jody Brickman read two early drafts and provided me with very helpful insights and suggestions. She also has provided me with encouragement from the very start.

My good friend Andrea Chasen was my writing buddy; we read drafts of each other's work for over two years, and she helped me see where there were holes in my story and made valuable suggestions for improving each chapter.

I also benefited from the expertise of Susanne Dunlap, whose professional services as my editor opened my eyes to the many ways I could improve the narrative. As a result of her careful and thorough editing and suggestions, I was able to see many ways to improve the book and make the story more readable and more interesting. To the extent the book still misses the mark, the fault is mine, not that of Susanne or anyone else.

In addition, Sharon Lippincott taught me how to use Word to turn my rough manuscript into a publishable format, and she introduced me to CreateSpace so that I could publish the book independently.

Finally, I could never have written this book without the loving support of my husband, Harvey Shrage. He somehow tolerated in good humor all the times I stared right past him because I was lost in the world of my grandparents and all the times I didn't hear what he said because my head was somewhere in 1910 New York. He has also always supported my genealogy endeavors by listening to my stories, reading my blog, walking through cemeteries, and traveling to Tarnobrzeg, Poland, where my grandmother's family had lived. Someday I will drag him with me to Iasi as well.

I wrote this book for my daughters, Rebecca and Maddy, and especially for my grandsons, Nate and Remy. I wanted them to know something about their ancestors and how hard life was for all those who came to America for a better life.

Nate and Remy live in Brooklyn, just three miles from where their great-great-grandparents Gussie and Isadore met on Pacific Street just over a hundred years ago.